CAPRICORN CONJURED

ZODIAC GUARDIANS BOOK 2

TAMAR SLOAN

TRICIA BARR

Jess
Connors
PUBLISHING

JARETH

F ire can be hard to paint.

But that doesn't stop Jareth from trying.

He steps back, assessing the wide expanse of wall before him. There's more to fire than people realize. More shades. More layers. More power.

Squatting down, Jareth starts low, where the fiercest heat would be. His fingers skim over the wall, the memories he doesn't want starting to consume him.

The first stroke is a bold one, sweeping straight across the bottom of the wall. The base is where the fire is the hottest, the most intense. The darkest in color.

He drops to his knees, his arm sweeping left then right. Maybe this time he'll be able to capture the moment. Capture the truth. His other hand joins the first, spreading across his canvas, pressing down hard.

This is the point the fire is being fed. This red is the color of hunger. Greed. Destruction. His arms spear out wide, sensing its need to be fueled.

Except it's not big enough. Not hot enough.

He jumps to his feet, energy thrumming through him.

The colors bloom, developing a life of their own like they always do. The deep clarets, the vivid crimsons, the shades of blood—dried blood, congealed blood, bright, oxygen-rich blood.

The higher he climbs, the more the flames come alive. Gut-ripping orange, sickly-scented yellow. It's terrifying and beautiful all at once.

Jareth pulls the stepladder over, and his hands blur as they dance across the wall and up to the ceiling. There's a roaring in his ears. His breath comes in pants. Just like last time, the flames will climb across the roof. The smoke will billow like clouds. If he keeps going, he can cover the whole room in flames. Maybe, if he tries hard enough, the fire will drown out the screams.

Their screams.

The doorbell ringing pierces the silence. Jareth looks around, his chest heaving. The scent of acrid smoke slowly clears from his throat. He's almost surprised to find himself still in the living room. To see the complete lack of damage and destruction.

Fire leaves behind charred coal and gutted rooms.

And shattered lives.

The doorbell rings again, twice this time. Jareth turns away from the carnage he splashed across his lounge room wall. It never looks right, anyway.

It never does the moment justice.

Flicking his hair back from his eyes, he shrugs as if he can shake off the helpless anger. Wishing he could ignore the visitor standing on the other side of the door, he opens it.

Shandra's bleached blonde hair startles Jareth every time he sees her. Maybe it's the sharp, pageboy cut. Maybe it's the lacquered way she plasters it to her skull. Maybe it's the harsh contrast to her rounded, ebony face.

She smiles. "Hello, Jareth."

Jareth opens the door wider even though he wants to slam it shut. "Hey, Shandra."

Just like he knew she would, she takes that as the invite to come in, hitching her over-sized handbag higher up her shoulder. Jareth supposes if social workers waited for a verbal invite, most of their home visits would be done in driveways.

She walks down the hall, familiar with the layout of the house after several visits, already fishing her notebook out of her handbag. She stops in the lounge room, looking around then doing exactly what Jareth knew she would.

She scribbles in her notepad.

Jareth leans a shoulder against the doorjamb that leads to the kitchen, waiting.

Her smile expanding across her round face, Shandra looks up. "So, how have you been?"

"Good."

Somehow, that justifies far more scrawling in the notepad than the single word he used.

"Wonderful!" Shandra exclaims like Jareth just told her he's joined a social club. Another quick glance at her surroundings and she indicates the table nearby. "May I?"

Jareth jams his hands in his pockets, not entering the room. "Of course."

It would get tiring writing all those notes without something to lean on.

Shandra lowers her bulk onto a chair, smoothing her too-smooth hair. "Thank you, Jareth. I always appreciate your hospitality."

Jareth's brows spike up. Was Shandra having a dig?

This is her fourth visit since he moved into this house. They've always been short, cordial, with lots of scribbles in that darned notepad. She checks he's still alive, she leaves.

He prepares his rote responses. *Yes, I'm eating more than*

pasta after you went through my kitchen cupboards, tsk tsking. Yes, I've washed my clothes more regularly after you commented that I need more than two changes. Yes, I've stayed in contact with all my old friends. He'll even say that last lie without blinking.

But this time, Shandra sits back, looks at him and sighs. She doesn't even glance at her notebook and whatever checklist is in there. "I see you haven't got a lot of furniture yet." She looks around, noting the battered wooden table and chairs she's sitting at, then takes in the rest of the room.

The place is open plan, which Jareth expected. His mother always loved open living spaces. Less corners to collect dust, she'd say. It means the dining area flows to the lounge room, a vast expanse of timber floor because his father had an allergy to dust mites and hated carpet.

Shandra's eyes keep scanning because there's nothing to catch her gaze. Nothing to stop and study. The walls are blank.

The room is empty.

"It's really…bare, Jareth. Have you thought of furniture? Maybe a TV?"

"I don't really watch TV."

He doesn't need a TV. His mind plays its own movies. Over and over and over.

"And the walls…" She looks away as if she doesn't like what's there. "They're quite bleak. Maybe some book-shelves?" Her face lights up. "Maybe some photos. They could really warm the place up."

Jareth glances at the wall that he just hurled his grief over. It's returned to being nothing more than a cream canvas.

He should've known his paintings would be a harbinger of what was to come.

The ability to paint with nothing but his hands had felt like a gift. But like anything that mattered in his life, his paintings disappear with time. They don't last.

Sometimes, it's like they never existed.

As if she's read his mind, Shandra leans forward, pressing a hand onto the table. "You used to like to paint, didn't you?"

"I did."

"It might be helpful to give it a try again."

What for? Those useless skills weren't able to save his parents.

Jareth shrugs, his hands still in his pockets. "Maybe."

Shandra sighs, leaning back and withdrawing her hand. Her face hardens in a way Jareth hasn't seen before. "The school rang me. They said you've yet to attend."

"I'm up to date with all my assessments. I got an A on my last assignment. I suspect that's better than quite a few others who are enrolled there."

"Attendance is a requirement of passing, Jareth."

And there's no one to home school him.

Jareth's life has come full circle. He's an orphan again.

He finally pulls his hands out of his pockets, only to cross his arms. "I can learn perfectly fine from home."

Shandra's face molds into another expression Jareth hasn't seen before. It fills with sympathy.

Jareth's spine stiffens. There are several reasons he's realized that keeping to himself is best. Avoiding pity is high up on the list.

"You know, you're not the only minor who lives independently. I have another case just like you."

Jareth doesn't say anything. Although it's sad that someone else has lost their parents and lives on their own, he doubts he has anything in common with this kid.

"It's quite unusual, actually, to have two cases so similar in the same area. He lives on his own, too, the sole beneficiary of a large estate." She leans forward. "But he goes to school. He hasn't isolated himself."

Jareth's muscles tighten. Yep, he has nothing in common with this boy.

Obviously, that boy didn't lose the people who were his world.

Obviously, that boy hasn't realized it's easier to stay separate. Less…painful. Safer.

Obviously, that boy wasn't the one who failed to save the two people who meant everything to him.

Shandra's eyes narrow. "I'm reducing my visits with him because my manager isn't breathing down my neck about it, saying words like post-traumatic stress disorder and support services." Jareth goes to say something but Shandra shoots her hand up in the air. "And foster care."

That silences him. *No one will ever replace my parents*, he thinks fiercely. *Ever.*

Shandra waits, her notebook sitting open beside her, the rest of her becoming as unmoving as her hair. She knows she's laid down the gauntlet.

She knows that page is waiting for her to record his decision.

When Jareth moved here two months ago, explaining that even staying in the same city he grew up in was too painful, child protective services had been willing to go along with it. Especially when his parents' portfolio had included a place in Mirror Point, the place where he was first adopted.

A new house.

A new start.

There's no way Shandra can know that Jareth was running away from more than just memories.

That maybe by staying away from others, Jareth's keeping them just as safe as himself.

And foster care isn't staying away from others.

Jareth's hands fall to his sides, cold, hard defeat settling in his gut. His gaze lifts to Shandra's. "I'll go to school."

2

VERONICA

The sound of the front door closing shakes Veronica out of her game of catch against her bedroom wall. She shoots up in her bed, ears twitching like a dog who's just heard the rabbit it's been stalking.

She tiptoes to her door, which is cracked slightly, and turns every ounce of her attention to her dad's voice.

"That kid just keeps surprising us," he says to someone on his cell phone. "Parents mysteriously die in a warehouse they had no business being in. And now he's fully emancipated and living on his own in a house the librarian left him in his will, after yet another mysterious death? I call bullshit."

Veronica knows who her dad's talking about. The boy he's been following for years.

Tristan Ayers.

Her dad is silent for a while as he rummages through papers in his office. How she wishes she could hear what the person on the other line is saying! Keeping Jack Cadbury quiet for any length of time in a discussion is quite the feat.

But the second she asks about his work, nothing but silence.

It's his own doing that she's had to stoop to sneaking around, picking the lock of his private office in their New York City apartment, going through his files, listening in on his phone calls. He's forced her hand. If she wants to prove to the world that he's not just some quack hell-bent on proving aliens exist, she has no other choice but to go behind his back and be his secret wingman. Wingwoman?

"Really? Another one? Are you sure?" The pitch of her dad's voice spikes, making Veronica press her jaw flat against the corner of her bedroom door.

There's another long silence, and Veronica hardly breathes as she waits for her father to speak again.

"Alright, I got it," he finally says. "Make sure we get a detail on her right away. I want to know everything about her."

Her. Who is this *her*?

The subtle *ding* lets her know he's hung up the phone, and not long after his footsteps carry down the hallway toward her. As swiftly as she can, she places herself back on her bed and throws her aged tennis ball at the wall, catching it just as her father sticks his head into the gap in her doorway.

"How you doin', Kitkat?" he asks, his five o'clock shadow matching the shadows under his eyes—another sign that he hasn't been sleeping. Again.

"Just the same old, same old," she replies with her characteristic bored tone. "Although school wasn't as monotonous today. Billy Crenshaw crashed into someone in the cafeteria, which naturally inspired a massive food fight."

Her father enters the room and sits on the edge of her bed. "And you managed to come out of it unscathed?"

"Yeah, I keep to myself," she says with a shrug. "I guess I'm like my dad that way." She throws him a playful smirk.

He shakes his head and sighs with a wearied smile. "Not

the best way to be, Kitkat. I wish you took more from your mother than just the dark hair."

Veronica giggles and sits up with her legs pretzeled beneath her. It's not often that he talks about her mom, so she needs to take advantage of it. "Tell me again why you call me Kitkat." To further persuade him, she flashes him her puppy-dog eyes, which isn't hard seeing as her eyes naturally take up most of her face, the way she sees it.

He chuckles and looks at the ball-beaten wall. "When we first started dating, she used to call me Egghead. Mostly because my last name Cadbury, but also because," he hisses between his teeth, "your dad used to be somewhat of a nerd."

No surprise there, Dad. She bites back a laugh.

"So when you came along, she kept the chocolate themed nicknames alive and you became Veronica 'Kitkat' Cadbury."

She smiles, wishing she could remember more of her mother than just her kind smile. "And why doesn't Logan have a chocolate themed nickname?"

He leans back on the pillow beside her and puts his arm over her shoulder. "You already know that. Your mom had Logan before she met me."

"Well yeah, but he should have been given a family nickname like us," she says. "I think we should give him one. How about…" she cups her chin and purses her lips. "Snickers."

Her dad chuckles. "I don't think your brother has snickered since he was ten."

"Ok, so we need a more prudish candy bar," she muses. "Maybe not even chocolate, because Logan isn't fun like chocolate. Oh! I've got it. Licorice!"

"Licorice?" he asks with a laugh.

"It's perfect for him. Old ladies love it and no one else can stand it."

Her dad bursts out laughing and slaps his knee. "Oh, come on now, your brother isn't that bad. Give him a break."

"Well, I am Kitkat. Isn't that my job?" She winks, making him laugh harder.

"How did I get so lucky to have such a witty daughter?" he asks.

"Like I said, I take after you."

He rubs the laughing tears from his eyes and angles off the bed. "Alright, as your dad, I guess I gotta feed you. What sounds good?"

"How about your specialty?" she suggests, gripping her painted toes.

"Hotdog spaghetti it is!" he announces as he heads out her door.

She smiles as she watches him leave. *I wish you were here, Mom.*

Once he's out of sight and his footsteps move into the kitchen, she slips stealthily out her door and down the hall to his office. It's locked again, but she's an ace at picking it by now. *Honestly, Dad, you really think you could keep me out if I wanted to get in?*

Veronica pushes the door silently open and sneaks inside. She needs to know what he and the person on the other end were talking about. Some girl. She needs to find out who. Her eyes scan over his papers, but everything is about the same as the last time. He would have written this girl's name down.

Veronica circles around his desk and finds what she's looking for—a post-it note stuck to the sleeping screen of his computer.

The note reads: BRIELLE PIERCE

3

BRIELLE

This is a dream come true!

Sitting in the passenger's seat of Frank's Prius on the way to school is just bliss. It's something Brielle's dreamt about for as long as she could dream. A loving father dropping her off at school, chatting in the car, him belatedly checking whether she grabbed her lunch with a rueful smile. No more empty, solo bike rides. And she's so grateful that Mirror Point High is on Frank's way to work in the big city. She'd hate to have to ride her bike all the way from their house on the outskirts of town.

Well, maybe "hate" is a strong word. She'd do anything to keep the family she now has, even ride her bike several miles at the crack of dawn to get to school. But this is so much better. For so many reasons.

"So, there's something I've been meaning to bring up," Frank begins, rubbing the back of his neck with his free hand as his left grips the wheel.

Brielle turns to him as they enter the main road of town. The past couple of weeks living with them has been everything she's ever wanted, and she's come to recognize Frank's demeanor when he's about to bring up what he thinks is a sensitive topic—almost everything about starting life together has been a sensitive topic.

"Sure, what's up?" she asks, trying to stifle the smile that blazes every morning on these drives.

"Bea and I have been considering transferring you to a school in the city," he says, flicking his eyes at her every few seconds to gauge her reaction. "I know this is your senior year, but there are some really good private schools there, schools that might give you a better chance at college."

Yep, definitely a sensitive topic.

"Oh," she stammers. "Um. That's very thoughtful of you both, but…" Tristan's face flashes in her mind—as it does regularly. Everything they went through a few weeks back comes flooding in. She's now fully aware of her purpose in life.

Find the other Zodiac Heirs. Prepare for Chardis's return. Save the Universe.

She can't do any of that properly if she goes to school in New York City.

But that's not the only reason she doesn't want to transfer.

Tristan…

Despite the truths that were revealed, she still feels a connection to him. He's the first thing on her mind when she wakes in the morning and the last thing when she falls asleep at night. And if that weren't enough, he fills every single hour of her dreams. Even if she wasn't part of this epic universal war, she'd still *want* to stay for him.

Even if she isn't his soulmate.

God, you're pathetic, Brielle.

"I'd really rather stay at Mirror Point High," she finally asserts. "All my friends are there, and like you said, this is my last year. I don't think a partial year at a better school would make a huge difference in my college application." She bites her lip and looks sidelong at him. "Can I stay?"

Frank pulls his eyes off the road and smiles. "Of course, you can!"

Brielle lets a slow sigh of relief out through her nose so Frank can't see it.

"And, of course, you'd want to stay with your friends and finish out the year with them," he continues, turning back to the road. "I just wanted you to know the option was there."

"Thank you. I really do appreciate the offer. And I don't think you have to worry about me getting into college. I think my resume is doing pretty good. I've had straight As all through high school, and I can apply much of my efforts at the orphanage as volunteer work." It's just the tuition that she doesn't have handled, and even though Frank and Bea are her parents now, she doesn't want the burden of paying that massive amount on them.

"That's great!" he says. "You're a smart girl, I had no doubts about that. I just want to make sure you can get into any school you want. Also…I want you to know that you *can* go to any school you want." There's that hesitant expression again.

Now it's her turn to look away awkwardly. She doesn't know what to say, so all she can do is nod. She needs an after school job. Desperately.

They pull up in front of Mirror Point High. This is Brielle's favorite part, even though it means she has to leave Frank.

"Have a good day, sweetheart," he says, using her favorite new pet name.

"Thanks, I will." She leans over the shifter console and hugs him, savoring the smell of his after shave. Then she waves and opens the door, saying "bye" before she gets out of the car. She longs to call him Dad, but it still feels too soon.

As she walks up to the front doors of the school, she wonders how long until it feels natural.

After English, she's eager to get to her second period class: Classic American Cooking. That's the class she shares with Tristan.

She goes to her station and sets her backpack in the seat that's been empty since the big reveal a few weeks ago. The betrayal still stings. It may never stop. Adalind was the best friend she'd ever had, and it wasn't even real. She was only interested in Brielle because she thought Brielle was a Zodiac Heir—and she'd been right.

It definitely hurts Brielle's ego. Tristan is now her only friend, and again he's only interested in her because of her Zodiac status.

Self-doubt increases as she wonders if she'll ever have a real friend, someone who doesn't want anything from her and only sticks around because they genuinely like her.

"Hey, is everything okay?" Tristan drops his bag on the floor by his bar stool, cocking his head at her frown.

She forcibly smooths her brow and offers a fake smile. "Yeah, everything's fine."

He glances at Brielle's bag on Adalind's empty stool. That's been its place ever since Adalind's...disappearance. He purses his lips. "The grief will pass eventually."

She looks away and nods. Tristan has grief, too. Even greater than hers. Does he expect his own mourning to pass so easily?

"How are things at the new house?" It's a loaded question, and she knows he'll understand the depth of it.

Turns out that Alden, the secretly sweet man that he was, had left all the wealth and property he'd amassed over the last seventeen years to Tristan in his will. Brielle hasn't tried to push for details, she just lets Tristan disclose things as he wishes. The transition to living on his own under the watchful eye of Social Services hasn't been easy for him. He doesn't show it, but she can sense it.

"It's fine." His face hardens. "Along those lines, can you come over after school today? I think it's time to begin your combat training. You never know who could be a Skin, as Adalind proved, and we need you to be prepared for a fight since your powers don't work on them."

Though Tristan's tone conveys no resentment, the same guilt and confusion writhe in her belly. The guilt that she's a pretty useless Zodiac Guardian because her powers don't work on Skins, and the confusion that her powers *do* work on Chardis, so much so that they sent him running with his inky black tail between his legs. Why is that? She kind of understands why the guilt amplification doesn't work on the Skins: they aren't in control of their actions, so there's nothing to feel guilty about. They are empty vessels devoid of souls, nothing more than robots.

But Chardis? From what Tristan has told her, he's sentient dark matter, a natural cosmic force and not human. So why would he feel guilty about the things he'd done? That's the part that just doesn't make sense. He looked pretty human in that warehouse. Why disguise himself as a person for their benefit? Why not come in his true form, which she can only imagine would be a giant mass of the same black smog he unleashed?

Brielle mentally shakes herself. None of that is important at this moment. Tristan just invited her over to his house! He's been so distant since his parents' deaths, and their dynamic has dramatically changed since they learned she's not the other Gemini. Even if he is only offering time with her to train her, she'll take it. Maybe it will help distract him from all he's lost, if only for a short time.

"Sure, I can come over after school." So much for looking

for an after-school job. But her training is more important than making money for college.

"Alright, class, everyone sit down and wash up," Ms. Brom says, closing the door as the final bell rings. "We're making something very special today."

Tristan leans close and whispers, "What do you think it is? Kraft mac n' cheese? Scrambled eggs? Maybe peanut butter and jelly sandwiches?"

Brielle giggles quietly. Tristan likes to complain that there's nothing special about American cuisine, and it's nice to see his playful side make an appearance now and then.

"You all know how much I love breakfast, and this is one of my absolute favorites." Ms. Brom claps her hands together excitedly.

"Cheerios!" Tristan whispers, making Brielle bite back another round of giggles.

"Waffles!" Ms. Brom announces as if a drumroll that only she could hear has just come to an end.

All play vanishes from Tristan's face as his expression turns stony and cold. Without a word, he picks up his backpack, slings it over his shoulder and walks right out the door.

"Mr. Ayers? Mr. Ayers!" Ms. Brom calls after him as the door closes.

Brielle is left sitting at her station alone, looking at the closed door with her brows pushing together so tight they ache.

What just happened?

4

TRISTAN

S omeone's following him.

Tristan surreptitiously glances over his shoulder as he crosses the road, striding away from school. If Ms. Brom hadn't gone straight for the jugular and chosen waffles as their cooking task today, he'd probably still be inside.

He wouldn't have seen the same guy in the nondescript gray car still sitting in the parking lot. The same one who pulls out as Tristan leaves.

Chardis will never give up.

Zarius's voice is in his head like he's never left.

Like he's not…gone.

Tristan shoves away the stabbing pain that always follows thinking of his parents. Instead, he focuses on the hot, simmering anger that's his other new friend.

A quick left past Creamy Dreams and Tristan's suspicion is confirmed. He's definitely being followed.

He's surprised Chardis already has more goons—he expected him to go lick his festering wounds for a little longer.

Come up with more of a plan.

At the same time, Tristan hasn't let his guard down. He's seen what that bastard is capable of. That no life is sacred.

That he'll target those closest to Tristan.

Which means losing this dude before he gets home. Before Brielle arrives.

Keeping his breathing steady, he picks up the pace a little, hunching like he's in a hurry. He takes a sharp right down the first street he comes across, glad to see it's still lined with shops and people.

The Skins would be super conscious of not attracting attention. Not after the warehouse. And the three dead bodies they didn't get to disappear.

Zarius.

Tess.

Adalind.

Tristan's hands clench in his pocket. At least if the Skins are back, he'll have something to take this bitter fury out on. Actually, he's looking forward to it.

But not now.

Not so close to home.

Unsurprisingly, the gray sedan rolls around the corner. Tristan purposely bumps into a guy walking toward him, spinning around with his hands up as he apologizes with a rueful smile.

"Sorry, my mind was on another planet."

The guy shakes his head, glaring at Tristan before stomping away.

But that's all that Tristan needed. In his brief pirouette, he got the information he wanted. One male. Dark hood.

Skins don't usually travel solo, but Chardis would know they need to stay under the radar for the moment…while he comes up with Plan B.

Looking ahead, Tristan makes his own plan. He's going to let this douche know that he's doing a crap job.

Seeing what he was hoping for, Tristan stops. Turning around, he finds the gray car has parked in front of a florist. He raises his hand, giving the guy a cheery wave.

Then, he turns and runs.

The alley is only a few yards ahead, and Tristan darts down it. Just as he was hoping, there's a chain link fence at the end. He hears the rev of an engine, jolting even more speed out of him. He runs at the fence and leaps. If he called on his suit, he could clear it in one smooth jump, but there are too many people around. His fingers looping through the holes, Tristan clambers up, vaulting over and landing on the other side.

A quick glance over his shoulder shows the gray car parked at the end of the alley. Tristan considers giving the guy the bird, but he jogs away instead. He has no doubt he'll be seeing that guy again.

Jogging the rest of the way home, Tristan realizes he almost welcomed the distraction. Two words accompany him, thumping out the rhythm of his feet hitting the pavement.

Find them.

Zarius's last words. What he and Tess died for.

And now that the Skins are back, the urgency has only increased.

Conscious he's running out of time, but clueless as to how to find the next Zodiac Guardian, Tristan's body clenches with determination. Training Brielle is what he can do now.

While he finds the others.

And his soulmate.

He's in front of Alden's house before he realizes it. In part because he was running like the Skin was still on his tail.

In part because Alden decided to buy a house not far from the main street of Mirror Point. Wisely, he knew that the more populated the area, the less the Skins were going to march up and want to discuss whether the Universe should be destroyed or not.

Panting a little, Tristan stops in the middle of a tree-lined street. He hikes his hands on his hips, taking in the two story house before him.

Alden's place is part high-end home, part bunker. It's somewhere both a rich lawyer and the army would be envious of. Pushing through the front gate, he strides up to the front door. No porch for Alden, just an open yard with a barely-there garden. No one was sneaking up on him.

Pressing his finger to the touch pad, the door silently swings open.

When the lawyer had finished telling Tristan the astounding news that he was Alden's sole beneficiary, he'd had him sign pages upon pages of forms and then handed him a manila envelope.

There were no keys. No "if you're opening this, then I must be dead" messages. All it held was a bound booklet full of endless instructions for all the technology Tristan is now surrounded by. The security around this place made Zarius's look like it came from a toy store. Not to mention the bomb-proof double-brick walls, the bullet-proof glass, the security screens that are everything-proof.

The door automatically shuts behind him, closing Tristan in his new home. It's big yet simple. It has everything a person would want in a house. A nice kitchen, a living area with a TV that looks like it wants to be a cinema screen when it grows up, several bedrooms that Tristan has yet to pick from. Heck, it even has a gym.

But as nothing but empty silence greets Tristan, the sting of loss spears through him. He's never felt more alone.

There's no one to greet him. No one to tell him he

shouldn't have walked out of class like that. No one to tell him this will all work out fine.

He misses Tess's cooking.

He misses Zarius's wonder at Tess's cooking.

He misses them, period.

Throwing his backpack beside the kitchen bench, Tristan flinches as the dull thud echoes hollowly through the open space. He probably should've stayed at school. The next few hours in this deluxe cavern, surrounded by the losses of his past and the pressures of his future, stretch out before him.

The bookcase in the living room is what draws Tristan forward. It's wide and heavy, the only adornment centered along the expanse of wall. Alden has a few books lined up on the shelves, although Tristan's never looked at them too closely.

The day he moved in and discovered the significance of this bookshelf, he put a framed photo of Zarius and Tess on the middle shelf. It was one of Zarius's first attempts at a selfie, taken when Tristan was a baby. Tess is in front of Zarius, laughing as her eyes glint with exasperation. She would've been telling him which button to press as he extended his arm. Zarius is half-frowning, half-grinning as he stares at the wrong place. The photo has always been one of Tristan's favorites. It's a candid shot of love and laughter.

With a sigh, Tristan reaches behind it and presses the timber panel. There's a *whoosh* as air sucks past him and the bookcase silently slides to the right. Before him, a set of concrete stairs are illuminated by recessed lights. Dipping down sharply, they disappear into the bowels beneath the house.

Tristan steps through, sensing rather than hearing the bookcase slide shut behind him. Running his fingers along the cool cement wall as he descends, Tristan remembers the awe he felt when he followed Alden's instructions and found the rooms downstairs. It's below ground level that the pretense of a home ends.

The lights automatically switch on as Tristan reaches the last step and he shakes his head like he has every time he's been down here. Alden may have perfected the cranky librarian persona, but at home, the guy was a high tech prepper. Decked out with every technological gadget a person could imagine, the place looks like a NASA bunker. Banks of screens flicker with life, several up on the wall rivalling the size of the TV upstairs. Computers and keyboards and things Tristan has yet to be able to name perch on desks, all seeming to look at him expectantly.

He sighs. "Yeah, yeah. I know."

Dropping himself into the nearest chair, he wheels himself closer to the computer on the desk in front of him. He scans the information on the screen, holding his breath despite himself.

Just like Zarius did, Alden has scans operating twenty-four-seven, looking for any shred of information about the Zodiacs. Pods. Special powers. People searching for others like them.

But just like the reams of information Tristan scoured when he first arrived, he finds nothing new.

Zip.

Zilch.

Zero.

Tristan rests his head on his arms. The same question that keeps haunting him weighs down on him.

What next?

His eyes flutter closed. He's tired. For some reason, choosing a room in this new house feels wrong. Like he's admitting this is now his home. The fitful dozing he does couldn't be called sleep, anyway. Whether he does it on the couch or with his head on the desk just like this doesn't really matter. It's enough to get him by.

Letting out a slow breath, Tristan's body sags. Maybe he could just rest for a sec...

When the doorbell rings, he jolts awake, the black mist that always invades his dreams clinging to his consciousness.

Leaping to his feet, he finds himself in fighting stance before he's fully alert. His heart a freight train in his chest, Tristan realizes he dozed off. But as his hands drop, he acknowledges he's probably in the safest place in Mirror Point.

The doorbell peals again and Tristan registers the time. That would be Brielle arriving, which means he was out for a few hours. Rubbing his hand down his face, he jogs back up the stairs. No nightmares this time, so that's good.

There are only so many times you can relive the death of your parents without developing a hate-hate relationship with sleep.

Upstairs, Tristan opens the door, bracing himself. Just like he knew she would, Brielle smiles when she sees him.

His own smile is reflexive. So is the jolt in his chest.

Followed by the only time he feels like all is right in the world.

Something settles in him when he sees Brielle. If she'd been his soulmate, he could've easily explained it.

But she's not. Brielle's the Libra.

Tristan steps back, acknowledging the feeling, but not knowing what to do with it. It's probably the grief. Maybe it's finally finding one of his own.

That's it. Brielle's proof that all is not lost.

"Welcome to *Casa de Alden*," Tristan says grandly as he sweeps his arm out wide.

Brielle's smile grows. "It's not what I imagined."

He arches a brow. "Wait till I give you the full tour."

He walks inside, heading straight past the kitchen to the gym out the back. The tour can wait. They have more important things to discuss.

Brielle follows, her head snapping from side to side as she takes in the large house. "Yep, definitely not the bachelor pad I was picturing," she murmurs.

"From what I can tell, he lived on ravioli," Tristan throws over his shoulder. "There were shelves of it in the pantry."

Which now makes it Tristan's first food group.

He stops inside the gym, which looks more like a martial arts dojo. Thick mats line the floor while punching bags hang in the back corner. Weights of various sizes line one wall, while all the classic weapons—swords, bo staffs like the one Tristan already owns, knives—hang along the other.

Brielle's hands hike to her hips. "Wow."

"Yeah, not bad, huh?"

Brielle spins around slowly, taking it all in. Tristan averts his eyes. Brielle looks good in workout gear. Of course she does...

He clears his throat. "I was followed today."

Her eyes widen. "What?"

"I lost him, but it's a reminder that Chardis is already looking for us."

She nods. She was there when they learned how high stakes this is. "Let's get started then."

Tristan walks to the center of the mats, finding Brielle just behind him. He frowns in thought. It feels so long ago that Zarius started his training, and they had years to prepare. But time isn't a luxury they have anymore. If Skins attack Brielle, and Tristan's not around, she needs to be able to defend herself.

The thought of Chardis capturing her has shudders ripping down his spine. It also gives him an idea of where they should start.

"I think we'll start with grabs," he says. "You don't want these guys getting a hold of you."

Brielle nods, looking both nervous and determined.

Something in Tristan's chest smiles. *That's m'girl...*

But he quickly quashes the thought. Brielle isn't his girl. He's destined to be with somebody else.

"If someone attacks, you have two options. Break and escape." Tristan clenches his jaw. "Or break and batter."

Frowning, Brielle nods in thought. "If I break and batter, then I can escape if I need to."

Clever girl.

"Break and batter, it is. Let's start with a choke hold. It's the one they're most likely to use."

Brielle nods again, squaring her shoulders.

Tristan steps in close, clamping his hands around her throat. He feels her pulse leap against his palm. "Once they have you like this, you need to get out fast. I want you to spike your hands up in between my arms, and punch them out wide."

Concentrating, Brielle does as he described. The moment her forearms hit his, he flings them out wide so she can get a sense of what should happen.

Brielle frowns. "Again."

Tristan clamps his hands around her throat. This time, when she shoves his hands away, she does it with more force. He grins. "Good. Now, if you were escaping, you'd step back at the same time."

"Which I'm not."

Tristan's grin widens. "In that case, you're going to grab me behind the neck and ram your right knee up."

Brielle's eyes widen a fraction, but she does as he described.

In the slowest, most gentle way she could...retracting her knee before it even touches him.

Tristan grabs her again. "You need to do it like you mean it. Skins don't feel pain like we do."

And your life depends on it.

"And it doesn't matter where your knee connects, just that it does it with force."

Swallowing, Brielle bites her lip. A second later, her hands spear up, knocking his off, then they wrap around his neck, jerking him down.

Her knee has just brushed his chest when Tristan collapses theatrically with a groan. He drops to the mat, clutching his abdomen, moaning some more.

Brielle gasps, but it's quickly cut off. When nothing happens, Tristan glances up.

She has her hands jammed on her hips, her brow creasing as her lips twitch. "Good thing you have a suit to protect you in real life."

Chuckling, Tristan rights himself. "Let's try it again."

This time when Brielle frees herself of his grip she pulls back, winding up for the knee. But Tristan instantly moves in, stopping his fist an inch from her face. "You need to keep your attacker close. Never give them an opening."

Frowning, Brielle shakes her arms out. "Right."

This time, she does as he says.

And Tristan realizes he should be careful what he wishes for.

As Brielle draws him close, his awareness of her spikes. He can see the flecks of sapphire in her eyes, smell her shampoo, feel her fluttering pulse beneath his palms.

She glances up and freezes.

The chemistry that's not supposed to exist between them flares. It heats Tristan from the inside out, narrowing his world to just him and Brielle.

She sucks her bottom lip in, drawing Tristan's attention to their plump curves.

They're not supposed to feel like this…

And then she jerks him down and lifts her knee. She makes contact with his chest, the sensation reverberating through him, then steps back, lifting two fists before her face.

The way she's clenched her hands is all wrong, and she's holding them too far apart, but Tristan can't help but admire her tenacity.

Brielle's panting a little as her jaw tightens. "Again."

Tristan realizes he's smiling. No, he's grinning. That he hasn't thought about the blackness that's always waiting at the periphery of his mind. That he wants to keep going, too.

He flexes his shoulders. "This time, I'm not letting go so easily."

Brielle nods, accepting the challenge. "This time, I won't stand back while you're down."

As another chuckle escapes him, Tristan wonders how long being with Brielle will be a double-edged sword.

She's everything his aching heart needs.

And yet she's everything he can't have.

JACK

09:45

Jack slams the blinds shut in his office, cutting off the punishing morning light. His coffee's cold and his heartburn's already scorching its way up his throat. The last thing he needs is cheery sunlight.

Chewing on an antacid like it's the source of all his stress, he returns to his seat. It creaks as he leans back, his gaze boring into the name he just scrawled down.

Brielle Pierce.

She's a new one. One he's yet to figure out where she fits into all of this.

"Cadbury." Jack looks up to find his boss standing in the doorway. "We need to talk."

Behind him, the rest of the guys in the FBI headquarters have wheeled their chairs so they can peer around McNally's portly form.

Jack nods, waving toward the seat on the other side of the desk. He doesn't bother to ask McNally to shut the door. He has nothing to hide.

But as his boss scans the paperwork between them as he sits, Jack resists the urge to shut the file sitting open before him. There's a difference between being transparent and inviting a grilling.

McNally clears his throat. "I've got a case for you." His gaze sharpens. "A real one."

Jack clenches his teeth. None of his cases are imaginary. "Sure, whatcha got?"

McNally slides a file across the paperwork. "We've got something in Chicago."

Jack flicks it open, scanning the contents. Two homicides, a couple who were out on a country walk. Nice middle-class people, no criminal history. He looks up sharply. "Like Seattle and New Orleans?"

Those killing sprees were years apart.

"Yep. Same MO as the Triple Murders. We're at two."

Which means one to go before this bastard sinks into obscurity again.

Jack shuts the file. "I'll get onto it."

"You're the only one who's managed to lift a fingerprint from one of the crime scenes, Cadbury." McNally jerks on the edges of his jacket, trying to make it look like a power move. "I want you to get to the bottom of this one."

Of course he does. He's only months from retiring…his

waistline has been preparing for it for some time now. This would be a nice little win to boast about at his retirement party.

McNally yanks the file sitting below the one he just brought in. "And leave this poor kid alone."

Jack suddenly feels the need for another antacid. And maybe an aspirin as his head starts to throb. "Tristan Ayers is a national threat."

"And that's because?" McNally rubs his forehead. He's asked this question before.

And he's hoping for a different answer.

"He's an extraterrestrial."

The sniggers from beyond his office tell Jack everyone else is listening in. Probably waiting for just this conversation.

McNally glances over his shoulder, having heard the muffled laughter, too. "Jack," he says more gently. "You're throwing away a distinguished career over this."

"Or I'm going to save every one of your ungrateful asses."

These agents think their greatest threat comes from within the borders of their planet. Fools. The power to end them all doesn't even lie in this solar system.

McNally shakes his head sadly. "Keep that up and I'll be thinking you've bought a first class ticket on the crazy train, just like the rest of the guys do."

He turns to leave and the office beyond becomes a flurry of movement.

Jack pops another antacid into his mouth, grinding it into a paste.

They'll see.

He'll find out the truth about Tristan.

There's nothing he won't do to make sure Earth remains safe.

5

JARETH

"So, school sucks." Jareth brushes away a leaf resting on his parents' memorial. "No wonder you moved to California."

He imagines his mother shaking her head, the tiny bells on her earrings tinkling softly. "We moved to California for the Feng Shui. It was the only city that aligned with all our astrological charts."

Jareth feels himself smile. They also moved because his father got a promotion. He sighs, the brief glint of humor disappearing. "Well, Mirror Point High has terrible Feng Shui."

If they were home, his mother would get busy making chamomile tea, sensing his unhappiness. "Does it face south? South is best for light, chi absorption, and harmony."

Jareth has no idea which direction the large, square building faces. He's only been there two days and he's made sure he's as invisible as possible. He's trying to figure out how long he has to keep attending before he can get his social worker off his back.

"Have you given it a chance?" his father would ask, bushy brows low.

Jareth squats down, tracing their names with his eyes. "I don't need to," he whispers. "I already know I don't have anything in common with them."

Jareth imagines his father stroking his moustache. "It sounds like you don't want to give this a chance. Classic defense mechanism."

That's what happens when your father's a psychologist. You get a free psychoanalysis every time you chat. His piercing gray eyes would hold Jareth's until his gaze slid away, deciding to focus on the intricate patterns on his work shirts.

His mother would nod sagely, her thick bangs brushing her eyelashes. "You just need to find a kindred spirit."

If the talk were to continue, her face would light up. "Your heart connection. The one person who speaks to your soul."

Jareth's head would've fallen into his hands with a groan, his father leaning over, as he placed a gentle hand on his wife's shoulder. "That will come later," he'd say, his face soft.

His mom would place her hand over his. "We weren't much older than you when we met."

In a haze of drug-induced euphoria, Jareth had usually pointed out. His parents would chuckle, eyes alight with memories, as Jareth shook his head ruefully.

Abruptly, Jareth pushes up. That conversation won't ever happen.

Because they're gone.

Instead, their screams still echo in his ears, like they're coated with the thick, viscous sound.

Jamming his hands into his pockets, Jareth turns away. The fierce need to paint wells up. To somehow make this right. To be able to remember them without flames…

Hunching his shoulders, he strides away. He needs to go home. Home is solitude. And solitude is safe.

He's about to break into a run when he slams into another body. Bouncing back with an "oomph", Jareth looks up in alarm.

A guy, probably around the same age, has leaped back, his fists in the air.

Jareth's hands shoot up. "Whoa, sorry. I wasn't looking where I was going."

The guy's hands drop, and he rubs the back of his head sheepishly. "Sorry. I wasn't paying attention." He frowns, as if that's a bad thing.

Jareth takes a small step back, just in case the guy changes his mind and decides he still wants to deck him. He almost considers taking a second, larger step when he registers this guy is all lean strength and coiled energy. And good looking to boot.

Probably a football jock.

Jareth shrugs. "You tend to focus on one thing in cemeteries."

The guy's eyes flicker to the two tombstones he's standing before. "Yeah, how to keep moving forward when they're here."

Jareth blinks as the words slice straight through him.

The guy smiles as if the motion is natural and easy. Like it's something he does often. "Anyway, sorry I overreacted."

With a short wave, the guy walks away, even though he only just arrived. It seems he doesn't really want company while he's visiting, either.

Jareth frowns, not sure why he hasn't moved. Spinning around, he discovers the guy's already out of sight, despite the winding path back to the gates. There was something about him... If Jareth's mother were here, the bangles on her wrist would be jangling with excitement. Fate, she'd call it.

Serendipity. If she got really carried away, she'd start talking about kindred spirits again. His father would wrap an arm around her shoulders, squeezing her quiet.

Jareth glances at the tombstones he's now standing before. The inscription is simple, like his own parents' ones —just names and a date. *Zarius and Tess Ayers*.

And just like Jareth's parents, they died on the same day. Glancing a little closer, though, he does the math. They were relatively young, so even if they were this guy's parents, they were nothing like Jareth's parents. It's even possible they were the guy's siblings. Probably good friends who died in a car crash or something. Any sense of kinship that might've bloomed disintegrates.

"We have nothing in common," he mutters.

This guy's first instinct is to fight. Jareth hates fighting.

And he smiles. Jareth doesn't even remember what that feels like.

Jareth's alone, and he needs to remember that. It's the way it needs to be.

Suddenly, the drive to paint is back. The tall, stone fence that surrounds the cemetery calls to him. The rocks are pale, shades of dove and concrete.

It's like a yards' long canvas. Beckoning. Waiting.

And whatever Jareth paints will be gone before anyone can see it.

Another quick check to make sure he's alone, and Jareth unleashes the rage and sorrow trapped in his heart. It spears down to his fingertips, making them clench and twitch.

Pressing his hands on the stone wall, Jareth feels the cold hardness. This is what his parents' tombstones feel like. This is the color of their skin when they were dragged out of the house, lungs full of smoke. Digging his fingers in, he welcomes the pain.

His strokes start small and sharp. Just a little image. A splash of pain..

But soon, his hands are flinging out, starting low and finishing high. The rock grazes his palms as Jareth's movements become frantic. As the wall is transformed by his pain.

The fire is shades of black and red, like a bloody bruise. Dark. Bleak. Glinting with loneliness. His nails tear, his eyes sting, but he keeps going. All Jareth has to paint with are the ashes of everything he's lost.

He's a few feet down the wall when the need disappears as quickly as it came. Like always, the mural before him is wrong. It hasn't captured...the moment. In an instant, he hates it. He's glad it'll fade away, never to exist again.

Jamming his fingers through his hair, Jareth walks away, not glancing at what he created. He'll give school one more week. When Shandra visits next, she'll be back to her note taking.

And then he's not going to stop until he gets it right.

6

VERONICA

Whoa, what is this guy's deal?

W   Veronica watches from beside the thick trunk of
a large tree as this Tristan guy prepares to deck some poor
dude visiting a loved one's grave site. She snaps pictures,
awaiting the clearly inevitable fight. What a jerk he must be.

But he lets down his fists and the two talk for a moment.

Okay, so maybe he's not a total jerk. Just jumpy.

Her father was right about him, at least as far as this guy
is a problem case.

Tristan walks away, and Veronica waits for the appropriate time to follow.

But something stops her. The guy Tristan bumped into is
acting shady, looking all around as if making sure no one is
watching. So naturally, she hides further behind the very
helpful trunk. What's he up to?

He approaches the stone fence of the cemetery and all of
a sudden begins creating vibrant graffiti.

"What?" she jokingly asks herself as she switches to
recording on her phone. She's witnessing live vandalism and
this isn't even New York City!

Her eyes dart back and forth between the act itself and the image on her phone to make sure she's capturing it steadily. What was once columns of aged gray stone becomes a blazing fire. So real she can almost feel the heat.

And the pain behind it.

After a while, she forgets all about her phone and just stares as the masterpiece unfolds. She's completely mesmerized.

Huffing and panting, the guy steps back from his work. His raw emotion is tangible, radiating from the artwork he finished. It screams of sorrow and loss. How could this bright and beautiful fire make her feel so sad?

And then he does something she never expected.

He kicks the dirt, waves a dismissive hand at the fence and walks away, shoving his hands in his pockets. The look on his admittedly handsome face is all fury and disgust.

He doesn't like it. He created a masterpiece of street art, which she can greatly appreciate as a self-acclaimed street rat, and he doesn't like it.

Once he's out of sight, she runs to the fence and gawks at it up close. Every stroke is so perfect. Was he using spray paint? These look like brush strokes, but she didn't recall seeing neither a brush nor a can in his hands, let alone the amount she should have seen for all these vivid colors.

Veronica holds up her phone and plays the video back. The distance is too far for her to see clearly. Maybe he has some special airbrush preloaded with different colors? Either way, this is the most beautiful thing she's ever seen, and she got to watch it unfold.

She exits the video player and goes back to camera, ready to take pictures of each pillar.

Wait, wasn't this pillar covered a second ago?

She steps back and looks at the whole.

Before her eyes, the colors fade. She looks at one particular tongue of flame and it's vanishing right in front of her. How is this possible?

Anxiety closing in, she takes as many pictures as she can before the fence returns to its melancholy gray. A moment later, she stands in front of it, not a wink of color remaining.

Is there such a thing as disappearing paint? Is it one of those special paints that you can only see with a black light? Somehow, she doesn't think so; maybe thanks to years of going through her dad's alien conspiracy notes. But when she touches the stone, she feels nothing but cold roughness. Paint would leave a film, a texture she could recognize. It's as if there was never anything here, let alone a breathtaking spectacle.

Tristan Ayers is one thing, but her gut tells her this new guy is worth watching. She goes to the memorial he'd been standing at before he ran into Tristan.

Meredith and Jacob Stone. Died a few months ago. They must have been his parents. This was the pain and loss she felt in his work.

She needs to find out who this young Mister Stone is.

7

BRIELLE

The last training session was good, but Brielle knows she needs to do better. And, okay, it's not like she expected to become a black belt in one lesson, but time is literally running out! Skins could come at any moment, and she can't be the liability that gets Tristan killed. She needs to be able to handle herself so he can do his superman thing.

She arranged with Frank to pick her up from the Swiss bank/house Tristan inherited from Alden, and since Tristan left school early again—for whatever reason—she's taking the bus.

She sits at the bus stop, her only companion the pigeon that won't stop pecking at the empty Cheetos wrapper on the ground next to the garbage can. She stares blankly at the pigeon, the same question going through her mind since Tristan told her about the call from Alden's attorney.

Why didn't he leave anything to her?

Better yet, why didn't he adopt her?

Alden had all this money he acquired by trading gold—a cheap mineral on his planet that made up most of the electronics in his pod. He was able to buy a nice house and equip it with everything a Zodiac Guardian would need. He'd watched over her his entire life, thinking she was an Heir, and yet he never made contact, never tried to adopt her. Why?

Sure, the nuns of Grace Orphanage wouldn't have easily adopted her to a single male, let alone a lowly librarian with a missing eye and a questionable demeanor, but with his money, he could have at least tried. Why didn't he?

Or at the very least, why didn't he leave her his estate? Not that she questions Tristan is the better option, but according to Tristan, Alden had just found out about them that very day. And he left him everything?

Brielle isn't normally one to question her blessings. She loves, more than anything, that she finally has a family. A good family. One that loves and supports her. It's all she's ever wanted. But ever since Tristan told her the truth about Alden—that he'd been watching over her all her life and at least guessed what and who she was—she can't help but feel...rejected.

Oh, great. More guilt. But this time, it's her own, which makes it worse.

A stranger sits down at the edge of the bench next to her. He's a major upgrade to the pigeon, so she glances at him. A young guy with black hair, bangs in front of his face, shoulders hunched. She obliges the silent request to be unnoticed and turns away. She knows the value of being invisible, more than anyone else, so who is she to stomp all over his façade?

But try as she might, she can't ignore her new partner in public transportation. He keeps fiddling with a piece of paper, and the crinkling is so loud that she can no longer focus on her own thoughts.

She glances sidelong at him. He's staring at the crumpled slip of paper like it's the only thing in the world. And he keeps flipping it between his fingers, as if it's about to spontaneously combust and blow them both to kingdom come.

What the heck is he doing?

As she watches his quick finger movements, the crumpled piece of paper turns into a dollar bill.

Her eyes widen.

Did she just hallucinate?

She blinks several times. The object in his hands is still a dollar bill.

On her life as a Zodiac, that paper was not a monetary currency until just a second ago. It was trash. She's not crazy. Tristan and Alden proved that. She knows now to trust her eyes, and this stranger just turned a scrap into cash.

Before she can postulate further, the bus pulls into the stop, and the guy gets on, using his trash as passage.

With enlivened determination, Brielle leaps onto the bus, slides her pass, then finds a seat close to *him*.

Not right next to him. That would be weird. She has enough social skills to recognize that, especially in a bus that's mostly empty. But she sits adjacent behind him, the perfect spot to see if he transforms anything else.

She questions why she's so avidly watching him.

"How will I know?" she'd asked Tristan, when the topic of other heirs had come up repeatedly.

"Just look for any signs of things out of the ordinary," he'd said.

Well, if a guy turning paper into money isn't out of the ordinary, Brielle doesn't know what is.

She stares at him unblinkingly. Literally. Her eyes start to sting. But she doesn't want to miss anything he might do, even though all he's doing is sketch in a notepad.

The digital screen announcing the next stop dings, and the guy shuffles, gathering his things. Brielle's not about to miss a moment, even if this is two stops before hers.

She grabs her bag and follows him off the bus. But,

clumsy as she is, she trips over him as they get off, and his school papers scatter all over the pavement.

"I'm so sorry," she says as she helps him scrounge it all up into a cohesive pile.

"It's fine," he mumbles, scooping them up with her.

Brielle can't help but recognize her school's logo at the heading of most of his papers.

He's a student at Mirror Point High!

She arranges her stack into a neat pile and offers them back to him.

"Hey, um…" She has no idea how to do this. How does Tristan pull it off so seamlessly? "I noticed something…odd back there."

He accepts the stack and scowls at her.

"Um…I saw you change a piece of paper into a dollar bill," she finally spits out. "It's okay, I won't tell anyone, I just don't understand how you did it," she rushes to say.

He silently tucks his papers into his bag and starts to walk away, leaving Brielle bemused and totally lost.

He looks over his shoulder. "It's just a magic trick. I was practicing for a birthday party I'm hosting this weekend." He walks away down the sidewalk, not bothering to see what she has to say to that.

Brielle wants to follow.

But she can't think of a viable reason to. He gave her a proper excuse.

One she knows is a lie, thanks to her lie-detection superpower.

If she keeps following now, he'll think she's crazy.

Except she knows better. He just turned plain paper into cash, and he lied to her about it.

Did she just stumble across the next Zodiac Guardian?

8

TRISTAN

School feels like a total waste of time.

Especially when so much is at stake.

Now that Chardis is back.

Tristan yanks off his shirt, annoyed with the material sticking to his sweat-drenched body. He raises his fists, glaring at the wooden dummy in front of him like it has a face.

Like it's personal.

Zarius never let Tristan have one of these, no matter how much he begged. He'd always pointed out that a live sparring partner was far more effective. Then he'd grin and throw a punch. There was no time to point out that the rotating pole with wooden arms sticking out of it was great for so many things—correct angle of deflection, balance, accuracy, timing... Tristan would be blocking and counter attacking so fast there wasn't any chance to argue.

But he doesn't have a sparring partner anymore.

Which means the wooden contraption in front of him is all Tristan has. Dropping his shoulders, he pulls in a deep breath. The thick central trunk gleams under the lighting of the gym. The wooden arms jutting out at odd angles wait patiently. Tristan could've gotten the one with padding, but he didn't bother.

Skins don't have padding.

In a blink, Tristan goes from stationary to a flurry of movement. He strikes the first arm and the wooden dummy spins into action. The body of the contraption twists, the next arm flying toward him.

It slams into his forearm as he blocks it, his fist already aiming for the timber torso. A quick jab and he's deflecting the next strike that his momentum triggered. That's the beauty of the wooden dummy. It teaches you to execute blocks and strikes in concert with each other.

Parry. Counter. Each slam of wood against muscle is his cue to unleash the next strike.

Tristan develops a dizzying rhythm. He unleashes blow after blow. Strike after strike. To the head. The chest. The head again. His wooden assailant absorbs each one with a dull thud, rotating to throw the next unforgiving arm at him.

His knuckles smart with each hit. His forearms absorb the force of each block. It hurts, but that's a good thing. Tristan's strengthening his muscles. His bones. He won't always have his suit to protect him.

The doorbell chiming shocks Tristan out of his flow. He steps back, breathing heavily. The wooden dummy slows to a halt now that there's nothing to give the heavy body momentum.

For a moment, he considers ignoring the sound. There's still too much energy pounding through his body.

But a glance at the clock tells him he's been training longer than he realized.

And that Brielle's here.

Wiping his face with a towel, Tristan jogs through the house, grabbing a clean t-shirt from the laundry on his way through. With no bedroom, he has no wardrobe. He's yet to figure out why people bother with the middlemen that are closets. It's like making a bed knowing you're going to sleep it in that night. You're just going to wear the clothes again and they'll end up back in the laundry.

He's just pulling his shirt over his head when he opens the door. "Hey, I've programmed you into the system. Once we enter your fingerprint, you'll be able to just come through."

Brielle's eyes have popped wide open. "That's… ah…great."

Conscious that Brielle's cheeks have gone a little pink, he glances behind her. "Is everything okay?"

Brielle clears her throat. "You left school early again."

Tristan looks away. "I wanted to train."

Brielle enters but then stops. She waits till he's facing her again. "Would you have missed this much school…before?"

There's no way Tess would've let him skip classes unless it was something urgent. Something tangible like a Skin breathing down his neck.

Tristan heads down the hallway. "Things were different then."

He's halfway down when he realizes Brielle hasn't followed him. She clasps her hands, remaining beside the door. "I know this is hard, Tristan." She pauses. "But I'm worried about you."

Tristan's rooted to the ground. He wants to run the other way. Impossibly, he wants to take Brielle in his arms and collapse into the comfort she's offering.

Instead, he walks back toward her. He feels like his body's about to snap. "I learned some hard lessons that night, Brielle."

She nods, her eyes swimming with understanding.

Except the same night he lost his family, she gained one.

Tristan's hands clench, feeling hot. "I learned we're running out of time. We have to find the other Zodiacs."

Or others in this Universe will discover the loss he lives with.

"I think I can help."

Tristan bites back his denial. Brielle can't help him. Probably the only person who can is his soulmate.

"I saw a guy today. On the bus. He changed a piece of paper into a dollar bill."

This time, it's Tristan's eyes that widen. "What?"

Brielle's lips tip up. "Didn't you tell me you have great hearing?"

Grabbing Brielle's hand, he pulls her into the living room and sits them down. "Tell me everything."

She shrugs, but he can tell she's excited. "There's not much to tell. We were sitting at the bus stop. He was fiddling with a scrap of paper. When he got on, it was suddenly the dollar bill he used to pay for his fare."

Tristan frowns. He's spent most of his life reading too much into very little. Brielle's only just started to learn how much disappointment is involved in finding others like them. "It could've been a magic trick. A slight of hand."

"That's what he said. He said he was practicing for a kids birthday party this weekend."

Tristan stills. Brielle's power is the ability to sense lies. "And?"

"He wasn't telling the truth."

Tristan shoots to his feet, pacing the length of the room. "The lie could've been about why he was practicing. Who knows, maybe he's a con artist."

Brielle shrugs. "I don't think so. He was kinda...quiet."

"So, you spoke to him?"

"A little. I got off two stops early so I could."

Tristan's breathing is a little choppy. Another Zodiac Guardian... It feels too good to be true.

Something he hasn't felt in a while tingles in his chest.

Hope.

Sitting back down, he goes to grab Brielle's hands but stops himself. "What's his name? Where does he live? Did you get his number?"

Brielle's brow tenses. "I don't know. He didn't want to talk. He barely looked at me."

Tristan shoots to his feet again. He looks at Brielle in disbelief. "You didn't get his name?"

She draws back. "He wasn't exactly Mr. Talkative."

"He could be another Zodiac Guardian and you didn't even get his name?" Tristan has to work to keep his voice modulated.

This time, it's Brielle's turn to push to her feet. She clamps her hands on her hips. "He seems like a loner. He wouldn't have given me anything if I just struck up a conversation with him."

"He needs to know."

Doesn't Brielle realize? They need him.

She angles her head. "So you'll use the same strategy you did with me? Just blurt out words like princes and aliens and the fight to save the Universe?"

Tristan's mouth snaps shut.

Brielle was...different. He lost his cool. He was so sure she was—

He jams his hand through his hair. "Sorry. It's just really important that we find him."

"I know." Brielle's hands slip from her hips. "It's a good thing I figured out he goes to our school."

Tristan's hand drops in shock. "He goes to Mirror Point High?"

"Yep." Brielle smiles. "I think he might be new, I haven't seen him before."

Tristan's back to pacing. "Right. So, we'll keep an eye out for him. Then we'll talk to him."

"Maybe I should?"

"Why?"

"You don't have to do this alone, Tristan. We're a team." She shrugs one shoulder as her smile grows. "Plus, I'm less likely to scare him off."

Tristan's lips twist ruefully. "I was only like that with you."

Brielle blinks and Tristan turns away before she can ask any questions. He shouldn't have let that slip…

He steps toward the hallway. "I think your training will have to wait for today. I want to show you something."

Her face puzzled but curious, Brielle follows him. He stops in front of the bookcase. Reaching behind the photograph of Zarius and Tess, he glances over his shoulder. "Wait till you see this."

Brielle gasps as the bookcase slides away, exposing the hole in the wall.

She peers at the stairs leading down. "He has a secret room?"

"More like a secret floor." Tristan holds out his hand. "You could live down here for years."

Brielle takes it and Tristan ignores the jolt that spears up his arm. It could happen with any Zodiac Guardian for all he knows.

Leading her down the stairs, he watches her face as the headquarters—as he likes to call it—

light up.

"Wow," Brielle says breathlessly. "This is…"

"Like something out of a movie?"

Her gaze shoots to his. "Yes! That's exactly what I was going to say."

She releases his hand, entering with slow, measured steps. "Alden's been preparing for this for a long time."

Tristan heads to the desk he usually sits at. "It seems so. I'm still getting my head around all the technology." There's a good chance he might never know what some of the buttons on the panels do. "But I thought this could be helpful."

Taking a seat, he clicks the mouse and the screen comes to life. A few taps of the keyboard and he finds what he's looking for.

Brielle slides into the seat next to him. "Is that the Mirror Point High yearbooks?"

"Every one of them. There isn't a piece of information on this town that Alden didn't index."

Brielle's brows hike high. "Wow."

"I thought we could see if you recognized the guy in any of the photos."

Leaning forward as she stares at the screen, Brielle nods. "Good thinking."

They lose themselves in the maze of information Alden had on Mirror Point High. They scroll through photos, skim over school bulletins. But nothing has Brielle jumping up shouting *"That's him!"*

Brielle stares at the screen thoughtfully. "What about the orphanage?"

Tristan turns to her. "What about it?"

"Well, several other babies arrived when I did." Her cheeks pink. "They were all adopted."

Tristan's chest aches. It would've been heartbreaking to know everyone else was chosen.

And wonder why you weren't.

But he doubts Brielle will find any answers on the database. "Alden already thought of that," he says gently. "Despite the mountains of information he's managed to collect on the orphanage, he mustn't have found any leads."

Brielle's gaze flutters to the screen. "I'd still like to look at it."

Tristan nods, knowing she needs to do this. "Sure." He wheels his chair to the side. "Here, you drive."

Brielle shuffles forward, her gaze never leaving the screen. Chewing her lip, she starts sifting through the information.

Tristan sits back, watching her read through everything he's already checked out. Grace Orphanage is a converted nunnery. One of the oldest buildings in Mirror Point. It's been privately funded for the past fifteen years.

And that's where the trail ends. Adoption papers are highly confidential. Meaning the names of the children are impossible to find. And so are the people who took their humanoid bundle of joy home, clueless as to the baby's true origins.

Sometime later, Brielle's back sags as she leans away from the computer. For a little while there, Tristan wondered if she was going to climb in.

She sighs. "Nothing."

"Tess always said there's no such thing as a dead end. If you find nothing, then it just means that's one less path you need to explore."

"She sounds like a wise woman."

Tristan looks away. "She was."

Brielle's gasp has him spinning back. She's staring at the clock in the corner of the screen. "Is that the time?"

Tristan leans closer, confirming that it's later than he realized. "It's easy to lose track down here. No windows."

Brielle shoots to her feet, panicked. "I'm supposed to be home in ten minutes!"

She darts for the stairs, only to stop. The knowledge that

there's no way they can drive there in that time has her shoulders dropping.

She turns back to Tristan, biting her lip. "I didn't want to be late."

Tristan's seen how important Frank and Bea have become to Brielle. They're the family she's always wanted. She wouldn't want to be worrying them. Or letting them down.

He strides forward, grabbing her hand. "I have an idea."

His heart rate picks up as they climb the steps. Leading Brielle to the back of the house, he takes the next flight of stairs there.

"Where are we going?"

"I have something else I want to show you."

"I really don't have time for this, Tristan."

But Tristan ignores her. A part of him has been wanting to do this from the moment he learned about their suits.

There's a hallway on the second floor, and Tristan walks to the door at the end. He opens it, revealing another set of stairs. "We're almost there."

These steps are steeper than the others, going straight up. The door at the top is a heavy metal one, but a quick swipe of his thumb and it swings open.

Pulling Brielle behind him, he steps onto the rooftop.

The blackness that swallows them tells Tristan the clock didn't lie. They were in there for hours and it's now evening. The dark below is punctured with the twinkling of houses and streetlights. He's always found it peaceful up here. He points in a southerly direction. "Your parents' house is that way."

"It's a lovely view, but that's not going to help me get home."

"I know. And you need to be there in about seven minutes." Tristan grins. "That's why I thought we'd fly."

Brielle freezes. "You what?"

"You want me to shout it?"

Her eyes widen. "Fly?"

"It's dark. You need to be somewhere ASAP." His grin grows, excitement tingling along his spine. "And I've been practicing."

Every night. Under the cover of darkness. When he can't sleep.

Brielle turns to look out over the glittering lights. "We couldn't…"

Tristan slips in close. "We didn't do any training today. And you need to learn how to use your suit."

She turns to him, apprehension and anticipation swirling in her green eyes. "It's too risky."

"We can't afford for you not to know how to do this, Brielle."

It could be her only way of escape if she's surrounded by Skins.

"And now you only have six minutes," Tristan points out.

Brielle's answer is to lift her hand and grip her stone. "If I crash into any trees or powerlines, you're going to explain it to my parents."

With a chuckle, Tristan wraps his fingers around his tanzanite. They'll be flying high above either of those.

They say the word almost simultaneously. "Akash."

The suit envelops him, now a familiar and welcome feeling. He hasn't had a chance to blink before the flexible armor has become his second skin. Tristan flexes his shoulders, feeling the tensile strength. If only he could wear this all the time. With the suit on, he feels strong. Powerful.

Confident they stand a chance.

He notices Brielle looking down at her arms, clenching and unclenching her hands.

"They're pretty cool, huh?"

"They really are," she breathes, the sound right beside

Tristan's ear. Her head angles up, her eye hidden by the reflective shield across her face. "So, how do we do this?"

"Well," Tristan says with amusement. "I've discovered how you don't do it."

Doing the superman just had him glad it was dark as he stood on the rooftop, his fist pointed to the sky, looking like a fool.

And Peter Pan's theory of thinking happy thoughts just lifted his spirits…only for them to come crashing back down when he remembered those who made him happy are now gone.

Tristan steps forward, grasping Brielle's hand. Even through the suit he can feel the warmth of her palm. "Essentially, you jump."

"That's it?" Brielle sounds as disbelieving as she should.

"Yep. Jump, without the intention of coming back down."

Brielle angles her head at the edge of the building. "You do know we're two stories up."

Tristan hesitates. He certainly had a few false starts. And several tumbled falls to the ground below. He knows how to roll and absorb the impact. Brielle doesn't.

"Let's do it together, then," he suggests.

Brielle nods and Tristan can imagine her chewing on her lip again.

Releasing her hand, he steps behind her. Drawing her close, his eyes widen as her back molds to his front.

Her gasp is almost silent, but it's undeniable through their audio link.

Tristan just realized why this is a bad idea.

Full. Body. Contact.

And it's not going to end any time soon.

Swallowing, Tristan ignores the spike in his pulse. And the desire to draw her even closer. "Hold on."

A slight flex of his legs and they've pushed off the roof. This time, Brielle's gasp spears through him.

An arch of his back and they're shooting up to the sky.

Brielle's hands grip his arms and Tristan instinctively tightens them around her waist. Holding her tightly, he angles them forward.

And just like that, they're flying.

Except it's nothing like the few times he's soared above Alden's house. This time, he's not alone.

"Oh, Tristan…"

Brielle's voice is full of wonder as the houses below become little more than glitter. The night sky envelops them, warm and welcoming. There's nothing but the sound of the wind, their excited breaths.

They're slicing through the air, so close it's as if they're one person…and it's the most effortless thing he's ever done.

"I know," he murmurs huskily.

Brielle points out their high school. Creamy Dreams. Grace Orphanage. Each time her hands dart back to weave through his, holding him tightly.

A smile spreading across his face, Tristan can't help himself. A slight dip of his shoulder and they snap into a roll. The world spins, light black light black. Brielle's gasp morphs into delighted laughter. Her arms are holding his so tightly, it would hurt if it wasn't for his suit.

It's over in a few minutes. The streets and houses of Mirror Point fade away as they fly toward the Pierces' house. Tristan slows as they reach the end of the driveway, knowing they can't exactly land on the porch.

Their feet touch solid ground, and Tristan already wishes it wasn't over. He knows without a doubt that he'll remember this forever.

Clearing his throat, he steps back. "Home, safe and sound and right on time."

Brielle doesn't move. Tristan's glad he can't see her face. If she's as moved by this experience as he is, it's the last thing he needs to know.

She glances at her house in the distance. The windows glow with warm light, waiting for her. Welcoming her.

While Tristan will be returning to his lonely fortress.

He takes another step back. They're not soulmates and he has to stop looking for that connection with Brielle, no matter how much his heart is hurting. "I'll see you at school tomorrow."

Looks like he might actually spend the full day, this time.

"Okay," Brielle says quietly. In a flash, her suit disappears back into her stone. She lifts her hand only to let it drop again. "We'll talk to that guy. And even if he's not a Guardian, we'll find the others."

Tristan turns away. Contracting down, he launches into the sky.

They don't have a choice. They have to find the other Guardians.

Just like they have to find his Gemini Twin.

9

JARETH

Mirror Point was supposed to be a fresh start.

Somewhere Jareth wasn't the boy who lost his parents in a tragic house fire. The place where the friends he made would be able to look him in the eye and not stumble over their words, unsure of what to say. And the constant looking over his shoulder was supposed to stop.

But as he leans against the stand of lockers, the shadows cool and comfortable around him, Jareth realizes he was wrong.

Here, no one sees him, period. The invisibility he craves is his. And yet, the painting hasn't stopped.

If anything, it's happening more.

Kids mill about, making their way to the cafeteria for lunch. They all blur, a palette of smiles and shouts and too much perfume or aftershave.

His mother's voice slips through his mind. "Life is all about the little things, Jareth."

And she lived by that motto, too.

Every morning, his father would take a brisk walk around the neighbourhood before breakfast. He said it was centering. Each day, he'd bring back something for Jareth's mother. A smooth rock. A fallen leaf. His favorite were the daisies that grew along road verges.

They were also his mother's.

She'd smile with delight, as if it's the first time he'd brought her one. Taking the furry stalk and stroking the milky petals, she'd marvel at the fuzzy, butter-colored center. She'd tuck it behind her ear like it was precious, and not the weed most people considered it to be.

"Daisies are one of the most complex flowers in the world," she'd say. "This one flower is actually several clustered together. Every one of those cute dots is a little yellow blossom." She'd beam. "A hundred flowers in one. Isn't that beautiful?"

Except Jareth won't be in Mirror Point long enough to appreciate any of its intricacies. Coming here was a mistake.

His jaw clenches, glad to see the corridor is slowly emptying. Once everyone's gone, he'll go outside to eat. Then, he'll wait for the bell to ring, get the last two classes over and done with and go home.

Only a few more days.

Shandra is back on Friday. Jareth will leave on Saturday. Coming here has achieved nothing.

A *bang* has Jareth gripping the lockers beside him and scanning frantically, ready to run. It takes several panicked seconds for him to realize a girl dropped her books at the other end of the corridor.

That there's no danger.

Jareth sags against the wall. The whispers and stares he could live with back in California.

The permanent state of fear was something he was hoping to escape.

Social Services had requested he see a counsellor after the fire. More like mentioned repeatedly. More like made an appointment for him then arrived at his house so they could drive him there.

He'd told the kind-faced man everything. The unforgettable scent of three lives going up in smoke. The way fire singed everything, right down to the eyeballs. His mother's screams. His father trying to shout over the roar of the flames to get the hell out.

Trying to save them.

The endless questions from the cops because the cause of the fire was inconclusive: Do either of your parents smoke? Is there anyone who can vouch that you were in bed, asleep? Have you ever liked playing with matches?

Jareth glances around again, his skin prickling. He'd told the men in suits just like he told the counsellor. There was someone in the house. Someone trying to escape the inferno just like they were.

Then there were more questions. What did this person look like? Was it anyone you know? Did your parents have any enemies?

Jareth could only answer the last question. Everyone loved his free-spirited mother and compassionate, grounded father. Of course they didn't have any enemies.

"And this intruder?" they'd asked.

The counsellor was the last person Jareth told the truth to. He didn't see the man. Only the eddies of smoke as he moved. His shadow splashed across the bubbling paint.

And then he felt the exploding pain at the back of his head before everything went black.

The counsellor had nodded, his eyes filled with sympathy. He'd said things like "that must've been extremely difficult," and "grief is normal after the loss you've experienced."

Jareth saw his report. His social worker had left it on her desk as she ran off to deal with a commotion in reception.

Jareth is a sweet, sensitive young man who has experienced a significant trauma...

He'd skimmed most of it. Somehow, it'd felt like he was intruding. That even though the report was about him, it was too personal to be read. It was too little...far too simple to reduce the death of his parents to a typed few pages. And yet, it was too much...

He'd had to stop himself from crushing the sheets of paper. He'd been about to put them back when other words had caught his attention.

Hypervigilance.

An overactive imagination.

Ongoing support is encouraged to address Jareth's persistent anxiety. There are times he appears to believe he's still being watched. Without appropriate intervention, Jareth's anxious thoughts could develop into more significant mental health issues, such as paranoia.

Jareth never went back again.

But even a new house, a new school in California hadn't been enough to escape the memories. The *significant trauma.* The belief he was being watched.

And it seems Mirror Point wasn't enough either.

Jareth's about to push off the wall when a door at the other end of the hallway swings open. He freezes, shrinking back into the shadows. His eyes widen when he sees the two teens who step through. It's the guy from the cemetery. And the girl from the bus stop.

Jareth pushes back, barely breathing as he tries to become one with the wall. The guy and the girl stop, chatting. There's an intensity between them as they talk. The guy gestures with his hands. The girl nods as she points to the doors that will take them outside.

The doors Jareth wanted to disappear through.

The guy's shoulders droop as he agrees. Jareth watches

through the bangs that have flopped over his eyes as they push the doors open. He holds his breath, willing them to leave. They're the last people he wants to run into.

The guy's swallowed by the sunshine outside and Jareth's already plotting an alternative escape route. There's another exit at the other end of the building, past the science labs. The popular kids hang out not far from there, but it'll have to do. Besides, he's found that as long as he doesn't acknowledge they exist, they do the same with him.

The girl follows the guy as he holds the door open for her without looking back. He seems preoccupied with scanning outside as if he, too, would have the question of paranoia hanging over his head.

The door's about to swing shut when Jareth makes his move. The need to be out of here is overwhelming. Skimming over the wall, he slips around the corner. He doesn't glance back as he strides down the hall. He needs to be even more invisible than he has been.

He shouldn't have painted the wall at the cemetery. He's lucky no one saw him.

And he sure as hell shouldn't have used that scrap of paper to pay for his bus fare. Spending time at his parents' memorial had unsettled him.

All the more reason to leave Mirror Point as soon as he can.

Spinning on his heel, Jareth strides for the door that will take him outside. He'll find some more shadows to blend into.

And in a few days, this place will be nothing but a mistake.

BRIELLE

"Wait." Brielle interrupts Tristan's defense of Cassandra's latest snotty comment by putting her flattened hand in the air between them.

He seems taken aback. "Look, I know you two have history—"

"No, it's not about her." Brielle rolls her eyes, then points to the guy who's quickly walking across the hall in the opposite direction. She lowers her voice to little more than a whisper. "Look. That's the guy from the bus stop."

Tristan follows her finger to the student with black bangs skimming the wall of lockers like he's a chameleon and can blend into them.

"*That's* the guy you saw doing magic tricks?" Tristan asks, and Brielle doesn't miss the flash of recognition in his eyes.

"You know him?"

"Not exactly." Tristan shrugs uncomfortably. "We kinda ran into each other at the cemetery the other day."

"Oh." She doesn't want to pry any further. She's learned that Tristan likes to keep his feelings to himself. "Come on, let's follow him." She tips her head in his direction and starts walking, and Tristan follows.

The guy heads to the back of the building, toward the science labs. It's lunch time, why is he going that way? Cassandra's clique owns the yard behind the labs. Brielle is pretty sure he's not one of them.

He pushes through the doors into the open sunshine, then shoves his hands back into his pockets as he treks over the grass. Brielle and Tristan exit the doors a safe distance behind him, pretending to stroll as they watch him curve around the main building toward the back of the school where the cafeteria loading dock is.

What is he doing?

Brielle and Tristan exchange curious glances as they scale the wall to the edge and peek around the corner. The new guy paces up and down the dock, his steps turning into stomps. Then he grunts and turns furious hands on the empty wall along which he's all but trod a trail into the cement.

Brilliant color flies onto the stucco.

"He's a graffiti artist?" Tristan whispers, obvious disappointment at the new guy's less than nefarious behavior in his voice.

But the longer they watch, they see that it's not gang symbols or slang words or even pop art that he's spraying. A scene of vivid fire and dark ash comes to life before them. And it's beautiful in a way that's haunting. Brielle can almost see his tortured soul, as if it's burning in the flames he's painting.

Despite her wonder at his skill, she senses something about this scene is not normal. She stares at him, trying to determine what it is that's wrong.

"He's not using spray paint," Tristan all but growls like a wolf who's caught a scent.

Brielle squints at the new guy's hands and sure enough, they're empty. There's no tool in them that's applying the colors onto the wall, no spray cans, no palettes to create the vivid masterpiece. In fact, the colors appear to be coming right out of his fingertips. It's not possible, and yet it's definitely happening.

Tristan pushes off the wall and passes Brielle, but she grabs his arm. "What are you doing?"

"I'm going to talk to him," he says, jaw set with determination.

"I'm not sure that's such a good idea," she says. "Let me do it. Remember how 'the talk' went with me?"

"That won't happen this time," he argue-whispers back.

"How do you know?" she asks, making sure to keep her voice hushed.

"Because you were different." Then his expression falls and his face turns into stone. He looks away.

Good. So he can't see her heart breaking even further. She takes a deep breath. "Let me try. If I mess up, you can go."

He crosses his arms and, without meeting her eyes, nods.

She rounds the corner and tries to appear as casual as possible as she approaches the new guy.

"Wow, that's beautiful," she says.

He drops his arms and slowly looks over his shoulders, which are rapidly rising and falling with his quickened breaths. In this moment, with his black hair messily hanging over one eye, he looks more like an impassioned symphony conductor than a delinquent street artist.

"Are you following me?" he accuses.

Yes. She can't lie, but she can't admit it either or he'll run off. Evasion is always a good loophole around her curse—er —power; it's hard to start thinking of it that way.

"Look, I just recognized you from the bus when I saw you

in the hall and thought I'd introduce myself. I'm Brielle." She smiles and extends a hand.

He remains still, eyes locked on her face and ignoring her hand.

She frowns, closes her hand and withdraws it. "I just wanted you to know that I think your art is amazing. And I won't tell anyone about it, so you don't have to worry about me ratting you out."

He snorts a laugh and shakes his head.

What the heck does that mean? He's not worried about getting in trouble? Or is he making fun of her?

She shrugs off the obvious hostility he's throwing her way and steps closer, admiring the wall. "What does it mean?"

"Why do you care?" He shoots a glare at her.

"Can't someone genuinely be interested in you and what you have to say?" she retorts.

"I already have a counsellor for that." He picks up his bag off the ground and slings it over his shoulder, then starts to walk away.

She runs after him. "I'm not offering to give you therapy, I'm offering friendship."

"I won't be here long enough to need it, but thanks anyway." The period at the end of his sentence is loud and final, making her stop her pursuit and let him go.

She stands alone in the middle of the lawn, unsure of her next move, when a trickle of snickers sounds beside one of the lab buildings.

"Chasing another guy away, huh, Brielle?"

Not now.

Brielle rolls her eyes, trying to telepathically convince Cassandra to stop coming closer. Unfortunately, mind control is not the power Brielle was given.

Cassandra circles Brielle, then juts a hip and looks down

her nose at her. "Does Tristan know you're failing miserably at stepping out on him?"

"I'm not stepping out on him. He and I are just…friends." The word stings as it springs off her tongue.

"Really? With how much time you two spend together, I thought for sure you were together." Cassandra's eyes narrow in a tight smile. "Ah, I understand. You want to be more than friends and he doesn't. So you follow him around like a lovesick puppy. How pathetic."

Rage boils in Brielle's chest. "Shut up, Cassandra," she grumbles.

"And you think you can make him jealous by hooking up with the new hottie, but he rejected you, too," Cassandra continues. "When are you going to figure it out, Brielle? You're an orphan for a reason. No one wants you. Not your parents, not the new guy, and not Tristan."

Fury consumes Brielle, and it's so blinding she doesn't notice her hand lifting to slap Cassandra.

"That's enough, Cassandra," Tristan barks as he comes up beside Brielle and stops her hand before it can lift past her waist.

The blond lioness darts her golden eyes at Tristan, clearly unaware that Brielle was about to retaliate.

Brielle struggles to slow her breathing and quell her anger as the desire to do more than slap Cassandra throbs with every pulse in her veins. A coolness radiates from Tristan's hand on her wrist, calming, lowering her blood pressure. She both loves and hates his effect on her.

"Whatever." Cassandra flips her hair over her shoulder and spins on her heel, sashaying back toward her cronies leaning against the lab as they pretend not to have seen anything.

Tristan rounds Brielle to face her. "Don't listen to her. You know nothing she said is true. Your parents wanted you very much, and so do your new parents. And I..." He falters and his face twists in frustration.

"It's okay," she says, tasting the lie, so she stops there before she has to lie any further. "Let's just go back inside. I think lunch break is almost over, anyway. We'll catch the guy some other time."

He says nothing more as they mosey back toward the main building. She's glad he doesn't. Because Cassandra had it right in her own bitchy way. Brielle does wish she and Tristan were more than friends. A lot. It would have been almost better if he'd rejected her. But he didn't. Fate did the rejecting for him. She's not good enough to be his soulmate, his other Gemini, and that's so much worse.

VERONICA

Veronica sticks to the shadows of a small building and watches as Brielle and Tristan head back into the school after the blonde vixen's verbal assault.

Maybe Brielle isn't the bad guy here—or girl, for that matter. Villains aren't typically bullied by mean girls. Veronica would be more willing to believe that the blonde is the person of interest over Brielle, with whom she can't help but feel a sort of comradery. Veronica is often teased by girls like the blonde, but she doesn't take it like Brielle did; she usually fights back. At least the suspension has meant she's able to sneak over to Mirror Point High.

Once Brielle and Tristan are back inside, and the popular jerks have turned their attention back on themselves as is their MO, Veronica skitters across the lawn to take a look at the wall her person-of-interest painted.

The image is already fading. Unwilling to waste any more time and miss it altogether, she pulls out her phone and snaps more pictures. It's not long before the wall returns to its original cream-colored stucco. Veronica sighs and looks through the pictures in her phone. This painting is different to the one in the cemetery. The flames lick higher, the smoke is thicker and darker. But the style is clearly the same, just as beautiful, and inspiring the same emotions. This guy is a real man of mystery. She finds herself wanting to know more about him, and not just because of his strange disappearing art.

But why do Tristan and Brielle have an interest in him? They clearly followed him out here, and when Brielle spoke to him, Veronica was too far away to overhear what they were talking about. Whatever it was, he didn't bite.

Is the suspect duo interested in him just because of his vanishing graffiti? Could that possibly have anything to do with aliens? These fiery scenes, while haunting and mysterious, don't scream "alien" to her. What's she missing?

The first lunch bell rings, and the students all herd into the main building. Veronica waits until the lawn is completely clear and quiet after the final bell rings before she runs into the school. Although she doesn't attend Mirror Point High, the halls are empty with all the classes in session, giving her free reign to search for the administration office.

She scans the labels on the doors as she wanders, then finally finds the main office at the end of the west corner. Good. Now that she's found it, how is she going to get past the secretary and the principal to get to the student records?

Veronica chews on her bottom lip as she ponders, until an idea strikes. She remembers seeing a red Mercedes-Benz parked in the spot labeled "Principal" in the parking lot when she first arrived. That being her favorite car, she was questioning how a school principal could afford such a thing.

She pulls out her phone, Googles the school's main phone number and calls it. It rings once before the secretary answers. "You've reached the Mirror Point High Administration Office. How can I help you?"

Veronica deepens her voice and says, "This is Officer

Hershey of the Mirror Point Police Department. We've found a red Mercedes-Benz on fire in the alley behind Creamy Dreams and traced the plates back to the principal. We'll need him to come down to the station for questioning."

"Oh my goodness!" the secretary shrieks. "He loves that car! I'll let him know right away."

"Thank you, ma'am." Veronica hangs up and watches through the thin rectangular window of the door as the secretary rushes to the principal's office and tells him the news. Like a rocket, the balding principal shoots out of his office and toward the main office door.

Veronica squeezes flat against the wall behind the door as the two school officials sprint out to the parking lot. She knows it won't be long before they realize the call was a hoax, but it should be long enough to accomplish her goal.

As soon as they're out of sight, she runs into the office and goes straight to the filing cabinet labeled "Student Files". She scans down the drawers: A-H, I-P, Q-Z. She opens the bottom one and flips through folders until she sees the name Stone, the same surname on the memorial.

"Hello there, Jareth," she whispers after internalizing his first name.

As quickly as she can, she pulls it out and skims over the couple of pages inside. What she reads breaks her heart. His parents died in a house fire last year that he barely escaped. That's why his paintings are so full of pain and loss. Poor guy. She knows what it feels like to lose a parent, but to lose both? With no other relatives to care for him, Jareth has opted to try living alone as an emancipated minor. How awful it must be to have no one, to be completely alone.

The shouting of voices down the hall has her snapping the file shut reflexively. She shoves it back into the cabinet, closes the drawer and dashes out of the office just as the two officials approach the open door.

They all stop and look at each other for a moment. Before either of the adults can begin to speculate about her presence, Veronica puts her hand to her belly and says, "I'm looking for the Nurse's Office?"

The irritated principal shakes his head and barks, "Across the hall," pointing to the appropriate door.

"Thank you," Veronica says in a forced shaky voice before rushing away.

She looks back to see the two go into the office and loudly close the door behind them. That was close.

Still looking over her shoulder, she collides into a large body.

"Sorry," she and a familiar voice say at the same time. She looks up to see that she's bumped into none other than Jareth Stone.

Dark eyes look at her through a curtain of jet black bangs, and she's taken aback by how handsome he is up close. She didn't expect him to be handsome.

"If you're looking for the Nurse's Office, it's right there," she says, pointing.

"Actually, I'm headed to the Principal's Office." He nods his head begrudgingly in that direction.

"Well, brace yourself because I just came from there and he's not happy," she says with a laugh.

The shield of hostility he'd been wearing on his face wavers, and the corners of his lips tip upward. "You're doing, I take it?"

She shrugs coolly. "Maybe."

His lips curl into a full blown smile. "Thanks for priming him for me, I guess. As if getting in trouble for refusing to read in front of the class wasn't ridiculous enough." He scoffs and rolls his eyes.

"No one wants to read in front of the class, but why did you refuse?" she asks, unable to keep her eyes from wandering over the broad shoulders that hide under his baggy rock band t-shirt.

"We were reading Frankenstein and I hate the part where the monster gets burned," he says, still wearing the playful smile even as a spark ignites in his dark eyes.

Feigning ignorance and speaking over the lump of pity in her throat, she asks with the same mildly flirtatious tone, "Not his fault he's a monster. He didn't ask the good doctor to create him."

He flicks his black bangs backward, revealing more of his kissable face. "I like the way you think."

She smiles. "I'm Veronica. Do you also have a name or should I just refer to you as Trouble Maker?"

He chuckles. "Jareth."

"Mr. Stone," the principal barks, hanging out of the office door, glaring at him.

"Good luck, Jareth." Veronica waves her fingers coyly, inviting him to heed the principal's call.

He smiles, and she watches as he follows the principal into the office, appreciating the way his tight skater jeans hug his butt.

"I'll definitely be seeing more of you, Jareth Stone," she whispers to herself, then leaves the school.

12

TRISTAN

"You didn't even get his name?"

Tristan hoists his backpack further up his shoulder, gripping the strap like he wants to strangle it.

They're standing beneath a tree outside the school, watching as students pour out the front door after the last bell. The minute it had rung, Tristan had rushed out of Geography, raced to Brielle's History class and grabbed her hand. They were standing out here in two minutes, flat.

Watching and waiting.

Brielle crosses her arms. "He doesn't want to talk, Tristan."

"Well, he needs to. You saw what he was doing."

Painting without paint. If the dude's not a Zodiac Guardian, then he should patent whatever technology he had up his sleeve, because it was damned impressive.

"You want to have the talk with him, don't you?" Brielle asks, although her tone tells Tristan she already knows the answer.

"We need to know. Chardis losing Adalind will only be a minor setback."

Tristan keeps his eyes on the doors as more students walk out, the spring of freedom in their step now that school's over. None of them have the dark hair and hunched shoulders of the new guy.

He wipes his hand down his face. They don't even know his name.

"We have to tread carefully with him," Brielle warns in a quiet tone. "It's like he doesn't want anyone near him."

Tristan sighs. They don't have time for this. "What did he say?"

"That he's not looking for friends." Her eyes widen. "And that he won't be around long enough to need them."

Tristan curses. "He just got here and he's already leaving?"

Which only increases the urgency. Tension is weaving its way through every muscle in Tristan's body. His center of gravity shifts forward onto the balls of his feet.

"What are you going to do? Pounce on him?" Brielle asks wryly.

The edginess whooshes out with a huff. They've been training enough that Brielle can recognize when he's winding up for something. He slides a crooked smile her way. "If need be."

Brielle's face softens. "I know this is important. But we have to be gentle. This guy is skittish for some reason."

Not quite believing the words that are forming on his tongue, Tristan shakes his head. "You get one more chance. After that, I go in."

Brielle rolls her eyes. "It's not a bank heist."

The students coming out of the front doors of the school have reduced to a trickle. Tristan frowns. A guy incongruously wearing a suit jacket with shorts drops his book as he reaches the front step. Picking it up with a quick glance to see whether anyone saw him, he hunches down as he scuttles away.

The doors remain open. And empty.

"That's the last of them," Tristan mutters. "Dammit. He didn't come out the front doors."

Brielle's brow scrunches thoughtfully. "Now that I think about it, that makes sense. He avoids crowds."

Patience. Zarius's deep voice slides through Tristan's mind.

Yeah, well. Even Zarius didn't have to do this alone. He had Tess.

The cheery honk of a car horn has them both spinning around. Brielle's parents' car is in the parking lot, Bea waving from the driver's seat.

Brielle smiles. "Sorry I can't make training tonight."

Tristan shakes his head. He'd never interfere with Brielle's family time...even though it stings to know she's going home to a house that doesn't echo with loneliness. "Tuesday is family dinner night. I get it."

Brielle presses a hand on his arm and Tristan grits his teeth at the contact. Warmth shoots from that one point of skin on skin and spears straight to his chest. Warming it. Soothing it.

"You sure you don't want to join us?"

He wrinkles his nose, his eyes twinkling. "I've tasted your cooking, remember?"

Brielle's hand slides away as she shakes her head with a smile. Tristan instantly misses the contact and is relieved all at once.

"And here I was going to bring you some of the pecan pie we're making for dessert to school tomorrow."

"Well, if Bea and Frank don't have food poisoning tomorrow morning," he teases. "Count me in."

With a quick mock frown his way, Brielle dashes off to join Bea. Tristan watches as they chat, glancing at him. Brielle shakes her head and Bea nods with understanding, as if they've had this conversation before. With a smile and a wave, they drive off.

Once they confirmed that Tristan is still being a hermit, Bea would've asked Brielle about her day. They'll probably talk about what assignments are coming up, what they'll be cooking for dinner. Whose turn it is to set the table.

Tristan turns away. They'd set the table together.

As he starts the walk home, he acknowledges he's glad they're such a good match. Alden probably spent a long time trying to find the right parents for Brielle. And he did good.

Tristan's just taken the first corner when the hairs on the back of his neck prickle. He stops, kneeling down as he ties his already tied shoelaces. A surreptitious look over his shoulder confirms what he thought.

He's being followed. Again.

And it's the same car as last time—an unobtrusive, gray sedan. A single male in the driver's seat. Wearing a hoodie.

Standing, Tristan knows the trick he used last time won't work again. If he takes an alley, the guy's going to get suspicious. And Tristan isn't looking for a fight.

Not yet.

Ambling like he has all the time in the world, Tristan heads down the block. As he sees the sign for Creamy Dreams, he gets an idea. He's just about to enter when he sees a slip of cardboard has been taped to the front door, two words scrawled in black marker pen.

Help wanted.

Even better.

Inside, Tristan pretends to take time scanning the brightly lit menu. He must admit, the Razzle Dazzle Pomegranate does sound kind of good... At the same time, what is Moon Pie flavor? How is that even a thing?

An older woman steps up, razzle dazzling Tristan all over again with her lime green top and bright orange cap. The moment she sees Tristan, her eyes sweep him from head to toe. "Welcome to Creamy Dreams," she practically purrs. "Which frozen delight would you like to order?"

Tristan suddenly wonders whether he should've just faced the assassin. "Actually, I'd like to apply for the job."

The woman's smile dials up, her perky, bleached ponytail swinging with delight. "Of course. Great timing! Theo—the boss—is out the back." With a quick eyebrow wriggle, she spins around to the door behind her. "I'll be back in a sec, hon."

Once she's gone, Tristan jams his hands into his pockets as he leans against the counter, casually looking around. A fleeting glance out the large front window shows the gray sedan parked out the front.

The door swings open and the woman sashays through like she's entering a runway. "It's your lucky day," she purrs. "He said to come on through."

She lifts a section of counter and Tristan smiles at her as he slips past. "Thanks"—he glances at her name tag—"Madge."

"Anytime, hon. And don't let him scare you. He's a pussycat."

As the door whooshes closed behind him, Tristan wonders what that's supposed to mean. There's someone scarier here than Madge?

The back area of Creamy Dreams is just as Tristan expected it to be. Cramped and full of stainless steel counters and shelves. A quick scan shows him what he was looking for —the back door.

Another door opens on the left of the room, a mist of cool air flowing out. A man lumbers out, wiping his hands as it slams shut behind him.

This is the pussycat?

Theo is Italian and fat and hairy, although not necessarily in that order. He glares at Tristan. "You wanna the job?"

Hell no. Tristan grins at him. "I'd like to enquire about it. How many hours a week are you needing?"

Theo's thick brows shoot up. "You bringa your resume?"

Tristan shrugs. "I've never had a job, so there didn't seem much point."

The two furry caterpillars dive back down. "No resume?"

"I thought I'd ask some questions first. I can't work most weekdays and am only free on Sundays, so I wanted to check what shifts were available." Tristan smiles. "And does your staff discount include the diary free range? I'm lactose intolerant."

Theo's eyebrows do another leap across his forehead, but this time, they come down and stay down. "You is wasting my time, boy." He waves his hand at Tristan, turning away. "Get outta here."

Tristan nods. "You're right. I don't think this is going to be a good fit for me."

Theo's too busy shaking his head muttering something about "kidsa these days," so he doesn't notice that Tristan walks toward him rather than back out the door.

Tristan smiles politely as he tries to slip past. "Excuse me."

Theo looks up, his thick lips slack with shock as Tristan squeezes through the gap between the man's belly and the stainless steel counter.

With a jaunty wave over his shoulder, Tristan leaves via the back door.

Once he's outside, he shakes his head ruefully. "I should've just faced the Skin," he mutters to himself.

Breaking into a jog, Tristan heads down the alleyway he finds himself in. He wonders how long the Skin will sit out the front before he realizes Tristan's gone. He almost wishes he was there to see his face when he realizes he's lost his mark again.

Avoiding the main streets, Tristan makes his way back to Alden's. There's no way he wants to have gone through Madge and Theo only to still run into the Skin.

Once he's home, Tristan heads straight for the downstairs rooms. Being followed for the second time has only reinforced what Brielle doesn't seem to understand.

Chardis isn't waiting.

He isn't planning or scheming.

Chardis is coming.

Inside HQ, Tristan walks to the cupboards that line the far wall. Stocked with canned food and bottles of water, it's a prepper's dream. But baked beans aren't what he's after.

The final cupboard, the one closest to the wall, has a sensor like many of the doors in this house do. Pressing his thumb against it, it clicks open.

Inside, he pulls out a sleek black box. His heart thudding like it always does when he's near the Zodiac stones, Tristan lifts the lid.

Five gems sit nestled inside. Each waiting to be reunited with its heir.

Including the tanzanite sitting in the center, waiting for its twin.

Picking up the black onyx, Tristan holds it up to the light. It glints dully with obsidian fire.

Capricorn. Zarius's voice would always take on a hushed note when he listed the Zodiacs and their powers. *The power of imagination.*

Gripping the onyx in his hand, Tristan stares at his clenched fist.

Brielle has one more chance to talk to this guy.

After that, Tristan won't be waiting.

13

JARETH

J areth skips school the next day. As he was coating the walls of his house in flames the night before, he'd real-ized that if he's leaving, then there's no point in attending.

Shandra can threaten extra services and foster care all she likes, but none of that will matter if Jareth's not staying.

The need for food is what finally draws him out of the house. There are only so many peanut butter sandwiches a guy can eat. Especially when the bread starts growing furry little islands the color of puke.

He's just got off the bus at the main street, thinking he might get himself a fro-yo at the local place when he freezes. He hadn't noticed the time. School must've finished.

Surely he can't be that unlucky.

A girl has just turned the corner ahead. The same girl who's approached him twice, now. Brielle.

Jareth spins on his heel, hunching his shoulders up as he lengthens his stride. No amount of fro-yo is worth having to talk to someone.

"Hey!"

Jareth hunches down even further as he hears her call out. Please let her be talking to someone else.

But then light footsteps approach behind him. Jareth spins around, glaring at her. "I don't have time for this."

Brielle pauses, one eyebrow hitching a little. "Really? Where are you off to?"

Not willing to admit that was a lie, Jareth's arms explode out wide. "Why won't you leave me alone?"

Brielle opens her mouth only to close it. Glancing over her shoulder, Jareth is shocked when she takes his hand and pulls him into an alleyway. She steps back, giving him some space, although she holds his gaze as she speaks. "Because I have special abilities, too."

Jareth freezes. He's never met someone else like him. "What are you talking about?"

Brielle takes a step forward. "I know that you paint without paint. And I know that the thing with the dollar bill the other day wasn't a magic trick. My power is that I can tell when someone's lying. It's something I've always been able to do."

"I need to get going." Jareth stumbles backward. He doesn't want to have this conversation. "My parents are waiting for me."

Brielle studies him for a moment before her face softens with compassion. "I'm so sorry." She lifts a hand toward him. "I was an orphan too, for most of my life."

Jareth feels like he's been sucker punched to the gut. Brielle must see something because she takes another step forward, but he holds up his hand for her to stop. "I'm fine."

"I don't need my powers to know that's a lie."

Jareth glares at her. "My favorite color is red."

Brielle shakes her head with a smile. "That's a lie."

Jareth's lips twist. His whole world has been swallowed

by shades of blood. He hates the color with the same passion it inspires.

"I moved here from California."

"Truth."

Jareth crosses his arm. "My mother was once arrested for running through Central Park naked."

Brielle's eyes widen. "Your mom sounds cool."

Sagging against the wall, Jareth looks at the girl in front of him.

"So you're good at finding a person's tell," he shrugs. "Big deal. Knowing when someone's lying isn't exactly a superpower."

She purses her lips and nods. "On its own, I would agree. But it's only the tip of the iceberg. The sense is often accompanied by a vision of whatever the truth is. That's how I knew about your pa—that you're an orphan, too."

The inference behind her words is jarring. Is she saying that she saw a vision of his parents' deaths? He's not sure how he feels about that.

Someone else who has powers. He never thought he'd find a person like that.

And yet, it's too late.

He's leaving.

Jareth pushes off. "What do you want from me?"

Brielle shrugs. "I already told you, friendship. I have a feeling you and I are kindred spirits…" She looks at him questioningly.

"Jareth," he says with a sigh. "My name's Jareth."

Her smile is blinding and Jareth's struck by how pretty she is. What's more, Brielle seems like a caring soul, as his mother would say. "Friends?"

Jareth's own smile creeps up before he realizes it. He rolls his eyes. "Fine, then. Friends."

Brielle doesn't have to know he won't be here long enough for that to happen.

"Can I grab your number?" she asks, looking like he's about to give her the moon.

Jareth hesitates, but then recites it as she quickly types it in her cell. He rarely answers it, anyway.

Brielle glances at her watch. "I have to go or I'll be late for training." She steps out of the alleyway. "I'll see you at school tomorrow?"

Jareth's about to agree when he realizes Brielle will recognize the lie for what it is. He smiles and opens his mouth to respond, only to pretend his cell just started ringing and grabs it out of his pocket.

Brielle's gone before Jareth has to make a pretense of talking to someone. Which is a good thing considering that would've been just as big a lie as telling her he'll be at school tomorrow.

Feeling a little guilty, along with a strange pang of regret, Jareth returns to the bus stop. He's no longer hungry. He just wants to go home.

Except the house he's in isn't home. It's nothing but a giant canvas for him to relive the loss of his parents. Crossing the road, Jareth decides there's somewhere else he's going to go. A quick scan of the timetable tells him he'll only have to wait ten minutes.

That's a good thing. He hates being out in the open. It's too…exposed. Too vulnerable.

His fingers twitching, Jareth glances at the bus stop seat. It's red. He clenches his hand. He can't paint. Not here.

He's slipped up too many times already.

"Jareth?"

Spinning around, Jareth's brain tries to reconcile the change in Brielle's voice. But as he sees who's walking towards him, he realizes why she sounded different. It's not Brielle.

It's Veronica.

His first assumption is that she's following him, too. But he quickly shakes it off. His counsellor would tell him his inevitable spiral into paranoia has started.

The closer she comes, the brighter her smile blazes. Jareth stands rooted to the spot, captivated. Dark, wavy hair bounces around Veronica's shoulders, highlights of bronze and ochre catching the light. Her full lips tip up with pleasure, and yet her walk is more sashay than stroll. She's not particularly tall, but what Veronica loses with height, she makes up with presence. Jareth swallows. And with curves.

She stops in front of him, smiling. "Mirror Point can be annoying with how small it is, but right now, I'm not minding that so much."

Jareth finds his lips tipping up. "What are the chances, huh?"

Veronica leans forward. "It's like it was meant to be," she whispers conspiratorially.

Just like the first time they met, Jareth finds himself drawn to this girl. At first he thought it was her eyes—the pale hazel a sharp contrast to her dark hair. They felt like a kaleidoscope of no color and yet every color.

But he can sense that it's more than just her looks. It's her…energy.

She pulls back, wrinkling her nose up at him. "Did you get detention? I thought the principal was about to snap his biscuit."

"Just a lecture." That Jareth barely heard. It's amazing how much knowing you're not staying reduces your care-factor about the importance of class participation.

"Well, that's good news then."

Jareth raises a brow. "I suppose that's one way of looking at it."

A small shuffle and Veronica minimizes the space between them. "It's good because it means you're free…" Her eyes twinkle. "To take me out on a date."

Jareth doesn't know whether he should do a double take or admire this girl's sass. "I'm…ah…busy."

Veronica plants a hand on her hip. "Doing what? Do you do any sports?"

"Ah…no."

"Activities? Drama club? Chess? Art classes?"

Jareth's spine stiffens a little at the last one, but Veronica's hazel eyes stay wide and teasing. Yep, he's getting paranoid.

"Well, no. I don't do any of those."

"Awesome!" Veronica's whole body seems to be vibrating with anticipation. "So, Saturday?"

The day he plans on leaving.

Jareth shakes his head. "I'm not sure that's going to work."

None of this will.

"You say that, Jareth." Another step from Veronica and there are only a handful of inches between them. "And yet, you don't move away."

Because he doesn't want to. In fact, he wants to find all the colors in Veronica's eyes and lose himself in them.

Jareth's bus pulls up, the brakes squealing loudly. It startles them both, and Jareth steps back. "Veronica…"

"Saturday sounds great?" she finishes for him.

Jareth pauses on the first step of the bus. A part of him likes that she's not taking no for an answer. That part of him wishes he'd be here to see what a date with Veronica would be like. It means he finds himself smiling at her, not denying that if things were different, Veronica wouldn't have to chase so hard.

"I would if I could."

With that, Jareth jogs onto the bus, finding the driver frowning at him because he took so long. Jareth pays—real money this time—and finds his usual seat halfway down. Glancing out the window, he sees Veronica's still watching him. She smiles and waves.

He blinks. She just blew him a kiss.

The bus pulls away with Jareth shaking his head. A friend and now a date? He feels like he's stepped into an alternate Universe.

Jareth almost misses the stop for the cemetery because he's still trying to process what just happened. Walking through, he's glad it's empty. Company has been far too unsettling today.

Reaching his parents' memorial, Jareth feels reality sink back in. The orphanage insisted on building it as his parents were key financial supporters for so long. When he moved here, he thought it would be enough to feel connected to them. But the flat, gray headstone doesn't capture his parents' energy, their vibrancy. What they meant.

Another reason there's no point staying.

If they were still alive, he'd be at home now, his mom asking about his day. It was never a token question. She'd look at him, expecting more than a token answer.

Jareth sighs. There was little he kept from his parents. They were the only ones who knew about his ability to paint with his hands. He would've told them what happened. "I ran into two girls today."

His mother would put down her herbal tea. His father would grunt as he took another piece of date and oat slice. He worked from home, his offices at the back of the house. He always blocked out the half hour after school so they could have 'connection time' as his mother liked to call it.

"The first wants to be my friend. She's sweet, compassionate...trusting."

She knows about the painting. And she says she has powers like me.

His mother's tea would pause midair. "She sounds like a kindred spirit."

Exactly what Brielle said.

Jareth sighs, Veronica's unforgettable face rising in his mind. "The second, well, she's...hot. Smart. Sassy."

His mother would nod knowingly. "He likes this one." She'd turn to Jareth's father. "And if Jareth likes her, I like her."

His father would glance up from where he was eyeing the slice. "You like everyone, Meredith."

"That's because we're all connected, Jacob." She'd grasp his hand. "We've seen it."

When they did a shamanic retreat in their early twenties. Jareth never asked what they were smoking at the time.

He bends over, tracing their names. The cool marble is such a contrast to the inferno that took their lives. His gut clenches painfully. The inferno that stole their light from his life.

The sharp sound of something slamming into the tree behind him has Jareth shooting upright. He glances around, but the cemetery is empty. It's just him.

He turns around, knowing the noise was unmistakable. Jareth's jaw drops as his pulse skyrockets. Fear freezes him to the spot.

Another wild glance around confirms he's surrounded by nothing but graves. But he wasn't alone. He couldn't have been.

There's an arrow impaled in the tree behind him.

An arrow that was undeniably meant for him.

JACK

16:03

Jack stomps up the stairs to his daughter's bedroom, scowling. He hates having to go away for work.

But McNally insisted. The serial killer behind the Triple Murders hasn't completed his trifecta. And once he does, he'll disappear down whatever sewer he came from.

McNally had pinned Jack with a glare. "You know this case, Cadbury. And you're one of the best detectives I've got."

And using those skills to find out about aliens is considered a waste of time.

"I need you in Chicago, even if it's just for a few days."

Jack can already feel another ulcer forming. Logan took the news well. Veronica's the one who always worries.

Her door is closed so Jack knocks and waits. When there's no answer, he opens it slightly. "KitKat, you in there? We need to have a chat."

The room's silent. Peeking around the door, he finds it empty. Jack glances at his watch, his scowl returning. She's usually home from school by now.

Jack's just about to close the door when he sees a plate sitting on Veronica's bedside table. With a sigh, he goes over to collect it. No point in having mice move in for the few days he'll be gone.

But as he lifts the plate, the flash of a brightly colored photo catches his eye. It's an art work of some sort, graffiti from the looks of things. But it's the most vibrant graffiti Jack's ever seen. He lifts the photo to take a closer look.

And the one behind it flutters to the ground.

Realizing he's snooping, Jack almost flushes. He needs a warrant to do this in anyone else's house. And this is his daughter. He trusts Veronica implicitly.

Bending over he picks up the photo just as he hears

Veronica's footsteps on the stairs. He's about to slip it back under the first when he freezes.

The photo.

When Veronica bounces through her door, that's how she finds him.

Frozen. Holding a picture of Tristan Ayers.

Jack turns to his daughter. "Where did you get this?"

Veronica's eyes widen for a split second before she throws her school bag to the floor. "You were spying on me? Like I'm one of your cases?"

Jack can feel his blood pressure spiking. "I was looking for you." He shakes the photo. "And I found this."

Jack glances down, seeing there are more.

Veronica shoots forward as he picks the next one up. "Hey, that's private!"

But it's too late. He's already seen it. This photo is also of Tristan, but there's someone next to him. A girl Jack recently followed.

Brielle.

Veronica snatches the photos before he can look any further. But Jack's seen enough. He sits on the bed, feeling like his world just bottomed out.

"You're following them?"

Veronica frowns, looking at the pictures in her hand. Jack knows his daughter well. Right now, she's strategizing. Does she come up with some convoluted story that will go so long, he'll have to leave it or he'll run late? Will she get angry, the classic defense mechanism? If she's really desperate, Veronica will use tears. Just one or two, glistening on her thick eyelashes.

His girl is one smart cookie.

She flops onto the bed next to him. "I hate the way they talk about you, Dad." She says fiercely. "It's not right. I'm going to help prove these guys are dangerous."

Jack's brows hike up. Then shoot down. She went with the truth. Veronica's doing this for him.

To prove he isn't nuttier than a five-pound fruitcake.

He shakes his head. "This is dangerous, Veronica. We don't know what these people are capable of."

"But, Dad—"

Jack vaults to his feet, the need for her to understand spearing through him. "No, Kitkat. This isn't some private investigation into some...some..." He flaps his hands at the photos. "Into some graffiti artist." He pins her with a glare. "I want you to stay out of this."

Veronica opens her mouth again.

"No!" Jack modulates his tone. "Promise me, you'll leave all this alone."

His daughter's shoulders sag. "Fine, then," she mumbles.

Jack grasps her shoulders. "Promise me," he insists.

Veronica looks up at him, those eyes so much like her mother's. She nods with resignation. "I promise I'll leave Tristan and Brielle alone."

Relieved, Jack releases her. "Thank you, Kitkat. I don't know what I'd do if something happened to you."

"I love you, too, Dad." With a sigh, she rests her head on his shoulder.

Relieved they're back on familiar ground, Jack's chest loosens. "I came in here to tell you I've got to go away for work for a few days."

His daughter nods, her head still resting on his shoulder. "Okay."

Glad she's taking it well, he squeezes her knee. "Logan said he'd cook—"

Instantly straightening, Veronica wrinkles her nose. "He boiled an egg once for forty-five minutes."

"But there's money in the usual place."

"Good." Veronica gets up, throwing the photos in the

trash can. "Because no egg should have to go through that again."

Jack chuckles as he presses a kiss to her head. He doesn't need to glance at his watch to know he's running late. "I'll call every night."

Veronica rolls her eyes. "Not during Vampire Diaries."

Shaking his head, he makes his way down the stairs and into the garage. His bag's already on the back seat, the coffee he made in the hope he'd talk to Veronica and be back in ten minutes is still in the holder.

Jack sips the cold, bitter brew. His stomach revolts as he swallows, but he ignores it. Caffeine is his first food group.

Antacids are his second.

He's just turned onto the freeway when his cell rings. Pressing the button on his steering wheel, Jack barks, "Cadbury here."

"I've got some information."

The voice is quiet, a little muffled, like the person has their hand cupped around their mouth.

Jack's breath hitches. "And?"

"I looked into those deaths. Zarius and Tess Ayers. Cause of death is still unknown."

Clenching his teeth, Jack waits. He's not paying for information he already knows.

"There were three other people there. We got positive IDs on two of them, Brielle Pierce and Tristan—"

"Ayers," Jack finishes for him. "Their statements say neither of them were there."

He should know. He's read those statements a hundred times. Which either means his informant is wrong...or Tristan is lying.

"Not according to the fingerprints," the man says with glee.

"Payment will be the usual way," Jack growls. "Keep me posted."

The line goes dead but his mind is alive with questions. He glances in the rear view mirror, watching New York disappear behind him. He has a direct order to drive to Chicago.

But…

Veronica's come up with the crazy idea to start investigating this herself. Jack's hands clench around the steering wheel. Either that, or she's tired of hearing about her loony father.

Horns honk and brakes squeal as Jack swerves across two lanes so he doesn't miss the upcoming exit ramp. He ignores the cursing and the invites to go to hell.

One day, these people will realize that if Jack doesn't do his job, they'll be dealing with far more than bad driving. They'll be fighting for their lives.

With a quick flick, Jack turns his work phone off. The Triple Murders are going to have to wait.

This is more important.

14

BRIELLE

"Where is he?" Tristan is pacing outside the school front steps.

He's getting impatient, and Brielle can sense a building tension in him. Tension she doesn't know how to soothe. When she first met him, he was so cool and collected. But his parents' deaths have changed him. It makes her anxious to please him.

"I don't know," she says, chewing on her bottom lip.

She hasn't seen Jareth all day. Not that either of them have any classes with him, but they looked for him at lunch, and scoured the hallways for him between classes. He was nowhere in sight.

"Maybe he called in sick?" she suggests, calling his number for the umpteenth time.

Tristan snaps his head toward her, scowling like she's just said something stupid. "Zodiacs don't get sick! Haven't you ever noticed that you've never been sick a day in your life? Our genes are immune to illness."

"Oh…" She's never really thought about it. Yes. While her fellow orphans frequently had the sniffles growing up, she'd never once suffered even so much as a sneeze. She never questioned it. She had her own problems to deal with, and hide.

"Granted our digestive systems have a hard time with the inadequate food on this planet," he mutters, almost to himself. "Tess told me I was a sickly boy before Zarius came along. Humans put so many hormones and pesticides in everything… That's why she'd only fed me organic foods since…" His eyes are distant, but only for a brief moment, then he returns to his manic scowl with even more fervor.

She hangs up when Jareth's voicemail answers. "I'm sure he'll be back tomorrow. Something could have easily come up. Jareth is a…troubled person. We just need to be patient."

Tristan stops pacing and throws up his hands. "You know what? We've tried it your way, and it didn't work. We don't have time for patience! I'm doing it my way." Without looking back, he storms off down the sidewalk toward the main road.

Brielle stands there, wondering if she should go after him. It feels like he's going off the rails, and she doesn't know what reckless thing he'll do, or what the ramifications will be. He could scare Jareth off for good, and then they'll really be screwed.

Beep beep!

She turns her head in the direction of the honking horn. It's Bea. Brielle had requested for her to show up a bit late, so that she and Tristan would have time for a conversation with Jareth. But Bea is a punctual person. Five minutes is the latest her personality would allow them.

Brielle hangs her head in defeat, then picks it back up to paste a cheery expression on her face before running to the car.

"Hi sweetie, how was your day?" Bea greets as Brielle buckles into the front passenger seat.

"Fine," Brielle says in a forcedly chipper tone.

"I know you asked me to be late, but I was so excited, I couldn't help it," Bea giggles.

"What's going on?" Bea's buzz is always contagious, and Brielle already feels better just being around her.

"We have a very important dinner guest tonight," Bea informs, all smiles. "The best New York City firm has proposed a merger with Frank's, and the CEO is coming over for dinner with his family to discuss the terms!"

The high pitch in Bea's voice tells Brielle how huge this is for their family. The Zodiac stuff is monumentally important, but she can afford to take a break from worrying about it for the night at least. She needs to be the best she can for her new parents. She needs to help impress the crap out of whoever this CEO is.

Make a good impression. Be a good daughter. That's her job tonight.

Besides, it's not like she can do anything in regards to Jareth at the moment anyway. She can only hope that Tristan and his newfound impatience doesn't chase Jareth away.

Brielle has spent the last three hours since getting home helping to make the house and herself presentable. She and Bea scrubbed every surface, prepared a truly delectable meal if she does say so herself, and set the dining room to perfection. Now she's putting the finishing touches on curling her hair, which never obeys heated beauty tools for long. No matter how long she holds her stubborn wavy locks in the curling wand, it proudly laxes to its usual wide sinusoidal wave.

Gritting her teeth in frustration, she sets down the wand and yanks the cord from the wall outlet in her bathroom. To heck with it. At least her outfit of completely new—unripped —clothes do the job of portraying her as an upstanding member of upper middle class society. Something she's never been and feels an imposter playing the part.

The doorbell rings and she turns away from her mirror with a sigh of acceptance, ready to be as charming as she can manage. *Just smile, nod, and laugh at the corny dad jokes*, she tells herself.

She scampers to the living room to stand beside Bea and Frank before the closed front door, adjusting her posture to fit into the image of the perfect family.

Frank opens the door.

"Mr. Sinclair, it's an honor to have you in our home," Frank says, extending his hand to a man who looks disturbingly familiar.

Sinclair...

No.

The well-dressed man and Frank exchange niceties, then he and his wife part to bring forward their daughter.

No!

"And may I introduce my daughter," the man says.

NO!!!

The perfect doll of a blonde curtsies. "Cassandra Sinclair, sir."

15

JARETH

O nly a few more days.

As he slides down the living room wall and crumples on the floor, Jareth's glad. Coming to Mirror Point was a mistake. For the briefest of seconds, Veronica's face flashes through his mind, but he pushes it away.

They spoke of a date on Saturday. They hadn't even discussed a time or location.

And Jareth won't be here on Saturday.

A part of him wonders why he just doesn't get up now and go, but his exhausted body can barely lift himself from the floor. He lets his head flop back, hitting the wall with a dull thud.

The painting's become worse. Today, he started in the living room, then couldn't stop. He moved onto the walls of the kitchen, the dining room, the bedrooms. Even the cramped spaces of the bathrooms held blank canvases. He's learned fire spares nothing, so neither did the fiery colors coating the walls.

His phone had rung several times. No doubt it was Brielle. Wondering why her new friend wasn't at school.

Knowing he was letting her down hadn't been enough for him to stop. For him to take the call.

By the time he'd come full circle and returned to the living room, the flames he'd painted there had already faded.

Maybe that's what it was. He just needed to be quicker.

So he'd started again. And painted faster. Splashed the clarets and cardinals harder. Higher. Like a hurricane of pain, he'd covered every inch.

But he'd come back to the point of ignition and it was all gone. Like none of it ever happened.

Sliding down the wall, Jareth's exhausted muscles had given out. Eventually, his breathing had slowed. His heart rate had dropped.

But the feelings hadn't abated.

The fury.

The anguish.

The wish he could turn back time.

His head lolls, the lack of sleep and frenzied painting catching up with him. Jareth's eyes drift closed, not bothering to move in case he loses the downward trajectory into oblivion. Maybe this time he'll be surrounded by nothing but black.

The nightmare comes the same time it always does. Just as Jareth hits the point of no return, the place where sleep has dragged him under too deep to easily escape its trap. The place where the flames don't need him to create them.

And it's not one of those dreams where he stands back and watches.

It's a dream he's in. Seeing, feeling, living everything. One he relives over and over and over again.

Because the first time he experienced it, it was reality.

The images assault him with the speed of a machine gun.

Waking with a start, confused by the piercing beeping that's assaulting his ears. Standing up to find smoke has filled the top half of his bedroom. Thick and cloying, it draws into his lungs and stays there. He coughs, but all that does is draw more in, making him choke more.

He opens the door and flames explode into his room. The smell of singed hair burns his nostrils as he stumbles back. The entire hall is ablaze.

Spinning around, his arm wrapping around his face as he staggers to the window and yanks it open. His dad used to joke that one day Jareth would use it to slip out at midnight to join rave parties.

Jareth had always rolled his eyes, commenting that just because they did that, didn't mean he would, too.

Clambering through and scraping his shins but not caring as he sucks in lungfuls of fresh air, glad his parents insisted on a small, single-story house. More environmentally friendly, his mother said.

A few stumbled steps away before turning to look back. His blood freezing in his veins. Half the house is ablaze, crackling and roaring and pulsing with heat.

"Mom! Dad!"

Barreling through the front door and being engulfed in smoke. More hacking coughs dragging the clouds of ash into his lungs.

"Mom! Dad!"

Please...

"Jareth? Where are you?"

Sweet relief at the sound of his father's voice. "Dad! This way."

His hand on the wall, feeling the throbbing heat. If it wasn't for the smoke pouring past him and out the door, he'd lose all sense of direction. The house he grew up in is no longer familiar. Predictable. Safe.

"We can't see a thing in this blasted smoke! Get out! Call for help!"

His father coughing. His mother crying. Jareth just wanting to be there, with them, not here, surrounded by helplessness.

His lungs scream for clean air. His heart cries for the two people who are his world. Jareth forges forward.

He has to find them. "Get to the kitchen! I'll meet you there!"

Getting an idea, he paints hurried yellow circles on the walls, fluorescent suns meant to guide his parents to safety.

But they fade too quickly.

The smoke is too thick.

"Go, Jareth! Get to safety!"

"I'm not leaving you!" His voice is hoarse, his shouts muffled by the climbing flames. "Follow the lights on the walls!"

He paints again, not willing to give up.

"I see them!" shouts his mother. "There, Jacob!"

Elation rises alongside the flames. "Hurry!"

"We're coming, son!"

But then the smoke billows as if someone else is moving. Jareth spins around, seeing shadows that don't belong to the flames.

He's not alone.

Then pain. Blackness.

Nothing.

Waking up to flashing lights that hurt his eyes. News that slices his heart open and robs his life of love.

Then the questions. The feds looking at him like he's holding back.

At first, Jareth's defensive that they don't believe him. Then angry. Then...the same doubt on their faces crawls inside. Coating his mind in the same way the smoke has stained his lungs.

"Sorry about all the questions, son," says one of the men. "It's just that—"

The phone ringing has Jareth jumping awake. He answers it instinctively, only remembering that he's avoiding the person on the other line as he croaks out, "Hello?"

"Hey, Jareth."

But it's not Brielle.

It's certainly not Shandra.

"Veronica." Jareth rubs his hand down his face. His spine stiffens, the fear that was receding suddenly shooting back. "Ah, how did you get my number?"

She laughs lightly. "I was hoping you wouldn't notice." She pauses, her voice dropping. "I got it off Brielle's phone. That girl trusts anyone with her passcode."

Jareth recalls the trusting way Brielle believed he'd be at school, despite him not giving her a straight answer. He relaxes, pushing away the last tendrils of horror still clinging to his consciousness.

Veronica's not a threat.

He clears his throat. "What's up?"

"I had a feeling you'd be having second thoughts about our date on Saturday," she says teasingly, but then pauses. "Are you okay?"

"I'm fine. I just…ah…couldn't find my phone there for a second." He clears his throat again. "About Saturday—"

"Are you sure you're okay? You sound like you've just been in a round with the boogey man or something."

Rubbing his forehead, Jareth is suddenly tired of lying. "I just woke up." He hesitates. "I was having a nightmare."

There's silence on the other side, and Jareth instantly regrets his words. "Look—"

"My mom died when I was a kid. I wasn't even in the car when it crashed, but I had nightmares for years after."

Jareth blinks as compassion flows down the line and

through his body. Suddenly, the loneliness loses its sharp edges. Suddenly, he's not…alone.

"Yeah, well. It seems the ones you lived through don't go away so easy."

"Nightmares suck," Veronica states emphatically. "But at least if you had a bad dream, then it means I wasn't in it."

Against the odds, the corner of Jareth's mouth tips up. "That's true. You weren't."

"Well…" The smile in Veronica's voice is unmistakable. It gives it a teasing lilt. "If you were to have a dream with me in it, what would we be doing? Let's say, for our first date?"

Surprised by the question, Jareth gives it some thought. "I'd take you to the fields of white in California." His gaze loses focus, remembering it. "Daisies as far as the eye can see. Each one pure white, but like snowflakes, each one is different. Each one is unique."

"That sounds…amazing."

Jareth flushes. "It's not exactly the movies and dinner."

Which is what he should've said. It's what anyone else would've said.

"Been there, done that. And I couldn't tell you a single detail about any of the times." There's a pause. "But I doubt I'd forget a date like that."

Veronica's voice has gone husky and Jareth's hand tightens around the phone. The image of her laughing and running through the fields of white, her dark hair catching the light, her hazel eyes a kaleidoscope of laughter, has his gut tightening.

He needs to remember he's leaving.

"Yeah, well. We're not in California."

And daisies don't appear in Jareth's dreams.

"Daisies grow in other places apart from California, you know." The eye roll in Veronica's voice is apparent. "Anyway, maybe we can go find some on our date on Saturday."

Before Jareth can say another word, she purrs a goodbye and hangs up.

Jareth pulls the phone back, slightly bewildered. Why does it feel like he's been swept up by a tsunami?

And why is he smiling?

But as he pushes himself to his feet, the smile dies.

On the table sits the arrow that he'd yanked out of the tree at the cemetery.

It reminds Jareth why he keeps to himself.

It reminds Jareth of how the nightmare always ends.

The fed, the one called McNally, snapping his notebook shut. "Sorry about all the questions, son. Just routine stuff."

But as they turn away, the other one mutters. "Routine, my ass. The fire started outside his bedroom."

16

TRISTAN

T ristan glances at his cell for the gazillionth time. Since telling him she has something going on tonight, Brielle hasn't answered any of his texts.

Tristan glares at the computer in front of him. Doesn't she realize as Zodiac Guardians they need to be contactable at all times? What if something came up on the computers, saying they might've found another Heir? What if he's attacked?

What if she doesn't want to talk to you because you're being a douche?

Letting his head drop onto the desk with a thud, Tristan lets out a long sigh. The last scenario is the most likely. His mind is more of a mess than his life, right now.

And poor Brielle is the one wanting to help him untangle it all. Only for him to push her away if it feels like they're getting too close. He has to.

And yet, his aching heart is drawn to her. Her smile is the one light in the days that are blending into shades of help-lessness. Chardis is planning something, he can feel it. Evil is coming.

And Jareth is their only lead right now. One who's determined to be a dead end.

Clenching his fists, Tristan straightens. He told Brielle she had one more chance. And the guy ghosted her.

Which is what's brought Tristan down here to headquarters. He almost scoffs at the label he optimistically gave these underground rooms. HQ implies there's something to command. Moving parts that need to be monitored and coordinated.

Right now, it's him and Brielle. And they're stuck.

Tristan wiggles the mouse and the screen comes to life. "Let's see what you got, Alden," he mutters.

He needs to find out if he can hack Mirror Point High's network. If not, he's going to get as much information as he can so he can break into the school office. Either way, he's determined to get Jareth's address.

Then, he's paying the guy a visit.

Not sure which he's looking forward to less, Tristan starts clicking on files. Alden accumulated an encyclopedia of information on Mirror Point, all carefully sorted into folders and subfolders. Each one labeled under a code name so no one could tell there's an entire server dedicated to the town.

Tristan sighs. It looks like he has a long night ahead of him.

When a quiet beeping creeps through the silent room, Tristan freezes. That's the external alarm.

Which means someone's here.

His muscles coiling reflexively, Tristan wheels to an adjacent screen. He was sure he lost the Skin before getting home, but he mustn't have been careful enough. Dammit. He glances at his phone only to shake his head. It seems even if he's going to get attacked, he wouldn't call Brielle. There's no point putting her in danger.

He'll deal with them himself.

But as he zooms in with the camera pointing at the driveway, Tristan's brows yank up. A white sedan is sitting in the driveway. Since when did Skins just pull up like that?

The moment the woman steps out of the car, Tristan's brows slam straight back down. Double dammit. He forgot Shandra was visiting this evening. He'd almost prefer to face a couple of Skins.

Crossing his arms, Tristan considers pretending he's not home. What's the woman going to do? Make more notes about it? Beat him up with her overly large handbag the next time he sees her?

Shandra's only taken a couple of steps when she pauses. Riffling through the glorified suitcase slung over her shoulder, she pulls out a file. Stepping back to the car, she lays it open on the hood and proceeds to punch a number into her cell.

Knowing this conversation is probably private, Tristan turns away. Shandra can make her driveway phone call then try his doorbell a few times, after that she can make like a tire and hit the road. No doubt, it'll be his file she'll have open tomorrow so she can do this all again.

"Jareth, it's Shandra."

Tristan stills as her voice carries through the speaker. *Surely, not…*

"This is my third message. I'd appreciate it if you could call me back. I'll be there in about an hour."

She hangs up, huffing.

Tristan still hasn't moved. How many Jareth's can there be in Mirror Point? Especially considering Brielle said he'd lost his parents somehow. But he's with child services? And they share the same social worker?

By the time Shandra presses the doorbell, Tristan's already striding down the hallway. She's just lifted her finger to press it again when he yanks it open with a smile. "Hey, Shandra. Great to see you."

She startles, her own smile instantaneous. Tristan figured early on that there probably aren't many people who are particularly happy to see Shandra on their doorstep. It means he's made a concerted effort to be friendly with her...no matter how much he doesn't like seeing her on his doorstep.

He pulls the door open wider. "Come on in."

She hoists her giant handbag further up her shoulder. "Why, thank you."

Familiar with the layout of Alden's house, she walks alongside Tristan, assuming they're heading to the kitchen. But he takes a sharp right, startling her. "I thought we'd chat in the living room today."

Shandra covers her surprise well, settling her bulk into one of the chairs and placing her giganta-handbag down beside her feet. "How are you doing, Tristan?"

Crap. "Good, thanks. Yourself?"

"Busier than I'd like to be."

Apparently doing the same thing as Brielle—trying to get a hold of the ellusive Jareth.

She leans down, getting her notebook out and Tristan works to keep his smile up. Until today, he's never liked that notebook.

But now, there are other pages in it that he wants to get a hold of.

"So, I noticed you've had a few absences at school?"

Shandra's keeping track of his attendance?

Tristan rubs the back of his head ruefully. "Sorry. I've been making sure I get there the past few days."

Because he's looking for more Zodiac Guardians.

Shandra scribbles in her notepad. "That's great. Keep that up. And everything else is going well?" She glances around the room, no doubt noticing it's tidy...because he barely spends any time on the above-ground levels.

"Yep. Just laying low."

As he tries to figure out what a life without Zarius and Tess looks like.

Shandra leans down and Tristan tenses as her hand slips in her bag. Please don't let her pull out what he thinks she's about to pull out.

The shiny leaflet catches the light as she holds it toward him. "Maybe it's time, then? This is a great group, Tristan. You could meet others who've been through the same thing as you."

She always mentions the grief group. Somehow, he doubts he'd have anything in common with any of the other teens there. Tristan can just imagine it. Sitting in a circle. Everyone holding a can of soda they don't want just so it gives their hands something to do. All eyes on Tristan, waiting for him to share why he's here. *Hi, my name's Tristan. My parents' hearts were crushed inside their chests by the greatest evil man has ever known. And if I don't find the others like me, that could happen to you.* He'd take a sip of warm soda. *What about everyone else?*

"I'm not sure that would be...helpful." He angles his head, smiling. "Have you ever tried beetroot coffee?"

Shandra blinks at the rapid change of topic. Or the use of 'beetroot' and 'coffee' alongside each other. "I can't say that I have."

Tristan leaps to his feet. "It's an unforgettable experience. Alden has packets and packets of it."

Probably trying to make up for any nutrient deficiencies that can develop on Earth.

"I don't think—"

But Tristan's already heading for the kitchen. "Come on, Shandra. You haven't lived until you've tried a beetroot coffee. And it's not like you have to worry about the caffeine."

Shandra has no choice but to follow him or seem rude, and Tristan's banking that a social worker wouldn't want that. When she follows him, he smiles to himself. But when she turns back and grabs her handbag, the smile dies an early death.

Great. He's going to have to do this the hard way.

Shandra settles herself at the dining room table as Tristan busies himself with the kettle. Beetroot coffee is as disgusting as it sounds. It was only a desperate need to have anything apart from ravioli that had Tristan trying it.

Lukewarm beetroot coffee is going to be next level gag inducing. But Tristan turns off the kettle long before it reaches boiling point. He glances over his shoulder, acting like he's making casual conversation.

"I have a friend, Brielle." *I thought she was my soulmate.* "She comes over most afternoons."

So that we can train for an alien invasion.

Shandra writes something down. "Just one friend?"

Tristan raises a brow. "You think I should be throwing parties or something? Pack this place out?"

Shandra looks like she's already had a sip of the beetroot coffee. "No, that's not what I'm saying."

Tristan grins. "Just kidding, Shandra. But it was worth it to see your face."

Her features relax as she shakes her head, her platinum helmet-hair never moving an inch. "You're doing so well, Tristan."

Tristan's gut clenches. That's what she's writing in her notes? That he's coping?

He's just about to put the mugs of non-steaming beetroot coffee down when Tristan trips on the giant handbag beside Shandra's chair. Trying not to make it look too comical, he lurches forward, the contents of one mug splashing onto her front.

"Oh gosh, I'm so sorry!" Tristan gasps. "Quick, the bathroom's down there. That stuff can leave a serious stain."

Shandra rushes off, her face stricken. Leaving her bag behind.

Ignoring the twinge of guilt—Shandra won't be getting those purple blotches out anytime soon—Tristan quickly yanks out the handful of folders in her bag.

The top one is the one he's looking for. Jareth Stone. Pulling his phone out of his pocket, Tristan quickly takes a photo of the front page. He's tempted to rifle through the next few but the sound of the bathroom door opening has him jumping back. Tucking the file back in, he puts the bag back where it was.

When Shandra returns, she finds him mopping up the liquid with a tea towel. Tristan tries not to scrunch up his nose. This stuff doesn't even smell good.

He straightens. "I'm really sorry, Shandra," he says sincerely. No one deserves to be painted in beetroot coffee, especially a well-meaning social worker. He was hoping she'd leave her bag behind in the lounge room and he could've excused himself for a quick toilet break and gotten the information he needs that way.

She flaps a hand. "Oh, no harm done. I'm sure it'll wash straight out."

"I hope you didn't have anywhere to go after this. You'll want to wash that before it dries."

Especially when it looks like someone just threw a dead animal on her.

Her lips twist a little. "Nothing that can't wait."

Tristan picks up her bag and passes it to her. "Well, like I said. I'm really sorry."

When she smiles gratefully, Tristan almost winces. "I

don't think I'll need to see you for another couple of weeks. Is that okay?"

"Sure." That's more than okay.

Tristan sees Shandra out the door, then closes it. He stands on the other side, listening as she climbs into her car and drives off.

In the next ten seconds that pass, Tristan stares at his phone. He has Jareth's address.

He thought it would take days. Possibly some breaking and entering.

But it's staring right at him. Shandra's scrawled writing just sitting on his cell.

The car keys are still in his pocket. Along with the onyx.

As he slams the door shut and heads to his car, Tristan sets his jaw. If Brielle was around, he'd take her with him.

But she's too busy playing happy families.

And unlike Shandra, this visit can't wait for another time.

17

JARETH

Jareth frowns when his doorbell rings. The pizza that's going to be his dinner is already paid for. His instructions were very clear—leave the box on the front porch.

With a sigh, he wipes his hand down his face. He's done a great job of avoiding human contact today. It looks like his streak is about to be broken.

He opens the door only to freeze.

There's no pizza being held by a sullen teen. In fact, Jareth just lost his appetite.

It's the guy from the cemetery.

The one who was with Brielle at school.

Jareth goes to slam the door shut again but the guy steps forward and it bounces off his shoe. He grins. "Hey, Jareth."

"How did you get my address?"

The guy shrugs nonchalantly. "Look, not totally legally, but I think I just saved you from a Shandra visit. That's gotta count for something."

Shandra?

Jareth grabs the door, his hand tightening around the knob. "I don't know who you're talking about."

"Really? Helmet hair? A love of leaflets? Overzealous note taker?"

Jareth stays resolutely silent despite the accurate description.

The guy's smile fades. "Look, I know you don't want me here, but we need to talk." He holds Jareth's gaze. "It's important."

Why does Jareth get the sense this guy won't back off like Brielle did? That he's not here to respect boundaries?

As if reading his mind, the guy leans against the door jamb, tucking his hands into his pockets. His smile returns, all casual friendliness. He looks like he plans on standing in the doorway all night long.

Jareth narrows his eyes. "I'll give you ten minutes."

The smile grows to a grin. "I'll talk fast."

Spinning around, Jareth stalks to the dining table, glad he hid the arrow in the bedroom. He doesn't stop till he's at the other end, turning around and gripping the back of the chair. He watches the guy walk in, openly looking around.

"You like home decorating as much as you like talking, huh?"

Jareth doesn't answer, not caring that he's reinforcing the guy's assumption.

Not looking like he was really expecting an answer, the guy takes a seat on the opposite side of the table. He clasps his hands, looking at them for several seconds.

When he looks up, there's an intensity in the guy's blue gaze that almost has Jareth stepping back. "My name's Tristan, and I believe you're one of us."

Uneasiness crawls up Jareth's spine. One of us. It sounds like a cult or something. "I doubt it."

He doesn't belong anywhere. Or with anyone. His family is gone.

Tristan watches Jareth closely. "How do you explain your

powers? Your ability to paint"—he arches a brow—"without paint."

"I don't." And Jareth's paintings don't last. No one has proof they even exist. "There are a lot of unexplained phenomena in this world."

"Well, I can."

Tristan leaves the words out there, probably waiting to see if Jareth will pick up the gauntlet. But he doesn't move a muscle. There was a time that he was curious about the answer to that question.

But now, Jareth just wants to disappear. No one is safe around him.

Tristan continues, just like Jareth suspected he would. "It's the same reason Brielle can sense lies, and I see visions of the future."

Those words have Jareth blinking. Tristan has powers, too?

Tristan lets out a slow breath and a flicker of nervousness flashes across his face so fast, Jareth isn't sure he saw it.

"You're like me, Jareth. An alien sent to Earth for your protection."

An. Alien.

Jareth lets those two words try to filter into his consciousness. But they can't get past logic. Reality. Disbelief. "You're crazy."

"That's what Brielle said when I first told her. But she saw all too soon that it's the truth. My people oversee the Gemini quadrant. Brielle's the Libra Guardian. I believe you're the Capricorn. There are ten others out there, just like us."

Jareth doesn't bother pointing out Tristan's poor math. There are twelve Zodiacs and Tristan just said there's thirteen.

Jareth shakes his head. Aliens. And Zodiacs.

His mother would be getting her Tarot cards out and asking Tristan how they fit into all this.

Jareth takes a step back. His mother believed it was goodness that powered the world. Good is the foundation we all fall back on.

Her death proved her wrong.

"Look, I'm sure you believe all…that. But I'm not who you're looking for."

Tristan jams his hand in his pocket, pulling something out and sitting it on the table with a *clack*.

"I believe this belongs to you."

"What?"

Tristan's blue gaze is almost neon with its intensity. "Pick it up, Jareth. It'll prove whether I'm right or wrong."

The size of a walnut, the smooth black stone sits on the table in front of Tristan. The color of the deepest midnight, it seems to absorb and reflect the light all at once. Somehow, the small obsidian rock is both beautiful and terrifying.

Jareth doesn't move. "What is it?"

"Onyx. Each Zodiac Guardian has a stone that belongs to them." Tristan pulls up a purple gem that was tucked beneath his shirt. "Each one unlocks our powers."

For some reason, Jareth can't seem to drag his gaze away from the onyx. His breath halts when he swears he sees it tremble for a fleeting second.

He looks up, wishing he hadn't seen it. "No."

"All I'm asking you to do is pick it up. If nothing happens, I'll leave."

Jareth shakes his head resolutely. He's not going to give Tristan's crazy theory credence by touching that thing.

Tristan waits, but Jareth's willing to stand around for as long as it takes. He's not touching the onyx.

With a loud sigh, Tristan stands. "I'd dare you, but I have a feeling that wouldn't work," he jokes.

Except there's nothing to smile about. There's a crazy guy in Jareth's house trying to recruit him into his extraterrestrial social club. "Nothing you can say will have me touching that stone."

Nodding, Tristan picks it up. He stares at it in his palm for long seconds. "My parents died protecting this stone and everything it represents."

Which is why Tristan must know Shandra. He's a fellow orphan. Jareth's chest aches, knowing the pain Tristan must be living with, but he doesn't move. Tristan doesn't realize Jareth's doing this for his protection just as much as his own.

Tristan looks up. "There's nothing I could say?"

"Nope."

Tristan nods in an "I thought you'd say that" way. Something sparks in his eyes a second before he says, "But what if I do this?"

With a flick of his wrist, he sends the stone flying into the air. It arcs high, then dips down.

Heading straight for Jareth.

As if time has slowed, Jareth watches its trajectory. He knows he doesn't want to catch it. That it won't matter if it tumbles to the floor.

But his hand reflexively shoots out. It's almost instinctive. An ancient drive to touch it. To hold it.

The onyx drops into his hand, nestling into the center of his palm.

Jareth freezes, his eyes wide. The sensation is instantaneous. It's like a tidal wave of energy detonates from the one point of pressure on his hand.

It floods him, feeling warm and right and full of the magic his mother was so sure existed. It fills him, expands him... somehow makes him more.

Jareth stifles a gasp.

That's the last thing he wants.

In a flash, he drops it to the ground. Looking up at Tristan, he molds his face with the anger now scorching through him, burning away whatever it was he just felt.

"Get out."

"No, I saw—"

Jareth kicks the onyx toward Tristan. "I don't like being tricked." Breathing hard, Jareth returns his hands to the back of the chair. "Nothing happened. Now leave."

Tristan's jaw works for long seconds, but with a short, sharp movement, he spins around and walks away. The door closes with a sharp click.

Finally, Jareth sits. He barely makes it to the chair before his knees give out.

What just happened? Some sort of weird static electricity or something. A trick of the mind because Tristan seemed so sure something was going to happen.

Shaking his head, Jareth looks around the room. On the upside, for once, the walls don't call to him.

He's not sure he'll ever want to paint again.

Not if people are going to start thinking he's an alien.

When the doorbell rings, Jareth startles so hard his chair scrapes across the floor. He stalks to the door, deciding he's no longer going to be quiet and contained this time round.

Tristan needs to back off.

But when he jerks open the door, there's no one there.

Correction. There's a pizza box sitting on the front door step.

Picking it up, Jareth takes it into the kitchen and lays it on the counter. He's too angry to eat.

Of all the explanations for what he can do, that's what Tristan believes? Some conspiracy theory that they come from another planet and were sent here for protection?

Obviously, the guy's been watching too much Star Wars.

But as Jareth stalks to his room, hoping he can lose himself in a book, he pauses. When Tristan first started talking to him, he was worried he was talking about some sort of cult. And it's obvious he wants others joining him.

Does that mean Brielle believes his crazy theory, too?

18

BRIELLE

T he dinner with the Sinclairs has not gone at all the way Brielle expected.

She'd hoped that they'd be some random family she knew nothing of, that she could set aside her curse—er, power—for one night, and her past, and just be at the very least a pretty background member of her new family.

How could she be so naïve? When has her life ever made things that easy?

Not only does Brielle know for a fact that Mr. Sinclair is a wretched human being, but Cassandra has taken every opportunity to shove her perfection in Brielle's parents' faces. National Track Star, she boasts. In line for Valedictorian, she says casually.

Somehow, it would have been better if she'd been putting Brielle down as she normally does. Reveal herself as the cruel bully she really is. But no. Cassandra is nothing if not a cunning and wicked fox.

"Don't we go to school together?" she asks in the middle of dinner, cocking her pretty bobble head at Brielle like they're strangers.

"Yes, and we have since kindergarten," Brielle manages through gritted teeth, all pretenses of an obedient smile gone as she stabs her fork at her food.

Of all the families for Frank to make a deal with, why did it have to be THIS ONE?

And she can't forget the horrible things her curse had shown her about Mr. Sinclair. They flash in her mind now as if they were fresh, as if the curse were presently in effect. All the girls he'd mutilated and beaten. Some left for dead for his sick pleasure. His addiction.

She pushes them away as she shoves a bite of chicken into her mouth. No matter what she knows or feels for the Sinclairs, she can't ruin this deal for Frank. She just can't. It's not like Mr. Sinclair's perverse tendencies can hurt Frank in a business deal. Even if they were to come to light, business is business and neither company would suffer for it. The Sinclairs' firm would just put another face as their CEO and all would be well.

But it's still torture for Brielle to sit through this dinner.

"That was a truly splendid meal, Beatrice," Mr. Sinclair says, rubbing his hands down the chest of his tailored suit. "Frank, how about you and I share a cigar while our wives chat over dessert preparation and our girls get to properly know each other. I had no idea you two went to school together, how perfect!" He pats Cassandra's shoulder like she's the star son of the football team and not his academically superior daughter.

Cassandra simply smiles, as fake as her mother does, and they all go their separate ways.

Great. Now she has to endure Cassandra's full discrimination in private.

Brielle reluctantly follows her to the drawing room as the men go outside and the women go to the kitchen.

"So…" Cassandra purrs, menace in her voice. "This is the pathetic couple you tricked into adopting you."

Brielle's first instinct is to defend Frank and Bea, but that's not how this game is played. In order to get any sort of edge with Cassandra, she has to match the hostility. She can't allow herself to be a victim.

She opens her mouth, ready to make a catty remark that her parents are far better than the ones who adopted Cassandra as a second choice. But she closes her mouth. Escalating the rivalry will only make things worse for Frank. Cassandra could say pitch knows what to her father and ruin the deal. Brielle knows how important this merger is to both of them.

She inhales deeply, then finally says, "Can we just stop?"

Surprised, Cassandra turns to her as she fingers the top of the mantle of the fireplace. "Excuse me?" she says in her snotty, privileged tone.

"This," Brielle waves her hand in the direction of their parents, "isn't about us and our childhood quarrel. This is about doing what's best for our families. And this merger seems to be what's best. Can we just set aside our issues and agree to a truce?"

Cassandra looks down and snickers, prowling along the edge of the fireplace. "Let me get this straight. You try to sabotage my adoption, make it so I end up alone and pathetic like you, then you destroy my best friend's relationship, and now you want peace?" Her glossed lips curl into a snarl as she turns to Brielle.

Exasperated, Brielle throws her hands up. "Ugh, don't you get it by now? You were my best friend. I never tried to sabotage you getting adopted. I just didn't want you at his mercy —" she cuts off, biting her lips so hard she tastes the salty rust of blood.

It could be possible that Mr. Sinclair changed his ways,

that he never raised a hand to Cassandra, and thank pitch for that! But Brielle had only the purest of intentions. To protect a dear friend from a clear threat. But Cassandra will never see that, and Brielle can never betray how she knows it.

"At whose mercy?" There's a bright flicker in Cassandra's already bright golden eyes, and for a moment, Brielle could swear they glow. Like the sun.

Brielle shakes her head. "It doesn't matter. I swear that I was just trying to protect you. But the past is the past and, no matter how much I wish otherwise, there's nothing we can do to change it. I just would like for us to at least *try* to start fresh. For our families' sakes."

Cassandra stalks closer, looking ever more the predator she's become since their youth. "Like you said, the past is the past, and you made your choice. You can't take it back now because it suits you. I will make sure my father sees you, and your parents, for the charlatans you really are. *You* made an enemy of *me*, not the other way around. And I'll make sure you regret it every single day."

Brielle can feel the hatred in Cassandra's words, and it still stabs straight at her heart even after all these years. If only Brielle could tell her the truth. Even if Cassandra has not yet been a victim of Mr. Sinclair's urges, it's only a matter of time. People don't change. That much she's learned. They only become more of what they are, and what he is, is *dangerous.*

"You're making a mistake, Cassie," she says softly.

"Don't you *ever* call me that again!" Cassandra snaps loudly, pointing a painted fake nail at Brielle's face. "You lost that right. And you will always be the vile backstabber you were when we were kids. I *hate* you!" Then she storms off into the dining room, twitching her hips with greater frequency as she walks away.

Brielle returns to the dining room only when she hears

that everyone else has. She can't be in Cassandra's presence alone. It hurts too much. If only she could make her see that she's not the enemy. Not even now.

She sits through the rest of dinner, looking down at her plate and only barely listening.

"Is everything okay?" Bea whispers while the men discuss business matters.

Brielle fakes a smile. That seems her only and most important job tonight. Again, lying doesn't feel comfortable, even to such an innocent question. "I'll tell you later," she manages, although she isn't sure what she'll say to Bea when the Sinclairs leave, but it's the best she can do right now.

Bea smiles, but her eyes linger with a knowing look of concern, flickering to Cassandra before she returns to appearing fully involved in what the men are saying. Brielle has decided not to insert herself. It's too late to appear the trophy daughter. Cassandra already ruined that with her boasts of excellence, not to mention their argument. All Brielle can do is sit here amicably until this nightmare is over and she's free of Cassandra's presence.

But life is never that easy. Even with Brielle ignoring the discussion between Frank and Mr. Sinclair, she can't help but be triggered by the unmistakable alarm of a lie. Her attention springs back in full force, and she unwillingly listens to every single word that follows.

"Yes, your customers need not worry. They'll be fully honored in any previous loans and forgiven of any penalties," Mr. Sinclair says around a mouthful of apple cobbler.

Lie. Lie. LIE!

Brielle wants to call him out. Her gift urges her to. But her conscious mind tells her she can't. She fidgets in her seat, praying desperately for some reprieve, for some explanation to proceed this flagrant falsehood.

But nothing comes.

Frank just nods happily and indulges in another delicious cinnamony bite of her and Bea's cobbler.

Please, please, she begs the Universe for Mr. Sinclair to elaborate, to make his lie less abhorrent.

Nothing.

Her leg bounces all through dessert as the men chat and the women nod, and all she can do is suffer with the knowledge she can't explain.

When dessert is over, the Sinclairs head to the front door with Bea and Frank escorting them, exchanging well-wishes for the future.

Brielle can't just stand by and do nothing. She pulls Cassandra aside.

"What is your father planning?" she hisses.

Cassandra gawks at her. "What the hell are you talking about?"

"He's lying. About the existing contracts," Brielle whispers.

Cassandra jerks her arm away from Brielle's touch. "There you go again, creating problems where there are none. You really are a piece of work, Brielle."

Cassandra turns on her heel and joins her parents, the epitome of upper middle class.

And it's disgusting.

How is she going to explain this to Frank? How is she going to salvage any of this without explanation?

"I'll have our lawyer draw up the papers and fax them to you Monday morning," Mr. Sinclair says with the iron-clad shake of a hand.

Brielle's lids close like the strike of a judge's gavel. The deal is all but set.

"Excellent, I look forward to signing them," Frank says, then closes the door on the Sinclairs. "I think that went well, don't you?" he asks them.

And there's nothing she can say.

JACK

07:03

Jack stretches his neck and it crackles like popcorn. He's getting too old to do things like sleep in his car, but he's supposed to be in Chicago.

Not in some darned parking lot outside Walmart.

And Tristan wasn't home last night. Which means he'll be getting an early visit whether he's a morning person or not.

Jack's just about to turn the key in the ignition when his cell rings. Not his work phone, which he has no intention of turning back on, but his personal phone. And it's from an unidentified number.

"What have you got?"

"Something I suspect you're willing to pay handsomely for," glides the voice of his confidential informant.

Jack grits his teeth, his temples already throbbing. "Price is set."

"Names are always worth more."

Jack straightens in the seat. What other names could there be? "I'll pay," he snaps. If this guy knew this information could be the difference between life or death—including his—he'd be paying Jack to give it to him.

The CI chuckles. "You always did have deep pockets."

"Get to the point."

"There's been a positive ID on the third body. A girl called Adalind Shaw. She moved here a few months ago. Also good friends of Brielle Pierce."

Brielle. There's that name again.

"You got an address for her?"

"Of course I have an address. You're paying for quality information," the man purrs.

Jack grabs a notepad and pen and quickly scribbles the address down, frowning when he sees where it is.

"I'll double the usual payment," Jack says curtly before hanging up.

Staring at the few lines he just scrawled down, Jack frowns as his gut churns, demanding coffee. Then some antacids.

Adalind's home address is in Pennsylvania, and that ain't a stone's throw away. He can't have a quick chat and then head over to Chicago, saying he had a flat tire, like he was going to if he talked to Tristan.

But it's a lead. Something he hasn't had in a long time.

Grabbing his phone, Jack types out a quick text message.

Hey, KitKat. Investigation is going better than I'd expected. Hope Logan hasn't tried cooking. Love ya.

Then, jamming the car into gear, he heads to Pennsylvania.

19

BRIELLE

With her home finally Cassandra-free, Brielle checks her phone.

Tristan has called several times.

Crap.

After the night she's had, a call with him wouldn't be enough. She needs to see him. Yes, she's not his soulmate, not his Gemini Princess, but they're still best friends as far as she sees it. And she just needs to see him right now. Whatever he needed to talk to her about was probably more urgent than responding with a phone call anyway.

"Bea? Frank?" She approaches them in the living room. "I've missed several calls from Tristan. We have...a project we're working on together and he must need help with it. Would it be alright if I ride over to his house for a bit?"

Frank looks at the wall clock. Brielle already knows it's eight o'clock, and that a bike ride anywhere is probably out of the question, but she's hopeful.

"No, not this late," Frank says.

Her shoulders slump.

"How about I drive you instead?"

His offer has her head springing back up.

"I can drop you off and then grab a fro-yo," he explains further.

"Oh no, Mr. Pierce," Bea shakes her head. "You're not getting a frozen treat without me. I'll go too!"

"Great! We definitely need to celebrate tonight's success!"

"Perfect!" Brielle is surprised by how relieved she is, especially knowing that the success he thinks he's won is not so great. All she knows is that she needs to see Tristan. She can't handle the crap Cassandra and her dad laid on her tonight by herself. And that Tristan needs her too is all she needs to know to go running to him.

The three load up in the car, Brielle's backpack in tow for appearances. She's only glad they didn't dig about the so-called project she mentioned. As it is, referring to Zodiac business as a project rides the thin line between truth and lie.

They drop her off outside Alden's mansion, waving her off with requests for her to call when she's done.

She rings the bell, and her parents don't drive away until Tristan opens the door.

"Oh, sure, *now* you decide to show up," Tristan grunts, rolling his eyes as he lets her in.

This is not the warm welcome she was expecting.

"I'm sorry, Tristan," she says. "I came as soon as I saw your missed calls. You wouldn't believe the night I had."

"Oh really? So playing happy family wasn't a blast?"

The snide tone in his voice is like venom to her ears. What's gotten into him?

"Did I do something wrong?" She feels small as she asks.

He shakes his head, not an answer to her question, but a way of expressing his irritation. An irritation she doesn't understand.

He suddenly turns on her, anger radiating from him like heat from a furnace. "You don't seem to have any idea how important it is to get Jareth on our side. And now, he may never be!" He throws his hands up and walks away toward the kitchen.

She instinctively follows him. "What does that even mean? Did you do something?"

He turns around, scowling at her. "Of course I did something! You weren't getting anywhere with your take-it-slow approach. So I went to his house tonight."

"Tristan, you didn't," she sighs, a feeling of hopelessness settling into her chest.

"What choice did I have?" he snaps. "You don't seem to realize that time is running out. You've been a Guardian for, what, two weeks? I've been a Guardian for sixteen years! I understand that fate doesn't wait for cocktail parties with your pretend family."

"They are not my pretend family." Now it's her own anger that simmers. "What happened with Jareth?"

"I told him the truth."

"Yes, because that went so well with me." She can't help that her tone is catty, if only to battle the rage in his.

His scowl deepens. "I gave him his stone. He felt its power. And he rejected it. We're going to lose him, and all you care about is playing house."

"You have no idea what I care about!" Her shout echoes in the large empty kitchen, and it has temporarily stunned him.

They stand in silence for a moment, and the tension is thick as the butter she loves to cook with.

"For your information, my night was not all fun and family games," she says in a low voice. "Cassandra and her parents were our guests, and needless to say it was the dinner from Hell. I rushed over here as soon as I saw your missed calls. All I wanted was to see you, help you, share our grievances. I care about you, Tristan, and I'm with you in this fight a hundred and ten percent. But if you aren't careful, you'll lose a friend. How many does that leave you with?"

He leans on the counter and lowers his head so she can't see his face. "I'm better off doing this on my own." His voice is low, so low she can barely hear it over the hum of the refrigerator.

But it's enough.

Without a word, she turns around and heads to the front door.

Mostly so he won't see the tears brimming in her eyes.

She slams the door behind her and takes a deep, calming breath before calling Frank to pick her up.

"That was fast," Frank says over the phone. "Bea and I barely ordered our fro-yos."

"Yeah, I know, I'm sorry," she says, fighting the tightness in her throat and willing the tears to reabsorb to no avail. "I guess Tristan is already out for the night. I'll just catch up on the project another time."

"Okay." Frank's voice holds notes of concern and doubt. "Well, do you want us to grab you a fro-yo before we come?"

"Sure, sounds great," she says before she hangs up.

Might as well drown her sorrows with frosty goodness like the girls in sad romances do.

Only this one won't ever have a happy ending.

20

JARETH

J areth draws in a deep breath as he steps off the bus. He stands there, watching the other students make their way to the entrance of Mirror Point high.

He can't believe he's back here. He was so sure he wouldn't be returning.

But then Tristan visited and brought his crazy theories with him. And that stone.

Jareth doesn't know what Tristan had done to it, but for a split-second, the sensations had felt so real.

It's amazing what the power of suggestion can do.

Which is why Jareth's here. If Tristan has tried his tricks on Brielle, she might be mixed up with one hell of a crazy guy. And Brielle's too nice for that. Too gentle and sweet.

Hoisting his backpack strap further up his shoulder, Jareth grits his teeth. He'll check on Brielle, and then he can leave Mirror Point with a clean conscience.

Plus, if Shandra keeps hassling him, at least he can say with all honesty that he went to school today.

Jareth's only taken a few steps when he sees Brielle. She's standing off to the side, checking her phone as she frowns.

She looks up, scanning the students milling around her as if she's looking for someone, her brows sinking even lower.

The next turn of her head and she sees Jareth walking toward her. The frown washes away with her momentary surprise, and her face quickly blossoms into a smile.

She waits until he's stopped before her. "Hey. You came to school today."

Jareth glances at the large building not far away from them. "I wasn't planning on it."

"I'm glad you did."

A spark of warmth flares in Jareth's chest. He'd almost forgotten how good it is to connect with someone. But then his spine stiffens.

There's an arrow tucked in his wardrobe to remind him exactly why he shouldn't connect with anyone.

"I came to see you, actually."

Brielle's smile brightens. "You did?"

"Yeah. Tristan visited me last night."

The smile not only disappears again, but it's replaced with a scowl. "He did, did he?" Her tone doesn't sound surprised though.

"He said some...pretty crazy stuff." Jareth's hands tighten around the strap of his backpack. "I kicked him out."

Brielle raises her free hand to press against her temple. "I bet you did."

Her phone dings and she glances at her screen, her brows knitting even further. "Well, you won't be able to talk to him about it. Tristan's not coming to school today."

"That's fine. Like I said, it's you I wanted to talk to."

Actually, Jareth's relieved. Having to see that guy again was the big drawback of coming today.

Tucking her phone in her pocket, Brielle focuses back on Jareth, her smile returning. "Sure. What's up?"

"All that stuff Tristan said. Your boyfriend has issues."

Brielle blinks. "He's not," she says, her gaze sliding away. "My boyfriend, that is."

Jareth's brows jump up but she doesn't see. He only saw them together for a few moments, but there was definitely something between them. He recognized it because he saw it with his parents. An unconscious, almost instinctive, contraction when they were near each other.

Well, if they're not an item yet, it's only a matter of time.

Jareth frowns. Maybe that's how Tristan recruits girls. "But you believe everything he says, don't you?"

Brielle's gaze settles on his, looking as if she's holding her breath. "I do."

Jareth doesn't need lie detection abilities to see that Brielle's telling the truth. Her eyes shine with it. And conviction.

His gut clenches. She's in deeper than he thought.

"You need to be careful with guys like that, Brielle. He means trouble."

For some reason, that has her smiling. "Trouble certainly follows him."

"And that doesn't scare you?"

Brielle bites her lip, snuffing out the smile. "Sometimes. But Tristan's the good guy, Jareth. He might be intense, and a jerk sometimes, but there's a reason for that."

"Well, I didn't appreciate his visit."

Sighing, Brielle nods. "I'll tell him to back off. Everything he told you, it's a lot to take in."

"And it's all a load of crap," Jareth adds darkly.

Brielle needs to consider that maybe Tristan's lying to her.

The ringing of the bell has them both looking around as if they're surprised to find themselves still outside of school. The other students around them start making their way up the stairs, disappearing into the building.

Brielle turns back to Jareth. "Are you staying today?"

Jareth hesitates. Now that he's spoken to Brielle, there's no reason to.

Except, the prospect of spending the day at home, painting, doesn't have the same pull it did. Not since Tristan tried to explain why Jareth can do what he can do.

Brielle presses her hand onto his arm. "We could hang out at breaks. Debate which is the most memorable fro-yo flavor at Creamy Dreams."

Jareth grins. "Have you tried the pumpkin pie flavor?"

Brielle wrinkles her nose. "I avoid vegetable flavors when it comes to desserts."

Chuckling, Jareth finds himself following the flow of students into school. Tristan isn't here today. Shandra will make a happy note in her books for a change.

And now, Jareth has a little more time to convince Brielle that Tristan's going to be nothing but bad news.

They're just at the doors when Jareth's cell rings. He pulls it out of his pocket to turn it off when he sees Veronica's name lighting up his screen. He shows it to Brielle. "It's Veronica."

Brielle looks a little perplexed. "Cool."

Jareth presses the green button before it goes to the message bank. "Hey, I'm just at school with Brielle."

Brielle waves, indicating she'll meet him inside. Appreciating that she's giving him some privacy, Jareth slips back out the door and leans against the wall.

"Oh, is she still with you?" asks Veronica.

"She's gone inside. I'll tell her you said hi."

"No need," Veronica replies airily. "I'm catching up with her tomorrow." There's a brief pause. "What do you know about…Brielle?"

"Not much. I'm new, remember?" Jareth feels himself tense. "Why?"

"Oh, no reason. Somedays, I think she and Tristan are joined at the hip!" She giggles. "Anyway, this isn't why I called. I'm checking up the time for Saturday."

Jareth finds himself grinning. "You know, I never agreed to a date."

"You never disagreed," Veronica counters.

The second bell rings, strident in its reminder that Jareth's supposed to be waiting outside his first class. Glancing at the door, he pushes off the wall.

He's already decided he's spending the day here at school.

A few more days can't hurt.

"I'll meet you at five outside Creamy Dreams."

"Looking forward to it," Veronica purrs, sending shivers dancing down Jareth's spine.

They hang up and Jareth looks around, surprised at the bright, light feeling in his chest.

He'll give himself a few days to convince Brielle she can be free of Tristan.

He'll go on this date.

Then, he'll leave.

TRISTAN

S handra is possibly going to break a nail writing notes
on him, but Tristan doesn't care. He's not going to
school today.

Glancing at the clock, he realizes Brielle would be in
cooking class right now. When he'd woken up this morning,
his head feeling like a pressure cooker, that had been the one
reason he'd considered going. Cooking with Brielle is fun,
not to mention delicious. Quite often, it's the highlight of
his day.

But then he'd remembered the awful things he'd said to
her last night.

And how crushed she was by them.

Tristan wipes a hand down his face. Which is exactly why
he's now sitting in HQ, staring at a screen, wondering what
Brielle's making in class.

Knowing he'll never get to taste it.

Opening a web browser, Tristan wonders if he wants this
too bad. It's possible Jareth isn't a Zodiac Guardian. That
Tristan's stalking the wrong guy.

But he could've sworn he saw Jareth jerk when the onyx

landed in his palm. Then he'd stood there, still as a statue for several seconds.

Only to throw the gem away, like it was nothing. Like he never wanted to touch it again.

And what other explanation is there for what Jareth can do?

His fingers punching the keyboard, Tristan types in two words. *Jareth Stone*.

He quickly discounts the handful of social profiles that come up—too blond, way too old, wrong skin tone. Clicking to the next page, Tristan keeps scanning. There's got to be something he can use as a lead.

But the following page gives Tristan nothing, apart from learning that Jareth is the Goblin King in some movie about a labyrinth. And that there's some guy with the same name who records himself playing video games while listening to classical music.

With a sigh, Tristan tries the next page. The links to his search term become weaker, showing results for Jared Stone, the Rolling Stones, some artist called Meredith Stone.

Tristan pauses. Jareth is an artist. Figuring he doesn't have anything else better to do than disappear down the rabbit hole of the world wide web, Tristan clicks on the link.

It's a news site from some town in California, reporting on the tragic death of a well-loved local artist and her husband. Tristan scans their photos—the woman has long, dark hair and smiling eyes. There's a daisy tucked behind her ear. The man is balding with glasses, looking like your friendly neighbourhood professor.

And they died in a house fire.

Suddenly alert, Tristan devours the short piece. It seems Meredith and Jacob were local celebrities who were well loved by the community. The tragic house fire started somewhere in the early hours of the morning. The couple were found in the kitchen, clinging to each other. Burned to a crisp.

While Jacob was a senior psychology lecturer in the nearby university, Meredith ran a healing center from a small yurt in their backyard. Tristan's brows hike up as he keeps reading. It seems she was also an entrepreneur. She created intricate dream catchers out of nothing but leaves and bark, she grew her own oolong tea, and she was the creator of Zen Paints.

His lips pressed hard together, Tristan's eyes scan the next lines, a direct quote from Meredith herself.

Zen Paints are inspired by the art of living in the moment. Paint to your glorious heart's content, then as the water slowly evaporates, your art will magically disappear leaving you with a clean slate, ready for you to find new heights of painting transcendence.

Tristan quickly scans the last line, more than ready to shut the whole thing down. *Meredith and Jacob Stone are survived by their only son. Our hearts go out to him during this difficult time.*

Discouraged, Tristan sags back in his seat. Water-based paint that disappears as it evaporates. Although it doesn't explain the colors that Jareth created, it goes some of the way to explain his disappearing creations.

Clenching his hands so hard he has to release the mouse before he crushes it, Tristan jerks back from the table. Everything's going wrong. Jareth. Brielle. Finding a way they can win the inevitable war that's coming. Why the hell did Zarius and Tess think he could do this?

Standing up so fast the chair wheels away crazily behind him, Tristan decides he'll do the only thing he can. Train. Yesterday, the wooden dummy cracked him across the back of the head, apparently not appreciating the kick Tristan dealt. Now, he has a score to settle.

If he has to be the only one who'll face Chardis when he shows his black hole for a face again, so be it.

But just as he's about to take a step, Tristan stumbles. His vision narrows, the edges blurring into nothingness. Blindly, he reaches out for the desk. Only the tips of his fingers connect with it, but it's enough. A few quick shuffles and he grips his one link to reality more tightly.

He hasn't had a vision since Zarius and Tess died. Although he's never really welcomed them, he knows he doesn't want to see whatever's coming. This is the last thing he needs.

As he exhales, the world dissolves.

With the next inhale, Tristan finds himself surrounded by flames. Roaring, fierce flames.

Instinctively, he raises his arms to protect his face, only to realize he can see the fire. Hear the fire.

But he can't feel the fire.

Lowering his arms, Tristan looks around. He's in a house, but not one that he recognizes, although it's hard to tell. The walls are moving waves of red and orange, the ceiling a roiling inferno. There's no way to know if he's standing in the very same room as he is now.

In the center is Jareth. Clinging to him is a curvy girl with dark hair. She presses closer as something crashes beyond the walls of heat they're surrounded by. Jareth draws her in closer, wrapping a protective arm around her head as he glances around frantically.

Suddenly he looks up, dread stamped across his features. Tristan's gut clenches. He heard it, too. The groaning of the ceiling above them.

Tristan shouts for them to move even though he knows they can't hear him. Even though they have nowhere to go.

He's seeing a future that hasn't happened yet.

Jareth curls around the girl even tighter, squeezing his eyes shut. "I'm so sorry," he whispers hoarsely.

As the roof collapses, the flames soar and surge for the sky like a monster who's suddenly been set free. The house becomes an inferno.

One nobody could survive.

Tristan's left panting as the vision recedes, clutching the table like a lifeline. He braces himself for what's coming next.

The second vision.

The room appears again, just like last time. Unrecognizable. Roaring with rage. Violently alive with flames he can't feel.

The ceiling collapses, the fire implodes and explodes all at once. All that's left behind is a concave shell of a house.

Tristan's legs almost give out. This time, there was no one in the room. No Jareth, no girl.

In this scenario, there will be no charred bodies for others to find.

Reality returns, feeling too quiet after what Tristan just experienced. He looks around the room, his mouth dry, beads of sweat cooling on his forehead.

That vision was like visiting hell itself. And there's no Zarius to talk him through it. No Tess and her eternal optimism to believe the second vision is the true one.

Wiping his arm across his forehead, Tristan sighs. There's no way he's going to let the first vision come true.

Because Zodiac or no Zodiac, Jareth's in danger.

Which means Tristan has to find a way to get through to him.

22

VERONICA

W hat is the connection between these three?
Jareth Stone. Brielle Pierce. And Tristan Ayers.
Any time she's seen Tristan, he's with Brielle. And the two of them seem awfully interested in Jareth.

Veronica needs to understand what the missing link is between them. She'd promised her dad she wouldn't investigate, but isn't it her civic duty to protect an innocent civilian —i.e. Jareth—from whatever Tristan might be up to? Plus, she never said she wouldn't investigate Jareth...

Having just gotten a text from her dad saying he won't be home anytime soon, Veronica knows she has time to hack into his computer and do some digging. She's done all she can do with Tristan—a bunch of clean records that say he's nothing more than an upstanding teen who just lost his parents in a mysterious warehouse slaughter. Basically, a bunch of nada.

But this Brielle character. She's on her dad's radar. Why?

That's her next step. Find out who Brielle really is and if she's any kind of threat.

Before she makes any move in edgewise, she pulls out her phone to text her brother.

Hey Bro, when you coming home? Whether or not you're planning to cook, I'm ordering pizza. No offense lol

She throws the tennis ball at the same spot on the beaten wall as she waits. It really is a wonder the paint hasn't flaked off yet.

The phone lights up on the bed beside her.

Studying with some friends. Go ahead and order. And don't get jalapenos this time!

She chuckles, then hops out of bed with a determination she no doubt inherited from her dad.

She's in his office sitting at his desk in seconds, having picked the lock in no time flat.

Using the password she figured out months ago—Logan's and her birthdays—she's logged into the FBI database. Her fingers rapidly type in the name Brielle Pierce, like she expects someone to walk in on her any minute. Speed has been bred into her when it comes to espionage.

Brielle's background info pops up.

Interesting. Brielle has only had the surname Pierce for a few weeks. Before that she was at the Grace Orphanage all her life.

For some reason, that makes Veronica's heart cringe. How awful it would be to grow up with no family. Sure, she lost her mother at a young age, but her father is everything to her. Hence, all this! She can't imagine having no parents, no home, no history but what you've lived.

She shakes off the twinge of empathy and focuses. No criminal history. No records at all but the addresses on the screen. Brielle's current home and the orphanage.

Veronica enters the latter into her phone and logs off, locking the office door behind her before heading out.

Her phone's GPS leads her to a quaint, gothic style orphanage that looks like it used to be a church.

Yet somehow, it still surprises her when a nun answers the door. The plump, handsome woman isn't wearing a comical habit, but there's a large rosary around her neck, and crosses all over the walls, along with paintings of various saints here and there.

She didn't realize Catholic orphanages still existed. And she just found her way in.

"Good afternoon, dear," the middle-aged nun says, giving her a curious look. "Can I help you?"

"Good afternoon, sister," Veronica greets, plastering a sweet smile on her face. "My name is Viv Styles and I'm writing a paper about this orphanage for school. I've been doing research online and at the library, but I figured, what better way to get to the heart of its colorful history than by speaking to some of its respectable nuns?"

The sister chuckles, her large belly bouncing slightly. "We'd be happy to help you with your assignment, but wouldn't you find abundant information more easily at the library or on the internet?"

Veronica isn't backing down that easily. Besides, she knows how to work older authority figures. "Well, this is closer to the shelter where I volunteer after school. And, truth be told, I'm interested myself in pursuing a life of piety. Knowing that there's a holy establishment such as this still in existence gives me hope." She widens her eyes and tilts her head slightly downward in a way she knows makes them sparkle.

The nun's face blossoms into a wide grin. "An aspiring nun, how splendid! Heaven knows we could use more of those. Come in and I'll do my best to answer any questions you may have." She opens the door and gestures for Veronica to enter and follow her to a loungeroom to the right.

Score!

They sit in opposite green loveseats that are stiffer than they appear.

"What would you like to know?" the nun asks.

"Well, Sister…?"

"Sister Agatha," the nun offers.

"Thank you," Veronica says. "Sister Agatha, I was wondering, why did this building transform from a church to an orphanage?"

Sister Agatha starts her explanation slowly at first, but then brightens up as she retells the story of how in the nineteen sixties the orphan population of New York City was so large that orphanages were overrun and the death rates of infants especially were skyrocketing. The nuns of Grace Orphanage were compelled to take in as many orphans as they could just to help them stay alive, and possibly bring them over to the faith. After a few years, the Catholic Church realized the value of the cause, and the dropping numbers of patrons, and officially turned the church into an orphanage.

"Wow, I had no idea," Veronica says, feigning greater interest than she feels. She asks a few more questions, making sure Sister Agatha is fully wrapped around her finger before she gets to the crux of the matter.

Before long, the stiffness in Sister Agatha's round shoulders loosens, the wrinkles in her cheeks crease in a wide smile. She's got her.

"You know, Sister," Veronica begins. "The reason I even decided to write my paper on this orphanage was because I have a friend who resided here."

"Oh?" Sister Agatha cocks her head, intrigued. "Who?"

"Brielle," Veronica replies, batting her eyes to increase the charm. "Brielle Pierce. She's such a sweet girl."

A twinkle brightens the nun's stern eyes. "Yes, she certainly is. I'm so glad she has you as a friend! I do worry about her."

"Really?" She's on to something now. "Why is that?"

The wrinkle between the nun's brows deepens slightly. "Well, as you may or may not know, she had quite a difficult time getting adopted."

Veronica didn't know. "I never understood why. She'd been here all her life, right? Since she was a baby?"

Sister Agatha nods. "Yes, the poor dear."

"Is it normal for someone here to get so close to aging out of the system?" Veronica pries, hoping to figure out if Brielle has any skeletons in her closet that caused the delay in her adoption.

"Well, Brielle…" The nun's eyes wander thoughtfully. "She was…a troubled young girl. She was well known here for her honesty, and I believe many of her peers didn't appreciate that honesty."

"She tattled on others?" Veronica asks. Not exactly a deplorable trait. Many of her dad's successes have depended on narcs.

"Not exactly. But when asked a direct question, she would answer honestly, even if she didn't want to. Almost like she couldn't bear to lie."

None of this is what Veronica expected to hear. And she doesn't quite know what to make of this information. None of it screams "aliens". She's certainly never heard anything about aliens being unable to lie.

And she still has no idea what the connection is between Brielle, Jareth and Tristan.

"Well, anyway, I'm glad Brielle has a good family now," Veronica says.

"How is she doing?" Sister Agatha leans forward, interest burning in her gray eyes. Veronica can almost feel the love the woman has for the girl who's a stranger to her.

"She's doing well," Veronica lies. "She seems happy. And she's making lots of new friends."

"Good, I'm glad to hear it."

Veronica stands. "Well, I've taken enough of your time. I should get going."

Sister Agatha stands as well and escorts her to the front door. "Thank you so much for coming. And if you need any more information for your assignment, don't be afraid to stop by."

"Of course. Good night, Sister."

The door closes behind her, and Veronica stands at the bottom of the steps, chewing her lips as she ponders.

So far, the only link she can see between the three teens is that Jareth and Tristan are now orphans and Brielle used to be one. It at least appears that Brielle and Tristan have known each other longer than the few weeks she's been with her new family. Could Tristan be targeting orphans, people who have no one else, to recruit them for some alien deeds?

Brielle seems like a sweet person, and Jareth is definitely a tortured soul. Those are often the types of people terrorists target.

The buzzing in her pocket stirs her out of her internal debate. She pulls out her phone to see a calendar alert. Her date with Jareth is in thirty minutes.

Perfect!

Maybe he can illuminate the mystery further.

But that's not the reason her heart skips a beat.

She's excited for this date for an entirely different reason.

23

JARETH

J areth adjusts the collar of his shirt for the fifth time, then checks his watch for the hundredth time. Ten minutes to go.

Scuffing his shoe on the pavement outside Creamy Dreams, he sighs. It seems without a mother to fuss over him, his brain is determined to do that itself. He'd swapped shirts several times, in the end wearing the first one he chose. He brushed his hair so it didn't fall in his eyes so much, and now he's glad it's flopped straight back to where it usually sits. It means he doesn't feel so…exposed.

He's not even sure what he's doing here.

By now, he should be on a bus back to California. But then there was Brielle's naivety and Tristan's craziness.

And then there's Veronica…

Scuffing the pavement again, a daisy catches Jareth's eye. Growing up through the cracks, the solitary flower looks like just that.

A single bloom.

Impulsively, he picks it. An everyday sight, yet it holds far more than most people realize. The petals are not really petals at all. The center is hundreds of flowers packed in together. His mother was always saying the daisy was a testament that everything is not as it seems.

"Hey."

Jareth looks up, startled and yet relieved all at once. She came.

He blinks. And she's beautiful.

One arm behind her back, Veronica bounces a little on her toes. Somehow, she can pull off a short, flared skirt along with black army boots.

She glances down, her smile growing. "Is that for me?"

Too late, Jareth realizes his hand is still frozen, clutching the small daisy. "Yeah, but you don't—"

Veronica's arm slips from around her back, a flush of her own tinting her cheeks. "I saw this and couldn't help myself."

She holds out her own daisy and something warm but indefinable blossoms in Jareth's chest. She reaches out, taking the flower Jareth's still holding as she swaps it with hers. Tingles dance across his skin at the contact. Then, with a sweet smile, she tucks it behind her ear.

Jareth blinks. One small gesture. And he can no longer deny why he's here.

He's drawn to this girl in a way he never has been before.

They both turn toward Creamy Dreams, yet neither move.

"Do you want to eat outside or inside?" Veronica asks.

Jareth hesitates. He doesn't like being around too many people. "I, ah, thought we might go for a walk?"

"Time alone. I like."

And there's that, too.

Veronica heads toward the door, a skip in her step. Jareth's heart seems to mirror the same joyous little leaps. Pushing the door open, he waits for her to pass through. Her eyes glinting her thanks, she slips past him, her arm grazing his chest. Heat spirals from the single point of contact, sweet and sharp. Before it's had a chance to fade away, Jareth's already wanting to feel it again.

For a split second, Veronica stills, and if Jareth wasn't so fascinated with every move this girl makes, he probably would've missed it. Ducking her head, she enters the café, leaving Jareth wondering if she felt it, too.

Inside, she scans the brightly lit menu above the counter. "I don't know why I'm doing this, I always get the same thing."

Jareth chuckles. "Once I discovered the pecan praline, I haven't moved on."

An older woman with bleached blonde hair steps up to the register. She looks from Jareth to Veronica and then back to Jareth, her gaze staying there. "Well, hello there. How can I tantalize your taste buds today, young man?"

Jareth's just telling himself he imagined the innuendo in the woman's words when he hears Veronica stifle a giggle. He works not to frown. Is this even legal?

"Ah, hi. Can I order a single pecan praline, and…" He turns to Veronica. "You want a double?"

Veronica wraps herself around his arms, her soft curves pressing up against him. "Can I have a triple, please. Cherry Cobbler on the bottom, Watermelon Wonder next, and Lemon Meringue on top."

The woman—Madge according to her name badge—seems to be more focused on the way Veronica just staked a claim on Jareth. "Sure," she mutters.

Veronica looks up at Jareth as Madge leaves to fill their order. "I call it Fruit Salad Sunrise."

Jareth shakes his head as he grins. "It's practically health food."

"That's what I tell everyone, too."

Madge returns with their frozen yogurt, Jareth's single

cup looking drab and small compared to Veronica's stacked shades of dawn. She passes them to Jareth with a wink. "There you go, handsome."

Jareth spins around and hightails it out of the café before Veronica's giggles can erupt. Outside, they've just passed the building when she bursts into laughter. Jareth shakes his head again, wondering how many times he's going to be doing the same thing throughout this date. "She..."

"Doesn't seem to think age is a barrier?" offers Veronica, fresh peals of laughter bubbling past her lips.

Jareth passes Veronica her fro-yo. "I think we never talk about that again."

Taking it, Veronica winks at him. "I think I might never let you live that down."

Pausing, Jareth realizes she's talking about future times they'll be laughing together. Future dates.

Jabbing his spoon into his pecan praline, he knows he needs to be honest with her. "I'm not planning on staying in Mirror Point, Veronica. It's why I didn't think this date was a great idea."

"So under different circumstances, you would've been up for it?"

Jareth blinks. That's what she decides to focus on? "Well, yeah. In a heartbeat."

Veronica's beautiful. Vivacious. She's a force of energy that's set his world in motion again, whether he wanted it to or not.

Her smile is instantaneous. And dazzling. "Well, that's all that counts for now."

One thought rises in Jareth's mind. *My mom would've loved this girl.*

Veronica looks at her fro-yo. "Oh, she forgot to give me a spoon." She throws a wry glance toward Jareth. "Probably too busy trying to recruit you to her harem."

She's gone before Jareth can reply, although a response hadn't exactly formed yet. Leaning against the wall, he watches her sashay back into the café. Few girls could pull off sashaying in army boots, but Veronica does it in a way that has him entranced.

With a quick smile over her shoulder, she disappears inside.

Jareth's responding smile is still intact as he idly runs his finger over the brick wall beside him. Without conscious thought, a little daisy appears on the rough surface. Small, delicate, beautiful. He realizes it's the first thing he's painted that isn't fire. Consumed by flames. Defined by death.

And he likes the way it looks.

"Got it," Veronica says as she approaches, holding up a long handled plastic spoon.

Jareth jolts upright, covering his impulsive painting with his shoulder. Thankfully, in a few minutes it'll be gone.

"Great. Is there anywhere worth checking out around here?"

Veronica sucks on a spoonful of the frozen dessert as she stares down the street one way then the other. "Not really." But then she brightens. "We could just wander aimlessly."

"Sounds like my life, so I'm in."

Jareth heads right, away from the business of the main street, and Veronica falls into step. They walk in silence, spooning fro-yo into their mouths. Jareth watches her from the corner of his eye, knowing he's probably supposed to be making small talk, but having no idea what that should be. She looks thoughtful, but not uncomfortable.

She turns, catching him looking at her. "Why aren't you staying, Jareth?"

Jareth shrugs. "I thought this place could be a new start. Seems I was wrong."

"Obviously you had high expectations of Mirror Point," jokes Veronica. "But how did it let you down so bad?"

They reach the end of the block, and Jareth takes a left, Veronica seemingly happy to go with the flow. He takes the time to think through his answer.

"Well, school's kinda lame."

Veronica snorts. "That's universal."

"I thought I'd stop missing my parents so much."

"My mom died when I was ten. I still miss her."

The street stretches out before them, tree lined and quiet, and Jareth slows down. He thinks of what finally had him wanting to leave. "And people here are crazy."

Even as he walks beside one of the reasons he's still here.

Veronica huffs out a laugh. "Fair call." She pokes her frozen yogurt, swirling together the sunrise hues. "Although the term crazy can be used rather liberally."

"I'm pretty sure talking about aliens is crazy."

Startling, Veronica looks up at him. "Aliens?"

Realizing he's just freaked her out, Jareth quickly clarifies. "It's nothing. Just something a guy from school said to me."

"Tristan?"

"Yeah. That guy is really something," Jareth mutters.

"What did he want?"

Jareth shakes his head. "You don't want to know. It doesn't matter anyway, I told him to leave me alone."

"Aren't he and Brielle a thing, though? And Brielle's your friend?"

"Yeah, that's the tricky bit. Brielle needs to stay away from him, too. He's bad news."

Veronica nudges his shoulder. "You sound like Logan— my protective older brother."

Jareth smiles ruefully. "Brielle's nice. She deserves better than getting caught up with someone like Tristan." He scoops up another spoonful. "But, enough about me. So it's just you and your brother and dad?"

Veronica scrunches up her nose. "I'd much rather talk about you, but yep, just me and those two lugs. The food's terrible, but I wouldn't trade them for anything."

Another left and Jareth realizes they're heading back toward Creamy Dreams. They've done a giant block, bringing them back to their starting point.

"Holy crap," Veronica breathes.

Jareth looks up in alarm, his heart hammering, but before he can see what's going on, Veronica's yanked him into a nearby shrub.

"What's—"

She clamps her hand over his mouth. "Shh."

Terrified, Jareth thinks of the arrow that impaled the tree at the cemetery. About the fire that killed his parents being forever labelled 'suspicious.' He glances out, seeing a silver sedan driving past, one male in the driver's seat.

A moment later, Veronica relaxes. "All clear."

Already? She slips her hand from his mouth, smiling sheepishly. "Sorry. My dad drove past."

"You dad?" Jareth croaks.

Brushing a branch from her face, Veronica nods. "He's been away for work, but it seems he's back early."

Now, Jareth's conscious of twigs poking him in the back, something jammed into his ribs, and a leaf tickling his ear. "He didn't know about our date?"

Veronica's hazel gaze can't meet his. "I may not have mentioned it."

"But you hid when he drove past. That's more than failing to mention it."

"My dad…he's got a lot on his plate right now. I just didn't want to stress him out before I knew where this was going."

"Right…"

Veronica's hands are on his chest, her body pressed against his. She frowns. "Your heart feels like it's on speed. Are you okay?"

Jareth goes as stiff as the branches around him. "Getting shoved into a shrub puts me on edge, okay?"

Jareth pulls away, stepping out of the bush. Veronica's closeness is…distracting. "It's probably a good thing your dad didn't know, seeing as I'm not staying."

Veronica follows him, pulling a leaf out of her curls. "Except you're not wandering aimlessly, Jareth. Everything we do is a decision. For example, you chose to walk this way, away from crowds"—she wriggles her brows—"obviously to get me alone. This date was a choice. Leaving is a choice." She holds his gaze. "But so is staying."

Frowning, Jareth starts walking again. The sudden yank into the bushes reminded him that he lives his life looking over his shoulder. That people he cares for die.

Except just being on this date has proven Veronica right. He wanted to be here.

Which now leaves him with the next choice to make…

They're almost back at Creamy Dreams when Veronica stops. "I had a really good time, Jareth." She smiles as she touches the daisy still tucked behind her ear. "And I have something to remember it by."

Jareth stops, too, finding himself next to the wall he stood beside while Veronica got her spoon. He pulls out his own daisy that he'd carefully tucked in his back pocket. "Me, too."

Veronica doesn't move, her kaleidoscope eyes seeming to hold a minefield of questions.

Will he stay?

Will he go?

But then her gaze flutters past her shoulders and that smile that takes his breath away spreads across her face. She moves in close, raising a finger to touch something on the wall behind him. Jareth turns and glances down, wondering what's caught her attention.

His eyes widen when he sees it. A daisy. Painted on the wall. Permanently.

"It's like someone immortalized our first date," Veronica murmurs as she touches it reverently.

Someone did.

Jareth.

Except it's not supposed to still be there.

Veronica takes a step closer. "Do you know what else would make it unforgettable?"

Jareth's gaze dips to her lips. A kiss…

He shouldn't.

It's not safe for him. Or for her.

But Jareth finds his head tipping forward, his body leaning in of its own volition. Three words whisper through his heart.

Meant to be.

He's only a few millimeters away when Veronica closes the remaining distance between them, impulsive and impatient as always. Their smiling lips brush. Something ignites.

Everything melts away.

Everything apart from the magic of the girl who's now in his arms. Their smiles dissolve. Veronica's hands return to press against his chest, curling into his shirt. Jareth draws her in, his world capsizing yet finding a new center of gravity all at once.

He pulls back as his arms tighten, instinctively wanting more. Veronica's eyes flutter open, the same dazed and delighted emotions he's feeling reflected there.

She steps back, smiling. "I don't know if you should stay, Jareth. But if you do, I'd love more daisies in my life."

Spinning around fast enough for her skirt to flare a little, she walks away, disappearing around the corner. Jareth stands there for long moments, trying to get his bearings.

His heart feels like it's soaring on a rainbow. A part of him wants to go pick every daisy he can find and bring them to Veronica.

But then he turns back and sees the single flower that's still on the wall. He touches it just like Veronica did. It's as real as the bricks it's painted on.

How is it possible?

Why is it still there?

Jamming his hands into his pockets, Jareth knows it's time to get home. Maybe subconsciously he didn't want this painting to disappear. It's the only explanation he can think of.

Crossing the road, Jareth stands at the bus stop. What the hell is he supposed to do now? His brain is screaming at him to leave. To run. To try and find some corner of this world where he can be safe.

But that would mean never seeing Veronica again.

And turning his back on Brielle.

The bus pulls up almost like Jareth willed it to get there so quickly. He climbs on, grabbing his usual seat in the middle and hunkering down.

He has a choice to make. Stay. Or leave.

But even as he arrives home, Jareth isn't any closer to a decision. As he slips his key into the door, Jareth's skin prickles. Telling himself his paranoid tendencies are being triggered again, he glances over his shoulder.

And freezes.

A silver sedan is driving past. Slowly. And the man in the driver's seat doesn't look like someone who could be Veronica's father. Even under his hoodie, Jareth can see the dark hair, the face only a few years older than him. He's too young to be the father of a teen.

The guy's gaze catches Jareth's, shocking him with the hot fury he finds there. With a threatening snarl, the guy accelerates and drives away.

It takes a few tries to turn the key because Jareth's hands are shaking so bad, but the moment he can, he slips inside. He presses himself against the door.

Surely, being somewhere far away, and alone, is the best thing he can do for everyone?

JACK

17:46

Jack straightens his tie then rubs his rough cheek. The small electric razor he keeps in the car never does a great job, but it's good enough to pull off respectable FBI agent.

Rather than rogue FBI agent.

Ignoring the twinge in his chest, Jack raps on the door in front of him and takes a step back. Dirty windows. Unkempt yard. Sagging porch.

The Shaw family don't put a lot of money into the upkeep of their place. They either don't want to, or they don't have the cash.

There are sounds of locks turning and chains rattling, and the door opens. Behind the screen stands a thin, limp woman. She takes one look at Jack's suit and crosses her arms. "Yeah?"

Jack pulls out his badge and presses it against the screen between them. "Good day, Mrs. Shaw. I'm Detective Jack Cadbury. I'd like to ask you a few questions about your daughter."

In a flash, the woman's shoved open the door. "You got news about my Adalind?"

Jack doesn't twitch a muscle, hiding his surprise. This woman doesn't know what's happened to her daughter? That means that Jack's the first official here since they ID'd the body.

And that Jack's going to have to tell the woman her daughter's dead.

"If I could come in?"

"Hell yeah, you can come in." She waves him in, straightening her gray cardigan. "Would you like a coffee or somethin'?"

Hell no.

Jack smiles. "I'm fine, thank you, Mrs. Shaw."

She flaps away the formality. "Just call me Darlene, hon. I ain't been a missus in years."

"Of course." Jack notes the cigarette stained curtains, the lack of furniture, the piles of rubbish in the corners of the room. He suspects Darlene fits into both types when it comes to home maintenance—she doesn't have the cash, but nor does she really care.

She takes a seat in a saggy chair that looks like a dog chewed off the end of one arm, indicating for Jack to sit on the discolored couch across from her.

Perching on the end, Jack smiles in thanks. "I'm afraid it's not good news, Darlene."

She blinks. "She's been missing for months. Did you know that? At first I thought she'd just run away." Her mouth twists. "We'd had another of them arguments over her phone. But she didn't come back…"

"She—"

But Darlene holds up her hand. "Then I figured she'd shacked up with her boyfriend, no matter how much I told her he was no good." She huffs. "Probably because I told her he was no good."

"Well—"

"But she would've rung me, eventually, you know. We may have fought like cats, but we were all each other had." Her shoulders sag. "But she never rang."

Jack waits, making sure Darlene's finished. That's she's as ready as she can be.

"Adalind died in a warehouse in New York, Darlene. She was found with two other bodies. We're still trying to ascertain the cause of death."

Darlene's eyes close, two tears leaking out and trickling down her worn cheeks. "So far from home. I already knew, but still, hearing it…"

"I'm very sorry for your loss."

Even as he says the words, Jack knows they're not enough. They never are. No matter how many times he's had to do this, he hasn't found the right ones.

He's pretty sure there aren't any.

Jack pulls a card out of his wallet, placing it on the sticky coffee table. "Here are some numbers and services which may be of help."

Darlene nods, her aged face now looking ancient. "Ah, thanks." She looks away. "Do you mind?"

She doesn't need to say what she's asking; Jack knows. With a nod, he gets up and leaves. Darlene wants to be alone with her grief.

The sobbing starts the moment Jack closes the door behind him. Climbing into his car, he thumps the steering wheel in frustration.

Another casualty chalked up to Tristan Ayers, as far as he's concerned. He's the reason Jack's here and had to have that awful conversation.

If Adalind was missing for months, then she had to be living with someone. Someone with enough influence over her that she didn't bother telling her mom where she was.

And it's what got her killed.

Jack's just about to put the car in gear when his personal phone rings. He picks it up the minute he sees the name on the screen.

"Hey, son."

"Hey, Dad." For some reason, even after years of Logan calling him that despite not being his biological father this has a shot of warmth spearing through Jack. "He's found another one."

Jack straightens in the car seat. "Who?"

"Tristan went and visited a guy. Name's Jareth Stone. Another orphan. I think he's also tried to get Brielle to befriend him."

Jack's hand tightens around the phone. Of course, Tristan has. Orphans would be easy targets and the more people he has on his side, the easier his job will be.

Ending the human race.

"Good job. Keep up the tail. I'll be home tomorrow."

"That's not all." Something in Logan's tone has Jack pausing. "Veronica went on a date with Jareth last night."

"Son of a—" Jack thumps the steering wheel with his fist. Looks like there won't be the lumpy motel bed he was looking forward to for him tonight. "I'm coming home, now."

"Thought you might say that. What's she doing with him, Dad?"

Logan expressed a desire to follow in Jack's footsteps from a young age. Except, now Veronica is, too. Jack shifts, the leather seat creaking under his weight. The thought of both his children being involved in this makes him uncomfortable.

"I don't know," he growls. "But she won't be with him for long."

Jack's just hung up when his cell rings again. He figures Logan must've forgotten something, except when he looks at the screen, he discovers it's a silent number.

It could be his informant. Although Veronica likes to do the same thing sometimes, like she's playing agent. He used to find it amusing until he realized that's exactly what she's been trying to do.

Until she went on a date with one of them.

Jack presses the receive button and the phone hasn't reached his ear before he realizes this is one call he doesn't want to take.

"Cadbury!" McNally shouts. "Where the hell have you been?"

Jack winces. He doesn't give this number out to anyone who's not deemed necessary—and work isn't under that category. McNally obviously went to some lengths to get hold of it.

"Hey, boss. I'm—"

"Not in Chicago!" Jack can practically hear McNally's teeth grinding. "You disobeyed a direct order."

The burning sensation is back in Jack's gut. "Listen, I think I've got a lead on this Tris—"

"Get back. Now."

McNally bites off the last word and spits it through the phone, then the line goes dead. With a sigh, Jack starts the car. Flicking on the indicator, Jack pulls out of the driveway.

He'll be hauling his ass back to New York.

24

BRIELLE

S chool feels...empty.

Yesterday and today, Brielle feels Adalind's loss more than ever. If the friend she'd believed Adalind to be was still here, Brielle would be telling her all about the BS Tristan said to her the other night—well, sans Zodiac business. And Adalind would be totally on her side, telling her everything she needs to hear.

But Brielle has no one. Well, there was Jareth yesterday, but she especially can't talk to him about Tristan. Not when he's convinced Tristan is a psycho.

Second period comes around, and Brielle prays that Tristan will be MIA once again. She doesn't want to see him. Doesn't want to endure anymore verbal abuse. His last words to her did more damage than he could ever know.

But prayers don't pay the bills.

Tristan is already sitting at their station in cooking class when she walks in.

Great. She closes her eyes heavily and sighs, resolute to be as platonic with him as possible. Today, they're just class partners, nothing more.

She doesn't look at him as she sits at her stool. Again, the tension in the air is like chilled molasses. And she has no intentions of cutting through it. Not now.

"Hey—" he begins before Ms. Brom interrupts by starting class.

Brielle listens intently to what the teacher says about their assignment for the day, and thank pitch Ms. Brom decides to have them watch a film about burgers—*Super Size Me* to be exact. No doubt their next project will be crafting healthy burgers.

Brielle watches the movie with a singular focus, pretending not to notice every nudge and whisper made by Tristan during the hour. She doesn't want to hear it.

As soon as the bell rings, she flies out the room.

But she's not so lucky during lunch break. For the first time, she begrudges that they share the same lunch hour.

He catches her just as she enters the hallway from her last class.

"Hey, can we please talk?" he asks, his hand gently gripping her upper arm.

She jerks her arm away. "Talk about what? How disappointed you are in your only other Zodiac Guardian?" She continues toward the lunch hall, debating what she can say to make him leave her alone without burning the bridge forever.

"Come on, Brielle, you know I didn't mean it," he coos as he pursues her.

"I don't think I do," she says without looking back. "You made your thoughts very clear."

He gently grabs her arm again, the tingling contact stopping her in her tracks. "I can't tell you how sorry I am about that. I was just upset. Look…with everything going on…I'm just struggling to find a balance."

"Uh-huh," she hums dubiously, rolling her eyes—her only

defense against meeting his. If she does, she knows she'll break. She'll forgive him everything and return to being the dog who comes running at his command.

She's better than that. She *deserves* better than that.

"Look." He combs his hand through his honey hair, an action she can't help but watch—and pine over. "Can we just…have lunch together? You were right, you're my only friend."

"Oh, thanks for reminding me I'm your only option."

"That's not—ugh!" He groans. "What I mean is, I don't want to lose you. We don't even have to talk. Just…have lunch with me."

She rolls her eyes again and sighs, her resolve weakening. "Fine."

She can feel his smile even though she refuses to look at his face. And she hates it. She hates that she's so attuned to his every movement, every emotion.

And yet she's not his soulmate.

Dammit!

He hooks his arm in hers, a gesture that means something at this school whether he realizes it or not, and she lets him guide her to the cafeteria.

They sit at their usual table, opening their prepared lunches in silence. Thank pitch for the silence!

Only it doesn't last long.

"Look, I really am sorry," Tristan says, putting down his Tupperware as if he's upset that it's not properly distracting him anymore. "You have to know that I didn't mean any of that stuff I said last night. I'm just struggling to deal with everything that's going on. Living alone in a house that shouldn't be mine without the two people that shouldn't be gone."

She slumps her shoulders, feeling like sad melting ice cream. "I know," she says.

"You also have to know that you really are my best friend," he continues, summer eyes twinkling with sincerity. "I couldn't do any of this without you, and I wouldn't want to. I need you."

Those last three words dissolve every last bit of stubborn resentment that had been holding on. They're everything she wants to hear him say.

"I'll always be here for you, Tristan." She smiles as if her heart is smiling through her lips. *No matter how many times you push me away...*

From the corner of her eye, she spots the dark and slinking figure that could only be Jareth, and she turns to see him escaping the cafeteria to the lawn.

She looks back at Tristan, who's already nodding in understanding. "Go ahead," he says. "You're getting farther than I have."

His response feels like an extra apology, emphasizing that he believes in her and trusts that she cares about finding the other Zodiacs as much as she does.

"Thanks," she says, packing her lunch back up. "I'll call you later."

"Looking forward to it," he says as she stands up and heads for the exit, his words sending a warm tingle over the skin of her belly.

"Hey stranger," Jareth calls from beneath their tree as she approaches.

"I wasn't sure you'd show up today," she says, plopping down beside him.

"Well, we never got to finish our fro-yo debate. How can you say vanilla isn't a flavor?"

"Because it's not," she rebukes, the playfulness of their conversation yesterday returning to her voice. "Vanilla is the base before they add flavor. It's the blank slate of flavors, and the most boring."

Jareth laughs and unwraps his sandwich of, from the smell of it, peanut butter and jelly.

"So, Brielle, what's your story?" he asks before taking a huge bite.

He chews for a while, looking at her, before she decides to answer.

"My story," she says almost in question, then snorts a laugh. "Well, I was an orphan for basically my entire life." She doesn't usually brag about that to people, but she likes Jareth, and she knows he can understand the darker sides of life. "I recently got adopted by the most amazing parents. Most people can't understand the impact that has for me."

He's silent for a moment, and she looks back at him.

"I can," he says, staring at the ground. "My parents died about a couple of months ago. I'm still struggling with their loss." He puffs a laugh through his nose. "In a way, my story and yours are opposites of each other. You just get a family after having none, and I lose one and am back to zero."

Just like Tristan, she can't help but think.

And her heart aches. For both of them.

"I'm so sorry," she says. "I just got a family I wished for my entire life. I can't imagine having one and them being taken away."

Jareth seems to hear the sincerity in her words, his eyes closing heavily for a moment.

Then they open, and a new fire sparks within him. "You know, for the longest time, I thought I'd never get over it. I thought I was doomed to relive that moment over and over again. But...you, and Veronica, have helped me see that life goes on. And we have the choice to wallow in our sorrows or rise above them."

He'd mentioned that name yesterday as well. Veronica. As if Brielle should know who that is. Is there a Veronica that goes to this school that she's unaware of? Maybe another new student?

Jareth looks at her. "I choose option B." He smiles, and she returns it.

She reviews her own options. She can go the Tristan way and bring up doomsday and Guardians and all that, or she can really get to know him, form a bond, then proceed if necessary. She, too, goes with option B.

"Tell me about California," she says with a friendly smile. "I've never been anywhere but this po-dunk town. Not even to New York City, which is basically right down the street. I'd love to hear about other places in the world."

Jareth happily indulges her, telling her all about how his parents moved him from Mirror Point to Los Angeles when he was just a kid because his dad was promoted, and how he both loved and hated it. He tells her about the city, the ugly and beautiful aspects of its rich culture. How there are gorgeous places like the flower district right next to hobo village where even the cops won't venture alone at night.

And she says nothing about Zodiacs or the end of the Universe. Because that's not what Jareth needs right now. That's not what she needs.

Right now, what they both need is a friend.

25

TRISTAN

Tristan watches Brielle walk away, wanting to follow her but knowing he can't. He wanted to say more.

He wanted to tell her about his vision.

He wanted some assurance that everything will be okay between them.

A movement from the corner of his eye has Tristan focusing back on the cafeteria and he sees Cassandra sashaying toward him.

She slides a chair around so she's sitting closer to him, blocking his line of sight to the door. "Brielle's walking away, and you're not following," she observes. "Seems she wants time alone."

Tristan arches a brow. "Or to be away from you," he says mildly.

Cassandra's glossy lips arch up into a smile. "That's just a bonus for both of us."

The door to the cafeteria swings shut and Brielle's gone. She'll probably go outside, maybe to the tree where they shared their first lunch. He almost envies Jareth and the uncomplicated time he can spend with her.

Cassandra leans forward, propping her chin in her hand. "A bit early for trouble in paradise, isn't it?"

Tristan frowns. "You need to back off from Brielle. Whatever you've got stuck in your head about her, it's wrong."

Cassandra's eyes flash with yellow fire. "That's what she told you? And you believed her?"

"Brielle hates lying."

"Doesn't mean she doesn't do it."

Tristan shakes his head. "She's a good person, Cassandra."

And Tristan doesn't know how to let her get close without pushing her away.

"Brielle's always been jealous of what I have. She's gone to some pretty extreme lengths to sabotage it."

Brielle mentioned they had a falling out at the orphanage just before Cassandra was adopted. That Cassandra's parents had considered adopting Brielle until Brielle saw that the father had a violent history.

Tristan's stomach clenches, and he reaches out, covering Cassandra's other hand with his own. "Do your parents... treat you well, Cassandra?"

Cassandra jerks back, fury practically shooting from her eyes. "See! She's still doing it! Telling people anything she can to destroy my life!"

Tristan backs off before she goes supernova. Whatever it is with Brielle, it gets under Cassandra's skin. "One day when you take a chill pill, maybe it might be worth considering Brielle's offer of friendship."

"No thanks. Trouble follows her like a rank smell."

Tristan stiffens, wondering if Cassandra means what he thinks she does—the night she was taken by the Skins and tortured. Relieved all over again that Cassandra isn't a Zodiac, Tristan watches her carefully. "That night, when we found you, it had nothing to do with Brielle."

Her gaze doesn't waver. "I wasn't talking about that. I told you, I don't remember a thing." Her chin wavers. "Nor do I want to."

Which is how they need to leave it.

Cassandra flicks her hair, her gaze sliding away. "Although, I bet she's relieved I don't."

Tristan throws his hands up in the air in exasperation. "Why have you got it in for her so bad?"

"Why do you defend her so hard?" Cassandra shoots back.

Knowing there's no way he can answer that, Tristan huffs out a half-laugh. "Touché."

Cassandra seems to unwind, her own smile springing up. "I'm happy to call it a draw."

"Would that mean you didn't come first in something?" Tristan asks in mock horror.

Pulling together a mock frown, Cassandra gazes at him thoughtfully. "We can't have that. Did you want me to tell you about the time Brielle told me Sister Daphne wasn't telling the truth about how much sacramental wine she'd had?"

Tristan's hands come up in surrender. "You get an A for stubbornness, if that counts for anything."

"I'll take it." Cassandra says with a grin.

Glad that the tension has dissipated, Tristan smiles back. If Cassandra could spit out whatever lemon she sucked on, she'd actually be fun to be around.

Except, then she leans forward again. Slower than last time. Something glinting in her eyes. "I actually came over here to tell you I think we should go out on a date again. One where you stay the whole time," she purrs.

Tristan softens his smile. "I think we could be great friends."

Cassandra's eyes narrow. "If you're waiting for Brielle, she's already moved on. She's been talking to that guy, Jareth. They look like they're becoming real close."

Tristan's spine feels like it just turned to stone. "Jareth's back at school?"

"Seems like he couldn't stay away."

No wonder Brielle didn't want to talk. She has someone else to commiserate with about Tristan's uncanny ability to lose anyone he cares about.

The irony is that Tristan asked her to talk to Jareth. To befriend him.

"Good for them," Tristan growls.

It's not like Tristan can stake a claim on Brielle. He's promised to someone else.

The bell rings, and they're surrounded by the sounds of scraping chairs as everyone heads to their next period.

Cassandra squeezes Tristan's hand before standing. "Good thing I got an A in stubbornness. It means I won't take no for an answer."

Before Tristan can object, she sashays out of the cafeteria.

Last period. Math.

Except Tristan can't stomach another hour in these walls. Tristan hasn't seen the girl who was with Jareth in his vision —as far as he can tell she doesn't go to Mirror Point High. Which means if Jareth's here, he won't be dying before the final bell rings.

All Tristan has to do is keep an eye on Jareth's house and any visitors who rock up. It'll give Tristan some time.

Time to figure out how the hell he can establish if Jareth's the Capricorn Zodiac.

Time to train because things are becoming life or death once more, and Tristan refuses to find himself dealing with the latter again.

Time to convince himself he's got this.

And maybe when he sees Brielle again tomorrow, he can be happy for her.

JACK

16:23

The moment Jack walks into the office, he knows something is up. Davidson can't meet his gaze. Flanagan toasts Jack with his perpetual half cup of coffee, that smug smile stuck on his face.

Jack pops an antacid into his mouth, then another. He's going to have to do some fast talking to get out of this one.

McNally's door is open and Jack raps on the door jamb. "Sir?"

He's writing something on a sheet of paper. He looks up, the only sign he's pissed is a tightening of his fingers around his pen. "Come in, Cadbury. Shut the door."

Doing as he asked, Jack sits in the chair across from his boss, instantly shifting to perch on the edge. "Boss. I know I should've been in Chicago, but things aren't stacking up with the Ayers case—"

"He struck again, Jack." McNally says the words quietly, but with barely contained fury.

Jack stills. "Who did? Tristan?"

But even as he asks it, Jack realizes who McNally's talking about.

McNally slams his hand down on the desk. "The Triple Murderer. He killed for the third time."

Jack wishes he'd gulped down half the bottle of antacids. He wipes his hand down his face, knowing what the third kill means.

McNally pushes forward "Now he's going to disappear

again. Until he tries for another trifecta. And all we can do is wait for him to kill some other poor chump!"

"I doubt I would've caught him in time," Jack offers feebly. The Triple Murder case has been going for years and apart from the one fingerprint Jack lifted years ago that led nowhere, no one's been able to crack it. It's like the guy's a ghost.

"We'll never know, will we? Because you weren't there!" McNally rises, his face turning a mottled red. "You disobeyed a direct order, Jack. You were uncontactable. And someone is dead because of it!"

"I'm sorry, okay? But I was onto something even more important than that. Something big is brewing. I can feel it."

McNally shakes his head, either in disappointment or disgust, Jack can't tell. "Your obsession with the Ayers kid has gone too far. You're suspended from further duties."

Jack shoots to his feet. "What? Look—"

But McNally sits down again, picking up his pen. "Get out, Cadbury. Before I fire you all together."

Jack shifts from foot to foot for precious seconds. He can't be suspended! Outside of his kids, his job is his life.

His job keeps people safe!

Except for the third victim of the Triple Murderer.

Shoulders slumped, Jack leaves the office.

Davidson has found something fascinating on his tie. Flanagan's already eyeing Jack's desk. Jack doesn't acknowledge any of them as he stalks out of the building. Most of them think he's a few cards short of a deck, anyway.

But as Jack unlocks his car, he realizes he has to go home.

That he won't be coming back here anytime soon.

What the hell is he going to tell Veronica and Logan?

VERONICA

V eronica never expected to like Jareth. He was just the loophole that would allow her to keep investigating for her father without breaking her promise to him.

But after the date last night, he's something else entirely. She looks forward to every text from him, and her body warms all over whenever she thinks about him. He isn't like the douche bags at her school. He isn't like any guy she's ever met. He's...special. Amazing. Talented.

Hot!

And as much as she craves to explore these feelings and let them burn like his fiery paintings, she wants to protect him even more.

Whatever interest Tristan Ayers has in him, it can't be good. The body count surrounding Tristan is precarious, and she doesn't want Jareth on that list.

Jareth had said he was planning to leave Mirror Point. Maybe it would be better if he did. Move back to California where Tristan can't get to him. His interest in Jareth can't be strong enough for him to follow him across the country, could it?

Veronica steps out of the shower, wraps the towel around her shoulders and looks in the mirror, her reflection silently judging her.

You should warn him, her reflection urges. *Tell him who Tristan really is and that he should run far away.*

And what about Brielle? There isn't a malevolent hair on that poor girl's head. She's every bit as innocent as Jareth, and who knows how far down Tristan's rabbit hole she already is?

"Veronica." The sound of her dad calling her name before slamming the front door makes her jump. That's not an "I'm home" kinda voice. That's her dad's "you're in big trouble, young lady" voice.

She squeezes her eyes shut and exhales, then throws on her bathrobe to walk the gallows to her dad, dreading what she may be in for this time.

She plasters on an innocent face as she descends the hallway to where he stands just past the door. "What's up, Dad?"

The expression he wears is one that can't be softened by her puppy-dog eyes. His brow is pinched together and his jaw is clenched, highlighting his ever-present five o'clock shadow. "You promised me you'd leave Tristan Ayers alone."

With unwavering composure and feigning confusion, she shakes her head. "I have."

"Oh really?" Her dad crosses his arms, all bad-cop in this moment. "Then why did I get a call from your brother saying that you were out last night with one of Tristan's known associates?"

She swallows, saying nothing and keeping her face blank.

"A Mr. Jareth Stone?" he prods.

So it hadn't been her dad she saw last night. It was Logan driving the family car. Apparently they weren't past him ratting her out. Frickin' goody two shoes!

That should have occurred to her before now, as her dad hadn't been home last night. But she'd been too preoccupied with thoughts of Jareth.

She cocks her head and frowns. "Huh, I didn't realize they were friends."

Her dad's face flares magenta at her response. "Don't give me that crap, Veronica! You deliberately disobeyed me. What do I have to do to prove to you that these people are dangerous?"

"Jareth isn't dangerous!" she protests.

Her dad rolls his eyes and scoffs.

"He's not! He's being manipulated by Tristan every bit as much as Brielle is."

Surprisingly, the magenta in his face fades to red. He shakes his head, looking away for a silent moment. "You're too much like your mother, seeing the good in everyone, even where there isn't any."

"You can't know that," she argues. "I'm not as easily fooled as you may think, which is pretty insulting actually. I got Jareth to trust me, not the other way around." A different issue sparks outrage in her gut. "Why can't you see that I could be useful? You recruit Logan to work for you, but you hardly trust me to order dinner. But I'm the one who's gotten into Tristan's inner circle. Why can't you let me help you like you let Logan?"

All the red has faded from her father's face, and his jaw releases its tension as he takes a few steps toward her. "You are so much more fragile than your brother. I don't want you to get hurt. Your mother would never forgive me—"

"I'm not some dandelion that will fall apart on a windy day." Where his tension eased, hers is just starting to build. She can feel the redness that left his face filling her cheeks. "I can handle far more than you give me credit for, if you'd only give me a chance!"

She crosses her arms and turns away, determined not to let him see the glistening in her suddenly wet eyes.

Neither of them says anything or moves for a long time. She can't move. She's too riled up to do anything, feeling too much like a kid throwing a tantrum and trying desperately not to look the part.

Finally, he comes close enough to touch her, but he doesn't. "I know you're not a delicate flower. You're my rough-and-tumble Kitkat. I pity any mugger who comes across you on a darkened street, but... we're not talking about people here. I know you know that."

She blinks, trying as hard as she can to suck the tears back inside where they belong.

"Well, Jareth is just a person," she murmurs. She sniffles then turns back to him, eyes sufficiently free of spillage. "He's not a villain." Or an alien. "He's just some poor kid who's unfortunately gotten on Ayers's radar. And if I can protect him from that, I will."

Her dad looks at her for several seconds, then lets out a heavy sigh and moves to the kitchen, popping a handful of antacids into his mouth before he grabs a glass from the cupboard.

"Well, either way, I won't be needing your services." He pauses at the sink with his empty glass, his back to her. "I got suspended today, so I'll have plenty of time to handle the Ayers case on my own."

Her defenses fall. "Suspended? For what?"

He fills his glass with water, then turns around and takes a sip. "That's for me to worry about."

She rolls her eyes, her walls rising again.

"You wanna know why I let Logan help me and not you?"

She crosses her arms, then hangs her head cattily in his direction. "Why?"

"Because he's an adult. He's finished school and is almost

through with college. He's on a career path that will inevitably lead him to the FBI." He takes another drink. "But you? You're still a kid. Your only job is to be a kid. Have fun. Go on bad dates with stupid boys, and learn from them. Get good grades and ditch classes without me finding out— which I do, by the way. Live, Kitkat. Just live. It's not your job to worry about the bills, much less catching extra-terrestrial terrorists. Please, for my sanity, just be a teenager. Give me a form of headaches I can handle."

She understands his argument. But that's not who she is. She's not the silly high school girl who gives a crap about being popular or getting a boyfriend. She couldn't care less about the latest smart phone or what celebrities are posting on Instagram. As much as he claims she's like her mother, she's her father's daughter.

"Alright," she says, jutting out her hip in defiance. "How's this for a headache you can handle? I'm dating Jareth Stone, and aside from locking me in my room, there's nothing you can do about it. No, scratch that, I can get out of that, too."

Then she turns and stomps stubbornly toward her room, slamming the door behind her.

She wouldn't put her dad past barricading it and barring her window, but she knows that won't stop her.

She's going to protect Jareth at all costs.

27

JARETH

As Jareth steps through the sliding doors of Mirror Point's library, he's taken aback for a moment. He blinks as he's assaulted with way too much color and cheer for a Sunday morning.

A large stand has been set up right in front of the doors, brightly colored letters dangling along a string saying *Reading is My Superpower*. Various drawings of superheroes are slapped around along with stacks and stacks of books, most of them with caped crusaders on the front. Stepping around a stack of Marvel comics, Jareth brings his surprised brows back down. Seems there's one heck of an enthusiastic librarian here.

Passing various shelves, each tacked with a *Welcome* sign in a different color, Jareth finds Brielle at one of the tables at the back. Frowning in concentration, she's making notes as she flips the page of the hardcover book in front of her.

Jareth pauses, surprised he's not having second thoughts. The decision to stay in Mirror Point—for now—wasn't an easy one to make, but once he did, his mind had felt like calm waters after a storm. He'd been relieved. Felt like he could take a breath deeper than a gasp.

For the first time since his parents' death, he's found something to focus on. Something other than the fear that's his constant companion.

Brielle. And making sure she's not mixed up with anything she's going to regret. If someone found a family at the same time he lost his, he wants to make sure Brielle doesn't lose hers, too.

Of course, there's also Veronica...but Jareth hasn't decided what he should do about that. Yes, he's never felt more drawn to a girl. Yes, their kiss was out of this world. Yes, he wants to see her again.

But they're all reasons he should stay away. He still doesn't know how much danger he's in...and how much is his colorful imagination, as his mother used to call it.

Was the house fire deliberate...or a tragic accident?

Was that arrow meant for him...or was it some douche in a backyard with crap aim?

Was the guy in the silver sedan following him...or just an angry young man cruising the streets?

Until Jareth has the answers to those questions, it wouldn't be fair to Veronica, or safe, to let their worlds touch any more than they already have.

Brielle looks up, a smile lighting up her face. "Have I given you enough time to decide whether you're going to stay for our study session?"

Jareth's own smile climbs its way up his face as he sits on the seat beside her. If he's staying for now, he needs to make sure he keeps on top of school work so he doesn't prompt more note-taking from Shandra. And more threats of support services...

"I was just deciding whether I wanted to do my ancient history assignment or my physics report first."

Brielle's nose wrinkles. "Tough choice." Her face clears as she shifts her notebook to make more room for him. "Although that's not what you were thinking."

Jareth opens his mouth only to shut it again. It seems Brielle can even pick up white lies. He arches a brow. "Showing off, huh?" He flicks a hand behind her ear, bringing it around to show a shiny silver coin. "But can you do that?"

Before he can retract, Brielle grabs the coin, shaking her head. "It's not hard to have powers cooler than mine."

Jareth detects the hitch in her voice, but he can't move. He watches as Brielle uncurls her hand, looking at the coin resting in her palm. Her smile fading, she passes it back to him.

At first, Jareth doesn't want to take it. If he touches it, it's undeniably real. But as Brielle's face morphs with concern, he quickly grabs it. "Thanks," he croaks out.

The hard metal digs into his palm. Just like the daisy he painted on the wall, the coin hasn't disappeared.

Brielle leans in a little. "Jareth, are you okay?"

Two shakes of his head and Jareth realizes he's wasting his time. Brielle picked up on his deflection only a moment ago. If he tries to say he's fine, she'll call him out for the liar he is.

He uncurls his fist, staring at what shouldn't be there.

"There was no coin," Jareth whispers.

Brielle glances at it. "Isn't that the trick though? Making it appear out of thin air?"

"That's what I used to do, make it look like there was a coin." A quick flick of his wrist and people would believe it had slipped back to wherever he hid it in the first place. "But there wasn't."

Brielle stills. "You didn't have a coin, did you?"

"No. I didn't."

Up until now, the coin's existence had been an illusion.

Brielle rests her hand on his wrist, catching his gaze. "See, so much cooler than my powers."

Her eyes are soft and smiling, not filled with horror and fear. Like they should be.

Jareth jerks his hand back, flinging the coin to the ground like it just burned him. His pulse is like a battering ram on his eardrums. His chest is too tight, his lungs fighting for air.

Brielle's warm hands grasp his own, gripping tightly despite their clamminess. "Hey, it's okay," she says evenly. "It's okay."

Jareth would shake his head if he could, but his body has turned to stone. It's why he can't breathe. Why he can't do what his mind is screaming for him to do.

Run.

Brielle presses closer. "I'm here, Jareth. I can help you."

Jareth blinks and her face comes into focus. Her calm, caring, sweet face.

She smiles. "That's it. Just breathe."

His chest loosens, the grip that feels like rigor mortis relaxing. He draws in a deep breath of cool air, his pulse retreating beyond his consciousness. The quiet sounds of the library filter in. Murmured voices, pages rustling, someone tunelessly singing louder than they probably realize.

Brielle stays where she is, watching him with serene intensity. "That's never happened before, huh?"

He shakes his head. "Anything I've ever created never lasted."

Brielle leans over to pick up the coin. "Well, now they are."

Just like the daisy he painted on his date with Veronica.

Tucking the coin back into his palm and wrapping his hand around it, Brielle looks at him, not letting him go. "Did it start after Tristan gave you the Onyx stone?"

Jareth's jaw slackens. Yes! And then it clamps tight. Tristan.

Again.

Before he can ask a question, a book drops to the ground with a *thump*. They both jump, pulling away as they turn around to see what's going on.

Tristan stands a few feet away, glowering at them, a textbook at his feet that he's not bothering to pick up. He turns his furious gaze to Brielle. "You planned this?"

Brielle shuffles, creating a little more space between her and Jareth. "Tristan, you came."

"Yep, like the idiot I am, you asked, and I came." He flicks a hot glare in Jareth's direction. "Sorry I interrupted."

Jareth arches a brow. "Are you?"

"Tristan—"

But he raises a hand, cutting Brielle off. "This idiot is leaving."

Spinning on his heel, Tristan strides straight back out, shoving away a paper Iron Man dangling near the doorway.

Jareth shakes his head. "Didn't you say you two aren't a thing?"

Tristan just played jealous boyfriend like he was born for the role.

Brielle shrugs helplessly. "We can't be."

Jareth's about to ask what that means when something else strikes him. "You lined this up? For Tristan and me to both be here?"

"I'd like for us all to get along," she says weakly.

Jareth can't see that happening any time this century. "Whatever's going on between you two, it's not...normal."

For some reason, that makes Brielle smile. "Says the guy who can create stuff with his mind."

"And you still think Tristan's theory explains that," Jareth says flatly.

Brielle nods. Whatever's going on between the two of them, it runs deeper than he thought.

"You know you could be threatening your adoption, don't you?"

There aren't many adults who will want someone in their house believing they're an alien.

Jareth asks the question quietly, gently. But Brielle still flinches.

She looks away. "I don't have a choice."

Curling back into the chair, Jareth shakes his head. Brielle's acting like it's too late. Like this life has already been chosen for her.

She starts to pack up her books. "I think I should go talk to him," she says apologetically.

Jareth sighs. He's not ready to give up yet, but it's going to take some time for Brielle to consider another perspective. "That's fine. I don't really feel like studying anymore."

Tucking the coin into his pocket, he admits he has his own problems to worry about. Like finding a way to explain what's going on.

In a way that doesn't include aliens and Zodiacs.

A young woman *tsk tsks* as she stops to pick up the book Tristan dropped, probably deliberately. She brushes the cover, the motion almost looking like a caress. Clasping it to her chest, she continues on, slipping behind the front desk and sitting down.

Brielle stands, tucking her books back into her bag. "You could come with me?"

"To Tristan's house?" Jareth asks incredulously.

"Yeah, we could—"

"No."

"But—"

"No, Brielle. Today's been tough enough as it is."

She nods, her gaze softening with understanding.

Grateful she's not pushing him, he indicates toward the door. "You could always go home," he suggests with a grin.

Brielle rolls her eyes. "I don't want any more misunderstandings between me and Tristan."

They make their way to the front doors, Jareth flicking one of the Welcome signs that's exploding out of a comical cannon taped to the wall. "This place sure is…welcoming," he says, trying to lighten the mood.

"The new librarian is really trying to get people back into the place."

Brielle says the words almost sadly, making Jareth pause. "People weren't using it much before?"

She almost smiles. "The old librarian wasn't the friendliest guy."

"So, shouldn't it be a good thing that there's a new one?"

"Alden died a few months ago. He…committed his life to this library and documenting the history of Mirror Point."

Jareth glances at her as they step outside. "You sound like you miss him."

Brielle shakes her head. "I barely knew him." She shrugs. "But it seems you can have friends looking out for you without you even knowing it."

They walk in silence to the bus stop only a few yards away. It looks as if Brielle's as deep in thought as he is.

Except she's been sucked in by a good-looking conman, all because she can do something no one else can. Well, so can Jareth, but that doesn't make him an extraterrestrial. And the girl who just helped him through a panic attack deserves better than that.

Jareth grabs her hand. "Hey, I just wanted to say thanks."

She looks up, whatever was troubling her clearing from her gaze. "That's what friends are for, Jareth."

He angles his head. "Why does it feel like we've been friends all my life?"

Brielle's the only person he has no secrets from, and yet that thought doesn't scare him. She's more like family than a friend.

"From what I can tell, the Zodiac bond is quite a special one."

Great. They're back there again.

"Help!" The word comes from behind them, tremulous and frightened.

Jareth and Brielle spin around, peering down the narrow alleyway between the two buildings there.

"Please, help!" A pile of rags that must be a person moves behind a couple of trash cans, only to collapse back down. "Please…"

They glance at each other. A second later, they break into a run. The homeless person is obviously in trouble.

They skid to a halt beside the trash cans. Jareth bends over, reaching out. "Hey, is there anything we can do to help?"

In a flutter of filthy rags, a man shoots to his feet.

"You could come quietly, for starters," he growls menacingly.

"Skins," Brielle gasps.

She grabs Jareth's arm, yanking him backward. He stumbles but quickly rights himself. Brielle's grip is hard. Full of fear.

A second man materializes making Jareth do a double-take. He literally appeared out of nowhere!

He nudges the first man. "He's the one we've been looking for."

Brielle moves in closer to Jareth, continuing to pull them backwards. "We need to run," she whispers urgently.

The first man's lips curl into a cruel smile. "You'll never make it." He flexes his neck. "I quite like this heightened speed and strength."

They're faster? And stronger?

The second man cracks his knuckles. "Although bringing you in alive is preferable, Chardis's instructions were clear. Kill them if they resist."

Adrenalin is thrumming hot and fast through Jareth's veins. The cold violence in the men's eyes is the darkest thing he's ever seen.

There's no doubt in his mind that they mean what they say.

Brielle is holding something hanging from her neck. "Go, Jareth," she whispers harshly.

What? He's not leaving her!

"They're not joking. They're here to kill us."

The first man takes a menacing step forward as if to verify her words, baring his teeth. "Unless you decide to come quietly."

Jareth's panicked mind tries to process what's going on here. Surely, this can't be happening.

But although Brielle's holding her ground, her grip on whatever she's holding is white-knuckled.

She's just as scared as Jareth is.

"It would be easier just to shoot them," the second man grumbles.

"You know our orders. No bringing attention to ourselves."

Cracking his knuckles again, the second man shrugs. "Fine."

The moment they move, Brielle shoves Jareth. "Go! Run!"

But there's no way someone else he cares about is going to die because of him. Whatever Brielle thinks this is, these men just said Jareth's the one they were looking for.

Just like they were when his parents were killed.

Jareth's hands come out instinctively. Desperately. This can't be happening again.

Images of the fiery flames that devoured his house explode through him, fed by his panic. Powered by the fear that he won't be able to stop this.

When that's exactly what bursts to life in front the men, they leap backward. Fire streaks across the alleyway, the flames swollen with fury.

Shock freezes Jareth, but he quickly shakes it off. He lifts his arms and the flames rise. He throws them out wide and they expand.

"Yes, Jareth!" breathes Brielle.

The men shout, raising their arms to shield their faces as they retreat further into the alley.

Heady power chases away the fear, and Jareth looks at first one wall then the other. Hungry flames erupt along the brick, alive and greedy as they were on the night Jareth lost everything.

Brielle grabs his arm. "Quick, we need to run."

They turn and flee, the men's shouts carrying after them.

"We need to get somewhere populated," Brielle gasps.

They run, both instinctively heading for the main street. A quick glance over his shoulder shows the men aren't behind them, but Jareth doesn't slow. For the first time in his life, the more people they pass, the better he feels.

Brielle finally comes to a stop, panting as she collapses against a wall. Jareth doubles over, his lungs working overtime to suck in oxygen. A few people wander past, probably looking at them strangely, but Jareth ignores them.

How many of them would know what it's like to literally run for your life?

When he looks up, Brielle's already getting her breathing under control.

She arches a brow at him. "Now do you believe?"

28

BRIELLE

P*ick up, Tristan. Pick. UP!*
Brielle's called Tristan three times since they got on the bus, and he still hasn't answered. Is he really that upset about her setting him and Jareth up Parent-Trap-style?

"I'm so sorry," Jareth whispers to her for the umpteenth time, looking out the window at the passing shops, as if he might see one of their pursuers on their tail.

She doesn't have the focus to question why *he's* the one apologizing. All she knows is that she needs Tristan. Right now. No, ten minutes ago!

"Urgh!" she groans as she hangs up on Tristan's voicemail again. "Why won't he answer?"

"Who?" Jareth asks, his neck poised over his shoulder, looking behind them.

"Tristan," she growls.

"Tristan?" His neck snaps back, eyes wide as he glares at her. "Why are you calling him?"

"Because he'll know how to handle this," she says through gritted teeth. "I...I can't fight them. I'm useless against them." She hangs her head in shame and disappointment.

He gawks at her, a look of curious outrage on his tanned face. "Of course, you are. They're trained killers! I fail to see how Tristan could stand a chance against them."

Every heady emotion she's struggled to hide for the past few days floods over Brielle like a riptide, and she feels just how truly helpless she is to all of it.

She laughs, having no other outlet. "You really have no idea what we're up against."

"I know that they're trying to kill me, and that they killed my parents in Cali," he says, exasperated.

"They're not human, Jareth," she hisses.

He rolls his eyes. "Here we go again."

"It's the truth! The truth you aren't willing to see. And the truth they are willing to kill for." Her chest is rocking with the heavy breaths she can barely keep up with.

"You really do believe everything that Tristan has said?" he asks, incredulous. "About Zodiac whatevers and aliens?"

She turns fierce eyes on him. "I don't just believe it, I've lived it, Jareth."

He shakes his head with a disbelieving smile and rakes his hands through his thick dark hair.

"I used to be just like you," she says, staring blankly out the window. "When Tristan came to me and told me all this stuff, I thought he was crazy, just like you do. But I *saw* those...those *things* with my own eyes. One of them I believed to be my best friend."

Her voice cracks at the last word, and she can feel Jareth's eyes on her though she's unwilling to meet them.

Adalind.

That sting will never die.

"She nearly killed me," Brielle continues, looking down at her lap, avoiding his examining eyes. "And she abducted Tristan's parents. Her leader, Chardis, is the greatest evil I've ever encountered. The most powerful being in the

Universe. And he killed Tristan's parents right in front of my eyes."

The pain of their death stabs at her anew, reopening the wound of that fateful night. Jareth's gaze is a spotlight on her, but she's unwilling to see the disbelief she's sure it holds. Tess and Zarius don't deserve that doubt. Their deaths, their lives, are too important for such a thing.

"He would have killed me, too, if I hadn't tapped into the power Tristan knew I had and sent him running back into the abyss." She turns to him then, a fire blazing in her passionate gaze. "You have that same potential, if you'd only be willing to see it, accept it, and hone it."

He's frozen for a moment, as if mesmerized by the intensity of her words.

Please, Jareth, she pleads silently with every tiny muscle in her face. *Please accept this and help us. Or we'll all die!*

His brows wrinkle, the unmistakable crease of doubt pulling at his brows. "So, you expect me to believe that I'm an alien?"

His criticism hurts, but not as much as the fear of losing him in this fight.

"Yes, because you are." She shakes her head. "You just made flames out of nothing, for pitch sake! And... I don't know how to explain it, but I can *sense* that you're one of us. The same way that I knew, even though I kept denying it, that Tristan was telling the truth when he told me the same thing." She looks at him with meaning. "The same way I know you can sense it."

He turns away, staring out the window. The silence buzzes between them as the fluorescent light flickers above them from the ceiling of the bus.

"We can't help you if you aren't willing to accept the truth," she presses, leaning toward him. "If you turn tail and run, they'll follow you, and you'll be defenseless without your stone and the skills only Tristan can teach you to defend yourself."

He shakes his head, still fixed toward the deceivingly peaceful view beyond the window.

"I don't know what Cool-Aid Tristan has you drinking, but those people aren't who you claim," he says finally. "They've been after me before I even met you. They killed my parents, burnt them alive in my house. And for whatever reason, they want me, too. I can't tell you how I know that, flames or no flames, but I do. But I'm no alien. And the fact that Tristan has brainwashed you into believing that you are...just makes me furious." He turns to her, his dark eyes lit with the same flames he scatters on walls. "You're too good for all of this, Brielle. And when I leave, I can only hope these bastards will follow me and leave you alone."

The bus stops and he stands, shoving past her and storming to the slid-open doors.

"Jareth!" she calls after him, but her cry falls on deaf ears.

He's already gone.

Brielle flops back into her seat. What's she supposed to do now?

29

TRISTAN

They were holding hands.
Sitting so close.
Obviously connecting.

Tristan's hands ball into fists. He's jealous. He can admit it. He can also admit he has no right to be. That Brielle has every right to start a relationship with whomever she wants.

But that doesn't stop the slimy green-eyed monster from rearing its ugly mug.

All it does is make Tristan feel even more guilty. Spinning around, he presses his forehead against the brick wall, his arms splaying out wide. "Could you be any more of a schmuck?" he mutters to himself.

The sound of footsteps coming down the path has Tristan looking up. He presses himself further into the shrubs by the wall of Jareth's house, peering out. Yep, it's him.

Jareth's walking toward him, hands in his pockets, shoulders hunched. He seems to be absorbed in the pavement in front of him, but Tristan sees the way his eyes dart beneath his bangs. The guy looks like Tristan does.

Like a Skin could jump out any second.

Jareth's shoulders relax down the closer he gets to the house as his steps pick up pace. He's obviously looking forward to getting inside.

But Tristan needs to know. Is Jareth one of them? Will the next Zodiac be Brielle's boyfriend?

He steps out just as Jareth pushes the key into the door. "Hey, Jareth."

Jareth jumps, the keys clattering to the ground. He spins around, eyes seeming to swallow his face. "Get back!" he yells.

Tristan steps backward, raising his hands and showing his palms. "Whoa, sorry. I didn't mean to scare the crap out of you."

Jareth shoves the hair out of his eyes, his face filling with storm clouds. "Get the hell out of here!"

Knowing this conversation just got off to a bad start, Tristan drops his hands and pulls up an apologetic smile. "I just wanted to talk."

"Go away."

Jareth picks up the keys, and Tristan notices his hands are still trembling. Internally, he frowns as he realizes how much he must've scared Jareth. The guy's obviously wound up.

Tristan leans a shoulder against the wall, letting Jareth know he's not going anywhere, but not wanting to be a threat. "You could be in danger."

His vision flashes through his mind, fresh and raw. He needs to find out what's the difference between the second and the first...where Jareth dies.

Jareth's arms explode outward. "I already was, you idiot! Have you even checked on Brielle?"

"What?" Tristan pushes away from the wall, everything on high alert.

"We were attacked by two goons not far from the library."

Skins! They found Brielle? But how?

"She's fine," Jareth huffs. "We got away."

Shame flushes over Tristan. All those phone calls after he left the library weren't wanting to talk. Brielle needed help. "Tell me what happened."

"If you weren't so busy jumping to conclusions, you would've been there to find out."

The truth is like a slap. Tristan even snaps his head to the side, unable to look Jareth in the eye. "You're right. I should've been there."

If Tristan wasn't so caught up in trying to let Brielle go, he would've been. His shoulders sag as he realizes he's failed. Again.

"What you need to do is leave *her* alone. For some reason, she won't stay away from you."

Tristan reels back. "Stay away from me? Why would she need to do that?"

"Because you're the one who's filled her head with all that stuff about aliens and Zodiacs!" Jareth pushes his face forward, his eyes intense. "You're going to ruin her life!"

Tristan flinches. "Despite what you may think, I care for Brielle."

"I'll make you a deal." Jareth's shoulders sag. "If you stay away from her, I will, too."

"What?" Jareth sure as hell didn't look like he wanted to stay away from Brielle when Tristan saw them in the library.

But Jareth's gaze is intense. Full of warning. "If you really do care about her, you'd want her safe. Today wasn't the first time I've been attacked."

Tristan stills. "When?"

Jareth looks away. "At the cemetery. It doesn't matter."

"Chardis has found you, Jareth." Tristan fills his voice with all the urgency he feels. It's quite possible the Skins were after Jareth, not Brielle. "You need to come with me."

"Like hell, I do. You can tie all this into your crazy theories all you want, but I know the truth."

Tristan's trying not to get angry, but he's definitely getting irritated. What the pitch is Jareth talking about? "Which is?"

Jareth snaps his mouth shut, his face twisted into a ferocious frown. "Like I said. Go. Away."

"But these men, they want to kill you!"

Jareth jams the keys into the lock. "Tell me something I don't know," he mutters. He yanks open the door, glaring at Tristan. "Next time you come here trying to recruit me into your sick little cult, I'll call the police."

Dammit. Tristan can't afford to have the cops sniffing around. Jack Cadbury probably has an entire satellite dedicated to scanning every wavelength he can think of, waiting for Tristan's name to be dropped.

His brows shoot up as he registers what Jareth said. Sick little cult? Jareth thinks he's running an alien-worshiping commune? He almost wants to laugh. Right now, Tristan can't get the two Zodiacs they have working as a team.

And if Jareth's the third, all Tristan keeps doing is pushing him away.

His mouth tipping down in defeat, Tristan jams his hands into his pockets. "Okay, I'll go. But let me give you my cell number—"

"No thanks."

Frustrated with being faced with another roadblock, Tristan spins on his heel. He has to hope that Brielle's got further than he has. That maybe she can reach Jareth…

Tristan walks down the path until he hears Jareth's door close. The moment it does, he breaks into a jog. He loops around the block and returns to his car. But instead of heading home, Tristan drives to the end of Jareth's street.

Crawling forward until he has a clear line of sight, he parks beside the curb.

Right now, keeping a watch on Jareth is Tristan's priority. As he settles more comfortably into the seat, he picks up his cell and dials the number he should've answered the first time it rang.

"Brielle…"

He swallows. He wants to tell her he's sorry.

That from now on, he'll try to get it right.

"Tristan!" Brielle's voice is part relief and a whole lot of annoyance. "Where the pitch have you been?"

30

JARETH

It's barely dawn when Jareth arrives at the cemetery. The headstones are as still and silent as the air as he makes his way to his parents' memorial. The place is as empty as a... well, a graveyard.

Which is just how Jareth wants it.

The moment he reaches the dual headstones, he collapses to his knees.

He slept even less than usual last night, his mind a carousel of two questions. Does he leave, for everyone's safety?

Or does he stay, and try to break the hold Tristan has on Brielle?

What does your heart say? his mother would ask.

That whatever it is that's blooming between him and Veronica could be the most beautiful thing he's ever seen.

Jareth shakes his head. This isn't about him and Veronica. This is about keeping people safe.

And the only way he can do that is to stay away.

His father would nod. *Things are never that simple, Meredith.*

Of course they are, his mother would instantly respond, her face serene with the knowledge that all of life's decisions can be made like this.

"I should've told you," Jareth whispers hoarsely.

The headstones stare blankly at him. He's never liked them. Their cool stone the color of bone never captured the complexity and beauty that were his parents. Their memorial should've been…more. Full of life and heart and color.

Jareth flops onto his backside, tucking his legs up and wrapping his arms around them. Last night was a night filled with memories thanks to Tristan's visit. Not memories of the fire, but of the day that led to its inevitability.

"I'm so sorry," he chokes.

He was only thirteen. It was becoming undeniable how different he was to other kids his age. To anyone, really. Although his mother told him that was something to celebrate, it sure as hell didn't feel like it.

Heck. She had to invent evaporating paint just to cover up how different he was.

He'd started painting, but with real paint. Because this painting was all about telling the world he didn't care what it thought about him.

The graffiti started small. Black suns. Crowns of thorns. Bleeding, clenched fists.

Then it grew. The phoenix was his favorite. The terrifying red bird was a symbol of strength and rebirth. He thought he was telling the world he could be whatever he wanted.

Looking back now, Jareth realizes he had no idea what that looked like.

As it turns out, it's where he got all the practice painting flames.

He even made a friend. Malachi was a homeless kid living in an abandoned apartment block with a bunch of other misfits. He loved Jareth's paintings, and showed the others. They'd asked him to decorate their peeling walls.

It almost felt like he belonged.

But he got caught. The first time had been a stern warning.

The second time had meant his parents had to pick him up from the station.

That's when he'd run away, filled with shame. Furious at the world. Telling himself that he'd find somewhere he belonged.

Jareth's head sinks onto his knees. His parents know all this. They thought the final time he got caught was why it ended.

The apartment block was in a dingy area of the city. Everywhere there were reminders why no one wanted to live there anymore. Garbage. Shopfronts that were long ago boarded up. Decay.

There wasn't even any grass or weeds working their way up through the cracks of the pavement, like they'd given up, too.

Jareth was standing beside a dumpster down a narrow alley, bags of rubbish piled around it rather than in it. He'd been wondering whether he should climb on top of it and paint something up high. Something big.

But there'd been footsteps. Determined, hard footsteps that Jareth had heard each time he'd been caught.

He'd leapt behind the dumpster, leaving his cans of spray paint where they were, and squatted down amongst the rotting black bags.

Three men had stopped in the alley.

One was gray-haired and in a suit. The other two were wearing black shirts, black pants, black scowls.

"Have you found it?" the gray-haired man hissed.

"Not yet," replied one of the others. "But we're working hard, boss."

The gray-haired man's voice had turned hard. "Do you have any leads?"

Silence. Just some feet scuffling.

Jareth had peeked over at that moment. Tucked behind the garbage bags, he'd had the perfect vantage point. A clear line of sight.

The gray-haired man had reached into his suit. "I don't think you realize how important the Staff is."

The first man had started nodding vigorously. "We know, boss. We really do."

The second had frowned. "What do you think we've been doing? Our nails?"

Jareth's eyes had widened when he saw the gun. He'd clapped his own hand over his mouth to stop himself from screaming.

The sound of the single shot had been muted. The man had barely groaned. His collapsing body had been little more than a muffled *thump*.

The gray-haired man had tucked the gun back into his jacket, then adjusted his lapels. "Tell the others that failure won't be tolerated."

He'd turned and walked away, his jaw tight. Jareth had curled up into a ball, terrified. He'd just seen a man shot! Killed!

There was more scuffling. A car driving away. Then silence as empty as death.

When Jareth's trembling muscles finally allowed him to stand again, to carefully creep from behind the garbage, there was no body. No sign that any of this had happened.

Jareth's counsellor had once suggested that painting could be a helpful way for the brain to cope with trauma. He was right. That's exactly what Jareth did.

There, on the dingy brick wall, he'd splashed the horror of what he'd just seen. There hadn't been any colors in the spray cans he'd brought, but then again, there was no one around. So he'd used his abilities.

The man. The gun. The hole in his chest.

The blood.

It was okay. It wouldn't last. It would fade and disappear.

He'd stepped back just as a soft *click* had fractured the still air. Jareth had spun around to find Malachi there, holding up his cell phone.

He'd just taken a photo of Jareth's artwork.

"Whoa!" Malachi had said in awe. "That's some serious detail you've got going on there. It looks so real!"

Malachi had looked at his screen, still marveling at the image he captured.

Jareth had rushed forward. "You need to delete that! Now!"

Malachi had looked up in surprise. "Why? It's really good."

"I don't care. You need to get rid of it!"

Malachi had paused, obviously seeing Jareth's panic. He'd frowned. "Well, if you insist…"

"I'm not asking, Malachi. Delete it. Right now."

Then there'd been more footsteps.

Jareth remembers the icy fear that the men had come back. That they'd found out he'd seen it all.

In fact, he'd been relieved when it was a couple of cops. He didn't even mind when they'd grabbed him because they'd seen the cans of spray paint.

By then, the painting had gone. Malachi had run.

And Jareth was taken to the local precinct. His chances had all been used up. They'd fingerprinted him. There was talk of court and juvie.

He was surprised, and touched, when Malachi turned up

with food. Apparently all the kids from the apartment block had pitched in to buy it. Jareth had tried to make sure Malachi had deleted the photo. That the evidence of what he'd witnessed was gone.

But Malachi hadn't let him speak. There was no time thanks to the burly cop already waiting to take Malachi straight back out. He'd pressed a foil-wrapped taco in Jareth's hand. "Dyad's going to take care of it. Your record's going to be wiped clean. Go home, Jareth. That's where you belong."

When his parents had turned up, regret almost had Jareth doubling over. But his mother had opened her arms, her sweet face already full of forgiveness. They'd hugged for the longest moments.

The court date that was mentioned never came. Malachi told the truth. Whoever Dyad was, they made his misdeeds disappear.

They'd gone home and the three of them had sat down with some apple and chamomile tea.

Just before his father took the first sip, he'd looked at Jareth over the rim of his cup. "We sure would appreciate it if you didn't do that again."

Jareth had promised he'd never, ever run away again. Whatever he was, he discovered he wanted to be someone they could be proud of. That Malachi was right.

Family is where you belong.

Jareth's throat works, wishing that's where the story ends. His bangs fall over his eyes as he hangs his head.

Malachi was found dead two days later. The bullet in his chest was put down to gang activity.

His parents moved to California a few months after. Jareth had welcomed it. No amount of apple and chamomile tea could stop him from looking over his shoulder constantly. From startling every time he saw a man with gray hair.

In the end, it hadn't mattered. He'd been found. It was his parents who paid the price.

Because of what he saw.

Hot tears track down Jareth's cheeks. Useless, hopeless tears.

He got his fire. He rose from the ashes.

And he's been running ever since.

Jareth imagines what it would've looked like if he'd told his parents the truth as they'd sat there, sipping their tea. His father would've insisted they tell the police.

He almost chuckles. His mother would've smiled as she stared off into space. "Isn't it beautiful that those kids, who don't even have a home, brought you something to eat?"

Jareth unfolds, looking up to find the sun has arrived. Golden light fills the cemetery, making the dew on the grass glisten.

His mother always saw the beauty in everything. The hope. The promise of something good. Jareth frowns at the headstones. That's why he doesn't like them. They represent his parents' deaths.

Not their lives.

Which is exactly what he's been doing with his painting. Commemorating their loss.

Not the gift they were.

His hands twitch. His brows sink lower. And then, he's on his knees. A flurry of movement.

Jareth molds. Sculpts. Creates.

The green stalks, as thick as an arm. The countless whorls of blossoms all packed into a sunshine-colored center. The florets, the petals, circling them, as wide as a hand.

And each one is a different color. The bubble gum pink of his baby blanket, because his parents refused to gender stereotype him. The sky blue of the wrapping paper around his last birthday present. The deep cheddar of his father's favorite cheese, the rosy blossom of his mother's cheeks as his father groaned when he bit into her coconut caramel slice, the pale caramel of the cardboard castle they built in the backyard.

Each one a precious memory that's now been immortalized.

Jareth's not sure how much time passes, but when he steps back, a tuft of daisies reaches almost to his chest. It's big and bright and magnificent.

Each one countless memories inside a memory.

He's panting as he realizes the daisies aren't a two dimensional painting. They have depth. Volume.

And they're not fading away.

Jareth waits, not sure if he should be marveling at his creation or scared of it. But it doesn't disappear. The daisies stand strong and proud in the bright sunshine.

His breath evaporates. He knows he should destroy them. That he just created something purely with the power of his mind. But he can't bring himself to. His mother would love these kaleidoscope daisies. His father would salute him with his cup of tea.

So, Jareth turns away and leaves the cemetery. At least he can feel like he left something good in Mirror Point.

The sun's climbing its way to a new day as Jareth heads to the bus stop. He'll go to school. He'll try one more time to tell Brielle she should stay away from Tristan.

He'll say goodbye to Veronica.

And then he'll do what he should've done in the beginning.

Run.

BRIELLE

B rielle isn't sure which emotion is stronger as she waits on the sidewalk: anger at Tristan's misplaced outrage and ignoring her calls during a crisis, or worry that Jareth will disappear without a trace, either because he wants to, or because the Skins do it for him.

A flurry of whispers war in her head as she taps her foot outside the school entrance, waiting for both guys with arms crossed.

Stupid Tristan, getting all worked up because I was doing exactly what he wanted me to do—attempt to bring Jareth into our inner circle.

Poor Jareth. I wish I could just make him see the truth. If we can't open his eyes, the Skins will get him for sure.

I still can't believe Tristan didn't answer my calls. We could have died! And probably would have if Jareth hadn't unleashed those awesome flames!

Jareth must be so confused with these new powers. Please, come to school today, Jareth, please!

She can't help but think back over her phone call with Tristan last night.

"Where the pitch have you been?" she'd asked.

"I'm sorry, I got...tied up," he'd answered vaguely. "Are you okay? I ran into Jareth and he told me you got attacked."

"Yeah, we did," she'd said, exasperated. "I can't fight off Skins, and I doubt our training sessions would have made even a dent. We needed you."

Silence for a moment.

"I know," he'd said, his tone dripping with shame. "I'm so sorry I wasn't there when you needed me. I'm just glad you're safe."

"We only got away because Jareth *created* flames, *actual flames,* and the Skins got scared off."

"He did what?" Tristan had asked, incredulous.

"If we were unsure he was a Zodiac Guardian, we can be sure of that now."

It was her turn to be silent as she gathered her thoughts, debating which question to ask.

"Why did you run out on us at the library?" she asked finally.

Another long pause. Even at that distance, she could feel the tension. Why was there tension? What was he hiding?

"I...it just struck me to see you both together, looking so friendly," he finally said.

"But that's what you wanted, isn't it?" she asked, her pitch hiking. "I don't understand why that got you upset."

"It's just that..." He made an odd growling sound. "I don't think it's a good idea for the two of you to be *too* close."

Wait, what? Did he think she and Jareth were a thing?

"I understand that, better than anyone." Her voice fell at the last three words. "Jareth and I are just friends. You have nothing to worry about."

"I know, he told me," he replied, deadpan.

How could he think that? Didn't he realize how deep her feelings for him dug into her? Could he really be so blind to that? It hurt to think that he'd completely written her off since finding out she was only the Libra.

Not his Gemini Princess.

And if that wasn't enough, it seemed he didn't want her to be with anyone else either.

Ouch.

"Either way, I'm sorry," he said again. "I promise I'll never leave you hanging again. I vow here and now to answer every time you call in the future. As long as you do the same for me."

"Of course," she said too quickly. Was it possible for her to deny him even the simplest request?

And now she stands here alone waiting for him like some obedient lap dog. Pathetic.

"Ah, now that's a sight I'm used to," Cassandra says as she stalks closer from the parking lot, clicking the lock button on her car remote with her overly bright pink polished fingers. "Brielle all alone. As it should be." She gives a fake pout. "What, did you chase off both guys?"

Brielle rolls her eyes, and the gesture feels so good. Anything to vent these flooding emotions. "What are you talking about, both guys?"

Cassandra stops, arching a perfectly plucked dark blond brow. "Really? Don't play dumb with me. I know the trick of pushing the jealousy angle when I see it. Tristan wasn't interested, so you suckered Jareth in. Can't say I'm surprised you're finally showing your true colors. And the sad part is that it's working on poor, innocent Tristan."

"J—" Brielle can't even voice the word, she's so shocked. *Jealous?*

Is Tristan actually…jealous? Of Jareth?

That makes no sense. She's not his soulmate. That lucky girl is hiding somewhere out there in the world, waiting for him to find her. He couldn't possibly feel the same burning agony of both being with her and not being with her like she does for him. So why would he be jealous?

Brielle can't speak to Tristan's jealousy, because she doesn't know if it even exists. But she can never say nothing in response to Cassandra. Call it her kryptonite.

"Once again, you've put your wicked mind to work and come to the wrong conclusion," she says. "There's nothing going on between me and either of them. Tristan is just a good friend, and Jareth is just badly in need of one."

Cassandra scoffs. "Like you have any idea how to be a good friend. That's why your little crony Adalind vanished, I presume. She found out what you really are and had her parents drag her to some other po-dunk town." She shrugs. "Whatever." She begins to sashay away, then stops and looks over her shoulder. "Oh, and I thought you should know that our fathers' merger was finalized this morning. I knew you more than anyone would be thrilled about the news." She winks and gives a cheeky grin before wagging her invisible tail up the steps of the school.

Brielle grits her teeth and turns back toward the parking lot, seething with hatred for Cassandra and her parents. Great, one more thing topped onto the ever-growing pile of things she needs to worry about.

"Good morning, Miss Pierce." An unfamiliar and authoritative voice draws her out of her ruminations, and she looks up to see a middle aged man, male pattern balding and all, in a black suit approaching her.

As if he could somehow have the wrong person, she looks around. But this early, she's the only one on the sidewalk. She shakes her head at her own foolishness. He used her name. He must be talking to her. But why?

"Uh…good morning," she replies questioningly.

The man pulls a leather wallet out of his suit pocket and flashes it at her, revealing a shiny FBI badge.

Her heart hiccups, and she's sure her eyes visibly widen.

"I'm Detective Cadbury," he introduces. "I'd like to ask you a few questions."

Her throat is dry, but she manages to croak out, "About what?" With Cassandra's comment freshly in mind, she's terrified it has to do with the deal between her new father and Mr. Sinclair.

"You're an acquaintance of Tristan Ayers, correct?"

Oh. Nowhere near what she expected.

Crap. It's worse!

"Y-yes," she stammers.

"How long have you known him?" he asks, his unflinching pale eyes seeing right through her like an x-ray.

"Umm, a few weeks, I guess," she says vaguely. "Since he moved here."

"Alright," he says, shoving his hands into the pockets of his slacks. "And would you say that the two of you are…close?"

Define close, she thinks to herself. She shrugs, hoping she's passing for nonchalant. "I guess." She narrows her eyes in faux concern. "Is he in any kind of trouble?"

"I'm just looking into the murder of his parents. Zarius and Tess Ayers. How well did you know them?" His gaze is fierce and penetrating, and she can't meet it for its intensity.

Well enough to watch them die in front of me. Does that count?

"Not well," she says honestly. "I'd only known him for a few days when they died." She pauses briefly. "Do you have any leads on their killer?" Not that she or Tristan were the villains in the situation, but she's terrified of either one of them being implicated. "I'm sure Tristan would sleep better at night if their killer was caught," she adds, once again rewording the truth to avoiding telling a lie.

Detective Cadbury sighs, rubbing the scruffy stubble on

his chin. "Nothing solid yet. That's why we're covering all our bases."

Lie.

Her sirens are going off, and suddenly her blind trust in this man is gone. Replaced by suspicion.

"How can I help?" she asks, filled with a sudden confidence that only comes when you know someone is lying to you.

"Well, Miss Pierce—"

"Please, call me Brielle," she offers. "I guess I'm still not used to my new surname." She fakes a bashful shrug.

The detective clears his throat and foregoes her invitation. "Have you noticed anything…strange about Tristan Ayers? Anything at all?"

Strange has a very loose definition. In her mind, there's nothing odd about Tristan, at all. He's pretty darn perfect.

She shakes her head. "No, not that I can think of. He seems like a pretty well-rounded guy. I just feel so bad for him, losing his parents. Especially as an orphan who never had any, I feel for him."

Playing the sympathy card was a wise angle, as Detective Cadbury seems momentarily thrown off.

"Alright," he says lengthily. He digs around in his suit jacket and comes out with a business card. "Well, if you think of anything that could be of use in our investigation, don't hesitate to call me."

She accepts the card and looks at the letters and numbers printed on it. "Like what?" She's fishing, trying to gauge exactly what this detective is investigating.

He looks away and shrugs. "I don't know. Anything odd you may have overheard about his parents. Any strange behaviors Tristan may have exhibited." He looks down at his feet for a moment, then right at her. "Don't you think it's odd that the town librarian, who had no affiliation or relation to

Tristan whatsoever, signed all his belongings over to Tristan in his will right before dying himself?"

A thousand questions swim in Brielle's mind, but there's only one worth voicing. "Is Tristan a suspect in his own parents' murder?"

The detective hosts a staring contest with her for long seconds, but she's not backing down.

"Just call me if you think of anything, okay?" he says, then turns around and huddles back to the parking lot as if he thinks he's invisible.

He'd make a terrible Skin, she thinks as he walks away.

She waits until he gets back into his silver car and drives away before pulling out her phone. It's seven-forty-eight, and though more cars are starting to arrive, there's no sign of either Jareth or Tristan. Whatever his issues, Tristan can't be so worked up as to miss school today, right?

She calls him.

Honoring the promise he just made, Tristan answers right away. "Brielle?"

"Where are you?" she hisses inadvertently, not meaning for her tone to come across so sharply.

"I'm tailing Jareth to make sure he doesn't get attacked again," he replies in a hasty, hushed tone.

She's relieved to hear that Jareth isn't completely on his own. "Tristan, an FBI agent just came *to the school* and questioned me. About you! About your parents!"

He says nothing, assumedly processing the information.

She sighs, unwilling to have this fight with him, especially from a distance. "Tristan, I'm worried about it. He was clearly lying when he said he had no leads about your parents' murder, and…and I'm certain his only aim in interrogating me was to gain info on you." She pauses, allowing him to respond, which he doesn't. "I think…you're a suspect."

Another long silence.

"We'll figure out what to do about this later. For now, I just need to make sure Jareth is safe."

Then the line goes dead.

She puts her cell back in her pocket and reluctantly slinks toward the school entrance. It's still twenty minutes before school starts, and though more and more students arrive, she's sure from Tristan's words that neither he nor Jareth will be coming any time soon.

It will all have to wait till lunch.

If Jareth even shows up.

Please, Jareth. For your own sake, don't run away!

32

TRISTAN

Tristan wipes his hand down his face as he steps through the gates of the cemetery. Jack spoke to Brielle. Asking questions about his parents' death. At least he got to say sorry before this next complication raised its head.

Jareth's bus drove away a few minutes ago, heading in the direction of school. Tristan leans against the rock wall, the rough surface digging into his shirt. He'll need to follow Jareth to make sure that's where he's going.

In a sec.

Coming to the cemetery is always hard. But seeing someone else living with the pain of loss that he does had felt like a sledgehammer to the gut. He'd discovered this morning that he and Jareth had far more in common than he realized.

Regret they can never undo.

As he'd watched Jareth crumple beside his parents' memorial, Tristan had stepped back around the wall surrounding the cemetery. He recognized the weight of grief pulling Jareth down. But not only that. The desperate wish that he'd done things differently was undeniable in his trembling jaw, in the way he struggled to keep his head up.

In the way he'd tucked into himself, as if wanting to disappear.

Tristan knew he deserved some privacy. His own chest had been caving under those same emotions.

Jareth had left not long after, striding out with his shoulders back, like he'd made a decision. That had made Tristan nervous. It was also an action he recognized.

It meant Jareth had a plan. A way forward that he's planning on seeing through, no matter what.

But Tristan's learned that grief blinds you. Isolates you. Has you believing you're alone with your pain, and there's no way out.

Brielle was right. What Jareth needs right now is a friend.

Pushing away from the wall, Tristan's taken two steps toward his car parked around the block when he stops.

You've got to be kidding.

A man's striding toward him, jacket flapping thanks to the determined speed he's built up.

Tristan considers turning around and doing his own power walk the other way, but he stops himself. He's never run from a fight, and he's not going to start.

The man's bald patè glints in the early morning light. His jaw is tight with righteousness.

Jack. Cadbury.

Tristan waits, tucking his hands into his pockets. In the past, he's had to stop himself from punching the guy in the jaw. Jack Cadbury is single-minded in his search for the truth. Unfortunately, he's getting too close.

Tristan's glad he's tucked his hands away as they clench into fists. Jack moved in on Brielle. That ticks him off.

Jack stops a few feet away, looking like he's consciously unwinding his muscles so he looks relaxed and friendly. "Tristan, it's been a while."

A lifetime would've been better…

"It's great to see you again, Jack," Tristan says in a way that conveys anything but that. "What have you been up to?"

"The usual."

Using FBI resources trying to prove aliens are a threat to the human race. Idiot. *We're the ones protecting you.*

For the second time, Tristan's glad his hands are deep in his pockets. The desire to cross his arms is overwhelming, but he refuses to look defensive in front of Jack.

Instead, he angles his head. "Spent any of your government funded time trying to figure out who killed my parents?"

"I have a feeling that case is going to be open for a while..." Jack muses, his quiet voice full of threat. He looks at Tristan, his eyes bright with certainty. "Do you know?"

An evil greater than you can imagine...

Tristan narrows his eyes. "I would love to bring the bastard to justice. Zarius and Tess were the only family I had," he grinds through clenched teeth. "They meant everything to me."

Jam that in the three-foot deep file you have on me, Jack.

Jack nods, and Tristan can almost see the gears turning in Jack's hairless head. If only he knew what conclusions this FBI bulldog was coming up with...

"What do you know about pods, Tristan?"

Tristan stops himself from freezing. His pod was destroyed by the Skins because they were looking for the stones. But every other Zodiac Heir had one, too. There could be another twelve round white vessels tucked away who-knows-where after bringing the others to Earth.

Still, there's no way Jack could know about the pods. He's bluffing.

"Like the ones you put in coffee machines?" Tristan asks, adding a good dose of mockery to his confusion. "Or the ones peas come in?"

Jack nods, like that's the response he expected—an answer he's disappointed with, but not surprised by.

He shrugs. "These ones are bigger. White. Like a giant egg, really."

Holy pitch, he knows what they look like...

Tristan grins. "Now, that's one hell of a chicken." He holds Jack's gaze. "I'm sure if they existed outside of your imagination, they'd look pretty cool."

Jack's eyes narrow as he pushes his face forward. "Your cocky act might fool others, but not me, Ayers. I'm getting closer, I can feel it. And when I discover the truth, everyone will know exactly what you are."

"E.T.'s cousin?" Tristan asks incredulously. "Either that, or you'll be even more of an FBI laughingstock than you already are, Jack."

Jack pulls back, his gaze stony. "I'll be watching. Waiting."

He spins on his heel and stalks away. Tristan wants to shout after him to stay the hell away from Brielle, but he keeps his clamped jaw shut. Jack doesn't need to know that Brielle's someone Tristan would give his life to protect.

Knowing that Jack might follow him yet, Tristan heads back into the cemetery. He'll take the back gate out and make his way to his car from there.

Gravel crunches underfoot as Tristan keeps his gaze averted from his parents' headstones. He can't afford to be pulled back into the pain of their loss right now. He's already learned what that means—increasing the likelihood of losing those who are still with him.

It's time to make Zarius and Tess proud.

He's just turned right into the small alcove that has the gate at the end, when he sees the gate's open. Tristan's senses sharpen. Anyone could've left it wide open like that...rushed out with tears clouding their vision, just wanting to get home...

But it's always been shut. He'd noticed before how seriously people took the little *Please Keep the Gate Shut* sign that hangs on it.

He deliberately missteps, his right foot taking a second longer to land on the gravel. That's when he hears it.

The crunch of stone grinding against stone. When his foot was in the air.

Tristan knows he has two choices. Run, hoping to reach the safety of people. Or stay and fight.

Planting his feet into the ground, he spins around. The decision was a no-brainer. He's been itching to pummel a couple of Skins.

They materialize as they run at him. Two men. Big ones. Angry ones.

Good. That's just the way he likes them.

He holds his ground, his fists by his side. The one who reaches him first slams into Tristan like a battering ram, grunting with satisfaction.

All the air is driven out of Tristan's lungs. It hurts. But the next grunt from the Skin is one of pain as Tristan drops low and raises both fists. They connect with the man's jaw with a *click*. A second later, the man's sailing through the air.

The second Skin quickly replaces the first, already swinging a kick at Tristan's ribs. He grabs the foot as it connects with his side and yanks so the Skin tumbles even closer.

He wants this fight to be up close. Dirty. He wants to deal some serious bruises. Maybe a few broken bones.

The Skins must sense something, though, because they don't give him his wish. The first man never returns, and Tristan sees him dart back out the gate from the corner of his eye. The second Skin shoves him away with enough force that Tristan stumbles back a pace or two.

The Skin glares at him over the few feet he just created. "Chardis told us about you."

Tristan's about to ask him whether he's as good-looking as their boss told them but the goon is already running at him again. Tristan locks every muscle, welcoming the next collision of body on body.

But at the last second, the Skin feints right, steps left and runs around Tristan. Straight toward the gate.

"Coward," mutters Tristan.

He goes from stationary to sprinting in a blink. It only takes two steps to catch up with the Skin, and one leap to spear him into the ground. A few twists and punches, and he's straddling the Skin, the man's arms trapped under Tristan's knees.

The man's panting hard as he stares up at Tristan, his face twisted in hatred. Up this close, the dark ring of black matter that circles a Skin's iris is visible. Subtle. But the undeniable mark of darkness that now controls him is there, as inescapable as the evil that's enveloped his soul.

Tristan slams his fist into the Skin's jaw. "Where's Chardis?"

The man turns his head back, smiling as if he relishes the pain. "Everywhere," he spits.

This time, Tristan ploughs his fist into the Skin's nose. "What is he planning?"

Blood gushes down the man's face, trickling down onto the grass. "Annihilation."

The next punch isn't a single. Left hook. Right hook, and the Skin's face is already starting to swell. "I just cancelled my plans," Tristan snarls. "I could do this all day."

The Skin spits out a mouthful of blood, then exposes his reddened teeth. "So, you're following the other one, too, huh?

Following the other one? "Who?"

Slam. His fist connects with the man's face.

"Who?"

The Skin's head lolls and Tristan waits, his chest heaving, knowing he doesn't want the man unconscious. Slowly, he turns his head back to look at Tristan.

"Tell me who you were following and this ends," Tristan growls. His thirst for vengeance is already waning. These men aren't the ones who killed his parents. They're nothing but puppets.

The man opens his mouth, his swollen lips starting to work.

Crack.

The sound of the shot is muffled. Muted by a silencer. But the impact is the same. Red blooms across the Skin's chest as his body goes limp. Tristan looks up to see the first Skin standing in the gateway, a gun in his hand.

With the next blink, he's gone.

"Dammit!" Tristan leaps to his feet, but when he gets to the gate, he sees what he expected to.

Nothing.

The Skin would've already made himself invisible. Who knows what direction he ran in. There's no way Tristan will be able to follow him so he can finish the interrogation.

Tristan glances back at the dead Skin. The other one will return to clean up his mess, which means Tristan could wait for him. Except he can't afford for Jack to still be loitering around. The last thing Tristan needs is to be implicated with more deaths.

"Dammit!"

He jogs out of the cemetery, heading back to his car. The Skins weren't here because of Tristan. They were following someone else…

And just like the Skin said, it's probably the same person Tristan was following.

Which means that's the second time the Skins have moved in on Jareth. Like they knew where he was.

Inside his truck, Tristan does an unobtrusive scan of his surroundings. No bald FBI agents with questions that are too close to home. No Skins with the answers he could actually use.

Flexing his hand, Tristan pulls out his cell phone, sending a quick text. Brielle will tell him if Jareth's at school.

Once they've sorted that out, they need to talk.

33

JARETH

Seeing Brielle's face light up as Jareth walks toward her hurts more than he thought it would. Sitting beneath the tree out on the school oval, she waves enthusiastically as she smiles. Jareth can't help but smile back. She was obviously waiting to see if he'd turn up.

His chest tightens. Although they've only been friends for a short time, it's going to be hard to tell her he's leaving.

Brielle lifts up the tub she has sitting on her lap as he approaches. "I made extra brownies in case you were here."

"I wasn't going to be."

Patting the grass beside her, she smiles. "I'm glad you are."

Jareth hesitates for a moment, but then folds himself and sits down next to her. Leaning his back against the tree like Brielle is, he reaches in and grabs a brownie. "These look amazing."

Brielle beams. "They're Tristan's favorite."

The fudgy slice stops on its way to his mouth. "Don't even start."

"He went and saw you again, didn't he?" she asks, although it's obvious the question is rhetorical.

Jareth leans his head back against the rough bark, closing his eyes. "He's persistent, I'll give him that."

Brielle sighs. "Those men who attacked us, they're Skins. Chardis's assassins. They want the Zodiac Guardians out of the way so they can attack Earth. We don't know what he's planning, but it's not good." He can feel her turn to him. "But you don't want to hear all this again, do you?"

Jareth hears the sadness in her voice. No, the disappointment. But he's not going to tell her about Malachi and why he knows otherwise. It would put Brielle in danger, too. Instead, he huffs out his own sigh. "No, I don't. I came here to tell you I'm leaving, Brielle."

"No…"

Although Brielle breathes out the denial, Jareth can tell she's not surprised.

"I'm being followed. Attacked." He looks at Brielle. "And now the people I care about are in danger."

Again.

But Brielle is already shaking her head. "Whether you believe us or not, going it alone isn't the answer, Jareth. You don't have to do this on your own."

Jareth opens his mouth but she raises her hand, her gaze determined.

"You lost your parents. Your family. I've seen what that did to Tristan—I know it hurts. But surely you can feel it. You could…belong here."

For the briefest of moments, Jareth hesitates. There's truth in Brielle's words. She would be the sister he never had. She has powers, too.

And then there's the sculpture he created at his parents' memorial…

But he shakes his head. The alternative is to face whoever wants him dead. And believe he's an alien.

Brielle crosses her arm. "So, you're going to run."

"I sure am."

"You'll be in more danger on your own."

Jareth simply stares at her mutely, thinking, *But those around me won't be.*

Brielle's brow contracts in frustration. "You're as stubborn as Tristan."

Jareth's lips twitch. "No need to get insulting."

"You two are far more alike than you realize," she huffs.

The buzzing of Jareth's cell phone interrupts the stalemate they were reaching.

He glances down at the screen. "It's Veronica."

He needs to talk to her, too, but he quickly silences it. She deserves to know he's leaving. But that's a conversation he wants to have in private, not with her friend sitting right beside him.

"Oh, the girl you mentioned the other day?"

Jareth frowns. "Yeah, Veronica. Short. Sassy. Likes to imitate a freight train."

Brielle smiles, looking puzzled. "She sounds cool."

"Isn't she a friend of yours?" He stills as uneasiness winds up his spine.

Brielle shakes her head. "No, I don't know a Veronica. In fact, there isn't a Veronica at this school as far as I know."

Shock slams Jareth in the gut, but it's short-lived. Betrayal barrels right over it.

Followed by the burn of anger.

Veronica lied about knowing Brielle. Why would she do that?

His phone rings again, but Jareth hangs up without even looking at it. How did Veronica know Brielle was a friend of his?

What else has she lied about?

Brielle leans forward. "Jareth, is everything okay?"

He swallows. No, nothing's okay.

Which is all the more reason to leave.

Jareth shoots to his feet, glancing around as if he's suddenly surrounded by the men who have been following him. A handful of students are standing around near the cafeteria doors, but apart from that, they seem to be alone.

Seem to be.

"Jareth?"

Brielle's hand on his arm has him startling. He glances down. "You could be one of them, for all I know."

She shakes her head. "But you know I'm not. No matter how crazy what I had to say was, I didn't keep the truth from you. I haven't lied to you, Jareth. I hate lies."

Because of her powers.

This time, when a cell rings, it's Brielle's. She hesitates, pulling it out to quickly glance at the screen.

She frowns. "It's the orphanage. Why would they be calling me in the middle of the day?" She shakes her head. "I'll have to call them back."

Jareth stops her as she tries to tuck it back into her pocket. "Take it." As she continues to look unsure, Jareth pulls up a smile. "I promise I won't bolt."

Giving him her own relieved smile, Brielle mouths a thank you.

"Hello? Oh, hi Sister Agatha. No, it's fine, I can talk."

Brielle's face pinches in concentration as she listens to the muffled voice on the other end. "Wow, it does sound amazing."

Another pause and Brielle nods. "Great idea, the orphanage is always looking for opportunities to raise awareness of adoption."

More nodding and Jareth averts his gaze as if that shows he can't hear every word.

"Yes, it would be great to have them there. Hmm, yes, I

can see you're short on time if you want to do it before you go on retreat."

Her gaze flies to Jareth's. "Jareth Stone? The memorial belongs to his parents?"

Jareth freezes. He's already shaking his head as a smile spreads across Brielle's face.

"It's your lucky day, Sister Agatha. He's standing right beside me! Yes, he'd love to talk."

She passes him the phone, eyes alight with mischief. And something else—triumph.

Staring at the black rectangle, Jareth wonders if he can bring himself to refuse. From the few words Brielle said, he knows he doesn't want to hear what's on the other end of the line.

But it has to do with his parents' memorial.

Crap. It has to do with the daisies.

Jareth takes the phone, regretting it even as he does so. "Hello?"

"Jareth," croons a matronly voice. "The last time I saw you, a beautiful couple were marveling at your thick head of dark hair."

The day he was adopted. "Ah, hi Sister Agatha."

"And what an admirable young man you've grown into. Your parents were wonderful supporters of Grace Orphanage, may the Lord bless their beautiful souls."

Jareth doesn't know what to say to that, so he stays silent.

"The reason I'm calling, " she continues, suddenly all businesslike. "As I was doing my morning rounds at the cemetery —blessing the dearly departed—I discovered someone has created a magnificent sculpture at your parents' memorial."

"Yes, the daisies." Jareth rubs his forehead. "I created it. My parents loved daisies."

"My, what talent, young man! It's like the Lord himself has shown us there's still light after the dark. What's more, this is the perfect chance to raise awareness for our wonderful cause. We'd love to coordinate a bit of an event. Get the local newspaper in, invite some of our sponsors, that sort of thing. We'd love for you to be there."

That sounds like a terrible idea.

"Ah," Jareth tries to stall. "When were you thinking of doing this?"

"That's the thing. Our senior nuns go on an annual retreat next week, which I'm loath to cancel. If we have the event this weekend, though, we can still do something to honor your wonderful parents' memory and your beautiful sculpture."

And get a few dollars in the coffer while they're there.

"It's just that—"

"The children of the Grace Orphanage, all sweet souls looking for a home just like you were, will thank you."

Jareth snaps his mouth shut. Sister Agatha sure knows how to push the guilt buttons.

Quickly, he does the math. The weekend is only a few days away. That will give him time to pack what little he has.

And get some answers. His mouth thins.

His gaze catches Brielle's as he replies. "Of course, I'd love to be there."

Brielle grins as she does an excited little clap. Sister Agatha goes all businesslike again as she reels off the details she's already coordinated. Jareth half-listens, making a mental note of what time he needs to be there.

And how soon he can disappear without too many people noticing.

He hangs up, shaking his head as he passes Brielle's phone back. "She's good, I'll give her that."

Brielle's grin only grows. "She has the Lord on her side. You never stood a chance."

Which Brielle knew.

"I'm still leaving afterward."

Brielle packs up her lunch and dusts herself off. "Not unless we can show you that I'm telling the truth—" before Jareth can put an end to the alien talk, Brielle gives him a quick hug. "We're your family, now."

A little stunned as unwanted warmth blooms in his chest, Jareth watches her walk away. With a quick wave, she disappears back inside the school. Family. It isn't a word he thought he'd ever call his own again.

Shaking his head, Jareth turns away. He's. Not. Staying. But now that he's stuck here for the next couple of days...

As he stalks away, Jareth pulls his phone out of his pocket, quickly dialing a number.

It rings once before the person on the other end picks up.

"Hey, Veronica," Jareth says warmly. "I hope that missed call I had was to organize our next date."

34

VERONICA

The bubble of excitement that bounces in Veronica's belly when Jareth returns her call is surprising, but she welcomes it.

She didn't expect to fall into a relationship during this investigation. She didn't expect to like him this much. She feels like she may have even found "the one", as corny as that sounds.

Veronica never pictured herself as the romantic type. She'd never witnessed real romance, only heard stories about her parents' love from her dad, and his stories are never that colorful, just all business. She's not even sure she ever believed in the whole "the one" theory—that there's only one person for everyone out there.

But as she walks up to the diner Jareth proposed for their date tonight, she can't shake the butterflies that are flying in a frenzy in her stomach. And though all kinds of warning alarms are going off in her mind—don't forget your mission; you have a job to do; save Jareth from Tristan Ayers—she can't help but savor the giddy sizzle flooding her veins.

She went all out on her appearance tonight, too.

Straightened her hair, mascara and eyeliner, clothes that hug her curvy form and flaunt all her best features. Her inner feminist is raging at her, but she doesn't care. Jareth is important, and putting in a little extra effort never hurt anybody.

She walks into the diner and instantly spots Jareth sitting at the corner booth. It was easy to do because the diner is mostly empty. A blush warms her cheeks as she assumes he chose this place for the privacy. *Good call, Jareth.*

He smiles when he sees her walking toward him, and that smile is all it takes to melt her insides.

"Good choice for a second date," she says, sitting on the bench across from him.

"I thought so," he says, his dark eyes boring into her with a strange intensity.

"Oh, I brought you something." Her heart flutters nervously as she pulls the freshly-cut daisy out from behind her ear.

His eyes melt, looking like liquid chocolate, as he takes in the daisy.

She extends her hand across the table to offer it to him. "The way I see it, the daisy is our flower."

His hand slowly rises to accept it, and a soft smile spreads across his lips. "Isn't the guy supposed to be the one to bring flowers?"

She shrugs, hoping her cheeks aren't as scarlet as they feel. "Yeah, well, I'm no ordinary girl. And you're no ordinary guy." She winks, but he doesn't see it. He's too focused on the flower.

A silence grows between them, and she feels the need to break it.

She laces her fingers in front of her and rests her chin on them. "So, what's good here?"

"Not sure, never been here before," he says. "I don't really get out much…but this place seemed quiet enough for some good conversation."

She flares her eyebrows, thrilled by the fact that Jareth actually wants to talk to her, cares what she has to say, just as much as she cares what he has to say. Heck, she's actually grateful for Tristan Ayers; if it weren't for him, she never would have met Jareth.

He furrows his brows, looking down. "So, I never see you at school. What classes do you have? Which lunch period?"

She didn't expect this line of questioning. At this point, she doesn't want to lie to him anymore than she has to—to protect her dad. She may have feelings for Jareth, but she never forgets that her dad comes first.

"I don't go to Mirror Point High," she answers, nonchalant. "I go to a school in the city. My dad thought it would be better for me."

"Oh," he says, taking a sip of the water he must have ordered while waiting for her. "But you were at Mirror Point High the day we met."

Damn, she's going to have to lie now.

"I was there to finish transferring some credits from before the move," she says with a shrug.

"Ah, so is that how you know Brielle?"

The questioning is getting deeper than she ever expected it to.

"Yes. We went to the same elementary school and just kept in contact since. I'm really glad she has a friend like you at school," she adds to take the focus off her.

He nods, but his eyes are distant. "So, school in the big city. What's that like?"

She rolls her eyes and frowns, mostly because she hasn't been going lately. "Tedious," she replies with a bored tone. "Definitely not all it's cracked up to be. Forty kids to a class, and the teachers don't give a damn. I actually wish I could go to a smaller school like Mirror Point High." But then, if she did, she couldn't get away with nearly as much… "How do you like the school?"

He shrugs. "It's fine."

She can't help but notice his posture and tone are different tonight. His body is much more tense, closed off.

Before she can ask if he's okay, the waitress comes up.

"Good evening, folks. What can I getcha?" The twenty-something woman hovers over their table with a bored expression, waiting to jot down their order on a notepad.

"I'll take the burger," Jareth says, eyes fixed on Veronica.

She's no longer sure if that's a sign of flirtation or…something else?

"I'll take the same," she says, turning away from Jareth's intense gaze to glance at the waitress. "And a strawberry milkshake, please."

The woman scribbles their order on her notepad and says, "Comin' right up," before skittering away.

As soon as she's gone, Jareth leans forward and crosses his arms on the table between them. "If you go to school in the city, why do you spend so much time here, with us lowly folk?"

Again with questions she's not prepared to answer. "Oh. Um…" She shrugs. "I guess I like the slower pace here opposed to the rat race over there." She's careful not to let slip that she doesn't actually live here. "Why do you ask?"

"I just figure there's more for a spunky girl like you to do in New York," he replies. "More interesting people."

She scoffs. "A bigger city doesn't mean more interesting people. A greater population just means more people without homes, and more crime. Spunky girls like me don't have time for that. I much prefer the artistic brooding types." She winks, radiating flirtation.

But he doesn't bite.

Something is definitely up with him.

She opens her mouth to ask, but he railroads her with another question.

"So how long have you and Brielle been friends?" he asks.

Veronica blinks a few times, trying to remember what she said earlier. "Since elementary school." Why does she feel like she's being interrogated? If she didn't know any better, she'd think she was sitting across from her dad. Is the old saying true? That girls are attracted to men that remind them of their fathers?

Thinking of Jack's receding hairline and beer gut, she shudders. She really hopes not.

He nods again, looking away.

What's going on in that mind of his?

"Do you have a thing for Brielle?" she asks before she can stop herself.

He nearly spits out the water he'd just sucked through his straw. He clears his throat and says, "No. She's more like a sister to me."

"Good," she says. "I'm definitely the jealous type." She giggles as a distraction.

She has to get him off this topic. If he keeps asking about Brielle, she won't be able to keep up the charade she's trapped herself into.

Once again, before she can get a word out, he cuts her off.

"What made you come up to me that day in Creamy Dreams?" His dark eyes are like a jackhammer, digging right into her.

She's definitely being interrogated.

She fights the stiffening in her shoulders, refusing to give in. "You seemed interesting. And very attractive. What other reasons should a girl have to approach a guy?" Now it's her turn to interrogate, and she can't keep her eyelids from lowering.

He chuckles dryly and looks away. "I'm sure there are much hotter guys that would appeal to a girl like you."

Jareth's odd and accusing tone ignites her characteristically short fuse, and she's done beating around the bush. "Is there something you want to say to me? I feel like I'm on trial here."

He shakes his head and bites his lip, then turns to her, all amusement gone from his expression. "I know you don't know Brielle. I mentioned you to her and she had no clue who you are."

All the blood drains from Veronica's face. She should've foreseen this outcome. But she let her feelings for Jareth cloud her reasoning.

"And if you lied about that," he says slowly, then shakes his head. "What do you want from me?"

The hurt and accusation in his tone stings more than she ever expected. What is she supposed to do now? Tell him the truth? Does he have any idea how dangerous Tristan is? And in relation, how much danger both he and Brielle might be in?

"I'm sorry I lied about knowing Brielle," she says, unable to look at him. "I know *of* her, and when I saw you two together, I..." She has to be as honest as possible. She hates lying to him. But she can't tell him the truth. He'd never trust her again. If he even does now. "Is it so wrong for someone to like you, Jareth?"

Her lip puckers, and she doesn't stop it. Even as she knows it's a manipulation tactic, it's also real.

He shakes his head again. "All I know is that I can't trust a word you say." He slaps a twenty on the table. "Enjoy your meal."

Then he gets up and walks out.

And she's left sitting there, feeling like her entire world just crumbled into nothing.

35

JARETH

J areth watches Veronica leave the diner from behind the corner of the building, his hood pulled low over his head.

She brought him a daisy.

And then continued to lie.

Her head is down as she types on her cell phone, her brow furrowed. Is she messaging someone? Another guy now that her deceit has been uncovered?

Hot jealousy spears through Jareth, even though he has no right to feel it. With a frown, he tells himself it's anger. Anger at being betrayed.

Anger at letting himself believe.

The bus pulls up at the stop, almost like Veronica willed it to come the moment she needed it. She climbs up the steps, her head still low over her cell. She doesn't glance back once.

Nursing his simmering anger, Jareth slips out from behind the brick wall. Veronica admitted she lied about not knowing Brielle. But the reasons she gave were flimsy, at best. He still doesn't know why. And now she's leaving, like none of it mattered.

The doors of the bus jerk as they start to close, and before Jareth's realized he's made the decision, he sprints forward. Slipping through the gap, he darts up the steps, a little surprised to find himself there. A quick glance shows Veronica only a few seats down, hunched over her phone.

Unaware he's followed her.

Not believing his luck, Jareth quickly pays and slips past her. Taking a seat a few rows behind her, he slides down, making himself as small as possible. The bus lurches forward, its giant, ancient engine seeming to struggle to accelerate. Jareth pulls his hood even lower. It's struggling because the poor vehicle is carrying more than just the handful of people on here. It's carrying every lie Veronica's told him.

And the hard, heavy betrayal each one spawned.

Anger is a wasted emotion. His mother's words creep through his mind. *It's quite destructive, really.*

His father would nod solemnly. *Mostly to yourself.*

Jareth crosses his arms, glaring out the window as they take a corner. Yeah, well, they'd drunk a whole lot more chamomile tea in their lifetime.

And the one person they fell for didn't betray them.

Something catches his attention from the corner of his eye, making Jareth spin in his seat. The bus straightens and the car behind them slips out of sight, but not before Jareth sees it.

A silver sedan. Single male driver. Wearing a hood just like Jareth is.

Because he has something to hide.

His heart rate picking up a notch, Jareth waits for the next corner. He has no idea where they're going seeing as he's never been on this route, but it's not long before the bus takes a left. A quick glance confirms Jareth's suspicion. Just like he's following Veronica, he's being followed, too.

Veronica straightens and Jareth instinctively ducks. With little more than a flick of her gaze, she reaches up and presses the button.

It seems they're getting off at the next stop.

Panic starts to grip Jareth with its familiar, frantic cords. They wrap around his chest, his limbs, his throat. He's done nothing but put Veronica in danger by coming here.

The bus's brakes squeal as it comes to a halt alongside the pavement. Trees and shrubs dot the peaceful looking suburb. Does he remain on the bus, and face whoever is in that car when he gets to the end of the route, and has no choice but get off? Strangely, the thought that this might finally be over brings a calming breath of relief along with it.

Unless the bastard who's following him knows Veronica means something to Jareth. Just like they did with Brielle.

And Malachi.

As Veronica steps off the bus, Jareth makes another split decision. He's going to make sure Veronica gets home safe.

Jareth's relieved to see someone else get off at the same stop. It means he slips behind them as they follow Veronica off the bus. Although, he's not sure he needed the impromptu human shield.

Veronica never looks up from her phone.

The unsuspecting person between them takes a left as Veronica turns right, leaving Jareth feeling exposed. He glances over his shoulder and the silver sedan is nowhere to be seen, but he knows it hasn't gone. The guy's waiting.

Veronica heads up the street, still clueless, and Jareth ducks behind a tree as he watches her. Her dark curls wisp over her cheeks, obscuring her face. He wonders how she's feeling. Did their conversation cut her as deep as it did him?

She turns a corner and Jareth hurries to catch up. A quick peek around the bend and he sees she's further than he expected, as if she's picked up the pace. He follows at a distance, seeing that she stops at a mailbox a couple of houses down. Opening it, she pulls out a handful of envelopes, flipping through them, then looking up.

Jareth darts behind the tree beside him, glad for all the shrubbery the street is lined with. When nothing happens, he checks and finds Veronica gone. The sound of a car behind him has Jareth freezing. A furtive glance tells him it's who he was hoping it wasn't.

The silver car.

Bolting forward, Jareth knows he's running out of time. He needs to make sure Veronica got inside okay, and then he needs to get out of here.

He's just reached the hedge that lines the front yard when someone barges him from behind. He cries out with alarm as he's shoved into the shrubs, sticks and twigs grazing his arms.

"Veronica!" he screams. "Run!"

He becomes a frenzy of fear. Shoving as hands try to grab him, trying to kick as his legs get tangled in the branches that surround him. This was probably his fate all along. But he has to make sure Veronica's safe.

"Jareth, it's me!"

Jareth stills, his chest still sucking in lungfuls of oxygen. "Veronica?"

Her kaleidoscope eyes blink at him in the green gloom. She's panting herself. "Yes, just me."

Jareth's hands go from trying to shove her away to pulling her close. "I'm so sorry, I thought you were…" His arms tighten. "You need to get yourself to safety. I'm being followed."

But Veronica just snuggles in closer, fitting her body to his. "I was the one being followed, actually. And by the way, you're terrible at it."

"You knew I was there?"

"From the moment you jumped on the bus. You're as subtle as a pink mammoth."

Jareth can feel his cheeks heat. He thought he was doing so well, too. He pulls Veronica back, gripping her shoulders. "That doesn't matter right now—"

"Why were you following me, Jareth?"

Jareth scowls. "You're asking *me* for the truth?"

Veronica's gaze slides away. "Fair point."

The sound of a car passing out on the street has Jareth's body tensing.. "It doesn't matter, right now your safety does. I'm being followed. I have been for a very long time."

Veronica's eyes widen. "What?"

"I don't have time to explain, but I've been attacked, twice. You need to get inside your house."

If the guy in the silver sedan saw Veronica shove Jareth into the bushes, then he's on his way here.

Veronica studies him for long minutes. Too long. There's no way she can realize the danger she's in.

"Fine," she agrees and Jareth lets himself sag with relief. "Come with me."

"No." His answer is hard and uncompromising. No one else is going to die because of him.

Veronica bites her lip, looking as if she's deciding something. "My dad's an FBI agent. He's been tailing Tristan for a while now." She shrugs sheepishly. "I thought I'd help out…"

Jareth's breath hitches. The feds are interested in Tristan?

But then it whooshes out like he was just sucker punched to the gut. Veronica was using him. For information.

The dates. The kiss. The daisies…

They were all as real as his paintings used to be.

Veronica's watching him closely, no doubt seeing the emotions play out across his face. Shock. Understanding. Pain.

She presses her hands against his chest. "But I was terrible at it. I got too close to the subject." Her eyes soften. "In fact, I fell for him pretty hard and fast. All it took was a daisy."

Jareth blinks. His mind is blank. His throat tight.

Veronica moves so she's pressed against him again. "Not a rose. Not a thousand roses. One sweet little daisy."

Holy hell, he must be an idiot. He wants to kiss her again. Despite the danger and the betrayal and the fact she could be lying all over again, he still wants to kiss her.

He shakes his head. "None of it matters if you're dead. Get inside your house, Veronica."

But she doesn't move. "If someone's following you, maybe my dad can help."

Jareth hesitates. The FBI. They investigated the fire and his parents' deaths. And Malachi's murder.

And came up with nothing.

But it seems they know something is going on with Tristan, too. Maybe Jareth can get some answers...

Veronica must sense his indecision, because she grabs his hand and hauls him out of the bush. Striding toward the front entrance of the house, she smiles over her shoulder. "Shrubbery seems to be a regular hang out for the two of us."

Before Jareth can answer, Veronica's grabbed a key from her pocket with her spare hand and unlocked the door. A quick glance over his shoulder tells Jareth the silver car is gone again.

For now.

Inside, Jareth draws in a steadying breath. Veronica's house is just as he expected—big, but not too big; lots of cool neutrals and straight lines. Jareth raises his brows. But messier. An overflowing hamper of clothes sits to his left, a stack of boxes stuffed with paper to his right. A bike is leaning against the wall further down the hall, a shirt hanging off the handlebars.

Veronica shrugs. "I'm not sure who's worse—me or my

dad and brother—when it comes to housekeeping." She glances at the large photo sitting on the hallway table behind him. "Dad says we used to drive her nuts."

The woman smiling from the picture is obviously Veronica's mother. She has the same dark curls and sassy tilt to her lips. "I bet dust never stood a chance in her house."

Veronica smiles broadly. "Dad says it gave her an unfair advantage."

Jareth glances at the stack of shoes beside the door. "Do you have a teepee in your living room?"

"Ah, no."

Jareth grins. "Then it's still more normal than my house was."

Her eyes widen with admiration. "Your mom sounds as cool as mine was."

Conscious that they're connecting again, Jareth looks away. He'd be a fool to trust Veronica a second time.

She slips past him, stopping at the staircase that goes to the second level. "Dad," Veronica calls out. "I've brought someone to meet you."

Veronica's father. The man she's obviously close to by the affectionate way she speaks about him.

An FBI agent.

The man who comes down the stairs is a little more portly and bald than Jareth was expecting, but just as shrewd looking. He blinks once when he sees who it is standing in his foyer, but apart from that, there's nothing that gives away that he already knows Jareth.

That Jareth is a 'subject.'

A smile spreads across his face. "Hi, I'm Jack. Nice to meet you."

Jareth shakes the offered hand. "Jareth Stone, likewise, sir."

Veronica moves a little closer to Jareth. "Dad, Jareth believes someone is following him."

Jack's eyes narrow imperceptibly. "That's because you've associated yourself with Tristan Ayers."

Jareth shoves his hands in his pockets. It's interesting that Jack assumed that's the case. He shrugs. "It's more like he associated himself with me."

"What has he told you?"

There's no way Jareth is getting into aliens and Zodiacs with Veronica and Jack. He's acting crazy enough as it is.

"Just that he thinks he knows why there are people after me."

Now that Jareth thinks about it, Tristan and Brielle were the first two people who never questioned that.

"Jareth…" Jack looks like he's weighing his words carefully. "Tristan is a dangerous boy and not someone you want to get yourself tangled up with. I can help you, but you need to tell me everything you know."

Veronica nods, her eyes pleading. "I don't want to see you get hurt."

Instinctively, Jareth takes a step back. Choices are starting to crowd around him. Each one with their own undeniable consequences. The air becomes heavy and suffocating, pressing in on his chest.

Turning on his heel, he yanks open the door.

Just like he always has, Jareth runs. He doesn't leave in the same direction he came, knowing that's where Veronica will look for him. He takes random turns up random streets, his path as erratic as his pulse.

As he starts to head east, instinctively seeking the direction that's home, Jareth realizes this time is different, though.

This time, he's no longer sure who he's running from.

JACK

17:26

Jack's still in the foyer when Veronica returns, huffing from her desperate dash after Jareth. Just as he expected, she's alone.

Her shoulders sag. "I lost him."

"I didn't like your chances. He had the hounds of Hades on his heels."

Veronica wraps her arms around herself. "He's so scared, Dad. We have to help him."

"Tristan's gotten to him, hasn't he?"

She nods, chewing her lip. "I think he's gotten to Brielle, too. She's been making contact with Jareth."

"Dammit."

Tristan's smart. He's got a pretty face on his side to help with the recruiting.

And Jack still doesn't have a concrete idea what he's building a team for. All he knows is it's dangerous. For everyone.

"Jareth's already lost his parents, Dad. He doesn't need fear on top of sorrow."

"He's a nice kid," Jack agrees. Jareth seems like someone who will talk, given the chance. Jack watches his daughter closely. "Easy to like."

Veronica's hands clench, knowing exactly what Jack's suggesting. Veronica's getting too close. She's emotionally invested.

"That's beside the point."

Except, it's not. If Veronica's developed feelings for Jareth, that's going to complicate things.

"You can't let your emotions get involved, KitKat. This guy could turn out to be one of them."

She lifts her chin in that way of hers. "He's not."

"You don't know—"

His daughter stomps past him. "I do. He's sweet and sensitive with a beautiful soul." She glowers at Jack over her shoulder. "And I'm going to add happy to that list."

Jack's ulcer burns like there's a cauldron of acid in his stomach. Tristan Ayers is doing nothing but making his life hell.

Now, it's getting personal.

36

BRIELLE

R elief washes over Brielle when Tristan opens the door of his house, and she wraps her arms around his neck before she can stop herself.

To her surprise, he hugs her back. His arms feel so good around her.

"You never showed up at school," she says. "I was worried."

He draws back and pulls her inside, then closes the door. "I needed some time to think, after I got attacked by Skins at the cemetery."

"What?" she exclaims.

Tristan leads her to the kitchen and they sit at the island.

"Yep, right after Jareth left," he replies. "And I don't think they were there for me. They bolted without much of a fight."

"Are you okay?" She looks him over, and though he looks unblemished, she needs his reassurance.

"I'm fine. But there's something we need to talk about." His light eyes swirl with a storm of brooding.

Honestly, there are a lot of things they need to talk about, so she's on the edge of her seat as she waits to hear which one he's chosen.

"What's up?" she asks when he doesn't immediately begin.

"I—I've had a vision. About Jareth." The words feel heavy as they hang in the air.

Brielle hasn't had much experience with Tristan's visions, but—like hers—they rarely reveal anything good. "What did you see?"

"In the first vision, Jareth died in a fire," he says. "In the second, the fire raged without him." He growls. "Ugh, why can't I have only one vision? I hate the double futures. I can never tell which one is true."

Panic floods her system at the thought of losing Jareth. "Were there any details in either vision that stood out to you? Anything we could trace to try and stop it?"

He shakes his head. "All I saw were flames." He thinks for a moment. "Oh, there was a brunette girl with him. But I've never seen her before."

A light bulb goes off above her head when she hears that.

Jareth has only ever talked about one other girl. What was her name?

"Veronica!" she almost shouts.

Tristan's eyes widen. "You know her?"

"No, but Jareth always talks about her." She remembers the strange conversation she and Jareth had at lunch. "For some reason, he thought I knew her. He seemed surprised to hear that I didn't."

Tristan frowns as he processes this. And suddenly, she can almost see the lightbulb over his head as well, right before he shakes his head and rolls his eyes. "Veronica Cadbury."

"*You* know her?" Brielle asks, intrigued.

"Not exactly," he says, pursing his lips in what looks like

irritation. "But I know who she is. I can't believe Jack would stoop so low."

Wait, Cadbury. She's heard that name earlier today. Jack.

"The detective?" She thinks out loud. "Veronica is his daughter?" Now she understands Tristan's reaction. "Omigod! She's tailing Jareth for her dad?"

"She must be," he grumbles, rubbing his knuckles as if they itch to hit something. "There's no way the two of them just happened to meet."

"Do you think she could be a Skin?"

Tristan snorts. "I doubt it. But Jack Cadbury is bad enough as an FBI agent. He doesn't need to be a Skin to be a problem. Apparently, neither does his daughter. The apple really doesn't fall far from the tree."

"We have to tell Jareth!" After everything Jareth has been through, she can't just stand by and let his heart get broken.

"And you think he'll believe us? He hasn't believed anything we've told him so far."

Tristan makes a good point. If Brielle tells Jareth his new gal pal is with the feds, he'd shrug off the idea like it's another one of her "conspiracy theories."

"Still, we have to at least try to warn him," she insists. "Especially if she has something to do with Jareth's—" she can't say the word, the idea hurts too much. "With your vision."

He raises his brows and nods.

She pulls out her phone and calls Jareth.

The phone rings three times before his voice answers, "Brielle?"

"Hey Jareth," she begins, suddenly unsure of how to continue. She'd been so determined to warn him that she hadn't thought about how to do it delicately without sounding like a lunatic. "Umm, that girl Veronica you mentioned earlier? Well, I found out something about her, and I just thought you should know…"

She pauses, expecting some snide comment or joke, but he says nothing.

She takes a deep breath before laying it all out on the line. "Sh-she's the daughter of an FBI agent that's been sniffing around. I… I think you should be careful."

"I already know," he says in a strangely soft tone.

"What?" She couldn't have heard that right.

"It's a bit of a long story, and," he sighs, "one that I don't really want to get into tonight." She can picture him raking his hands through his black bangs as he often does. "But I do think there are some things we need to figure out. Can you and Tristan meet me at the orphanage fundraiser tomorrow?"

Shock and confusion has her speechless for a moment. "Uh, y-yeah. Sure. We'll see you tomorrow. And Jareth?"

"Yeah?" His voice sounds so raw, so…vulnerable.

"Be careful," she says, praying the importance of her words carries through the phone.

"I will." Then the line goes dead.

It takes Brielle a moment to realize Tristan is staring at her expectantly. "He says he already knows about Veronica. And he wants us to meet him at the cemetery tomorrow for this fundraiser to celebrate his parents."

Tristan cocks his head in question.

"Apparently it's a long story," she says. "But anyway, he wants to talk to both of us. He sounded strange. I think he might finally be ready to listen."

"I hope so," Tristan sighs. "We can't lose our only other Zodiac Guardian."

But Jareth is more to Brielle than that. He's her only true friend. Outside of Tristan, of course, but then she's not really sure what she and Tristan are to each other.

She's sure now that Cassandra was right about him being jealous of Jareth. And if that's the case, he must have more than friendly feelings toward her. Even if she's not his destined soulmate. Fate can get things wrong sometimes, right?

She pastes on a playful smile. "Will you be my date to the fundraiser tomorrow?"

His tense jaw relaxes as he returns her smile. "Of course. Do I have to wear a suit?"

She giggles. "While I have a feeling you'd look very out of place, I'm sure I'd enjoy seeing you in one." Her cheeks burn with the words she didn't mean to say.

He leans closer, and suddenly all of her self-conscious-ness melts away. "And I bet you'd look amazing in an evening gown." His voice is deep, resonating with a warm vibration in her belly that only draws her closer, too.

She fights the urge to look down at her hands, because even though what she has to say is difficult, she doesn't want to break the connection with him she feels in this moment.

"Things have been a little weird between us lately." She pauses, holding his intense gaze and trying to slow her breathing. "And we can't keep dancing around the issue, pretending it doesn't exist. Pretending...we don't feel what I'm pretty sure we both do."

Heat rushes up her neck, and even as she tunes in keenly to her lie sensor, she's terrified he'll dismiss the idea, that he'll somehow confirm all of this is in her head.

He breaks eye contact, looking off to the side with a strained expression, and she braces for the rejection she's sure is coming.

"I have to admit, I am relieved to hear that Jareth has a girlfriend, even if she is a spy," he says finally, still looking away. "The thought of you getting close to another guy…" He shakes his head, grinding his teeth. "I'm a jerk for feeling that way."

She moistens her lips, relieved and thrilled at his confession. "Maybe when this is all over, you and I can," she shrugs, "maybe give *us* a shot?" She dares to reach her hand a few inches closer to cover his.

They stay like that for the longest moment, and she cherishes every second that their skin touches. The Pierces may have adopted her, but nowhere feels as much like home as being with Tristan.

Their faces are so close, it would only take her moving an extra inch for their lips to meet. And she knows she's not just imagining that he wants it, too.

But it has to be his move. He has to choose her. She can't push this on him.

So, when he doesn't close in, she withdraws and leans back on her stool. "I should probably get home. Big day tomorrow."

"Right," he says, looking a bit dazed.

"Pick me up at five?" she asks.

"I will."

She smiles, a gesture that means a thousand things in this moment, then heads for the door.

Tomorrow will definitely be a big day, but she doesn't know how she'll get any sleep with their unanswered question still sizzling through every fiber of her being.

37

TRISTAN

There are more people at the fundraiser than Tristan would've liked. Of course, he's never been keen on crowds, so even one person is more than he's comfortable with.

Each one of them clueless that the fight between good and evil has begun.

About forty people mill around the cemetery, their voices hushed like they're in a church. Nuns wander around with small, ornate brass bowls, murmuring prayers and thanks as they slowly fill up with dollar notes.

At least it's for a good cause. Brielle had said Sister Agatha was practically doing a highland jig when Jareth agreed to come to her impromptu event.

Except Jareth hasn't turned up yet.

Shifting his weight, Tristan works not to frown. A quick check on the way here had confirmed Jareth was still at his house. Surely, he wouldn't go back on his word?

Surely, he hasn't already left…

Surely, there's still a chance to make sure Tristan's first vision doesn't come true.

Tristan scans the area from his vantage point beside a tree. Brielle wandered away once her parents arrived, and now they're all standing around chatting with Sister Agatha. There's so much smiling that Tristan doesn't know whether to look away or give in to the impulse to move a little closer.

Brielle's their success story. Their unexpected happily ever after. He's not in the least bit surprised they want to make her happy—he loves watching her face light up.

"Maybe when this is all over, you and I can..." A delicate shrug. A sweet vulnerability. *"Maybe give us a shot?"*

The moment those words were out, Tristan's heart had leapt against his chest. *Yes! Yes! Yes!*

It had taken every shred of his willpower to stay where he was. This is one decision he can't make impulsively. He'd had to grip the benchtop not to go after her as she'd walked out the front door.

Us. He doesn't think he's ever heard a more beautiful word. Two simple letters that capture the coming together of Tristan and Brielle. How many times has he glanced at her lips, wondering? Felt her brush against him during training and wanted more?

And she wants it, too. She wasn't the one to move away. He was.

Brielle flips her hair over her shoulder, cocoa colored waves spilling down her back. The pale blue summer dress she wore for the occasion brushes against her legs in the gentle breeze. Tristan's breath catches in his throat as he studies her. She's…beautiful.

Although Brielle in her platinum pink suit is what really gets his pulse thrumming. For the moment, he's the only one who's seen her in it…

Pushing away from the tree, Tristan can't bring himself to tear his eyes away from her. What's the harm in seeing where these feelings could take them? There's nothing to say his soulmate is going to be more like a sister. That their bond will be little more than the connection that draws all the Zodiac Guardians together.

Especially considering pushing Brielle away hasn't worked.

His heart starts to thump as it registers he's actually considering this. He finds himself walking toward her, giving into the pull that's always been there.

Brielle's gaze flies to his and her smile widens when she sees him approach. It's almost like she's conscious of every move he makes.

Frank slaps Tristan on the shoulder as he joins the group. "We were just asking Brielle where you were."

Stopping beside Brielle, Tristan's conscious that his arm brushes hers. "Hey, Frank. Nice to see you again."

When Brielle doesn't move away, he imagines what it would be like to casually grab her hand. To look down at her with a smile that's just for her.

For her lips to curve up with one just for him.

He turns to look at Beatrice, pulling up a grin. "So, my guess is you guys baked for this."

Tristan's pretty sure Beatrice and Brielle bonded over their shared love of cooking. It's the nurturing in them, the endless well of giving.

Beatrice's eyes spark with delight. "Just a few finger foods."

Sister Agatha clasps her hands in front of her. "May the Lord bless both of you." She makes a sign of the cross. "The children of Grace Orphanage thank you."

"It was our pleasure," Brielle assures. She glances at Beatrice ruefully. "I think we may have over catered."

Tristan rubs his stomach. "Challenge accepted."

Brielle groans. "I take that back," she giggles. "We should've doubled the recipe for the mini quiches."

He arches a brow as he leans forward. "Did you make any sweets?"

Brielle seems to freeze, her moss-green eyes widening. "Baby pecan pies," she says quietly. Almost a little breathlessly.

"My favorite."

Her lips soften as they tip up. A smile. One that feels like it's just for him. "You said that about brownies."

"They're also my favorite."

They stare at each other for a long moment, the cemetery, their responsibilities, fading away. Tristan's gaze roams her face. Her smooth cheeks. Her parted mouth. Her eyes that seem to mirror the longing soaring through his veins.

Frank clears his throat. Then clears it again.

An arm shoots between them and Tristan pulls back to see Bea's smiling face looming just above it. "Shall we go get the food out of the car, Brielle?"

Tristan jerks back, unaware of how much closer he'd moved. He looks up to see Sister Agatha has her hands clasped just beneath her bosom, her fingers gripping the cross dangling from her necklace as she glares at him. She looks like she just had a shot or two of vinegar. Tristan considers moving even closer to Brielle just to really give her something to go all sour grapes on. When he glances just behind her, Frank is watching Tristan, his mouth subtly turned down.

Brielle pulls away. "Of course."

With an apologetic smile, she lets Bea lead her away. Tristan shoves his hands in his pockets, his mind feeling a little like mush. Why does he feel like he just got caught making out in church?

Frank claps his hands together jovially. "Sister Agatha, why don't you show me this wonderful new sculpture we're all here to appreciate?"

The rod that had just shot up Sister Agatha's spine softens. "Of course. It really is quite remarkable."

With a short nod in Tristan's direction, Frank follows Sister Agatha as she heads toward the memorial.

His brow furrowed, Tristan makes his way back to the tree he just left. The tree that he feels like maybe he shouldn't have left. Over at the memorial, Sister Agatha's hands are moving animatedly, while Frank looks at it pensively. His gaze flickers to Tristan before quickly darting back. He points something out to Sister Agatha, who launches into another excited monologue.

Leaning his shoulder against the trunk, Tristan's frown cramps his brows in full force.

How much do Frank and Bea know? Do they know about the prophecy of the Gemini Twins? Because if they do, they'd know Brielle is the Libra.

Brielle and Bea return, each carrying a large platter of food. Tristan's stomach rumbles at the prospect of anything that resembles homemade. Alden's ravioli feels like it's starting to glue his insides together.

But he doesn't join them. He doesn't give in to the draw to be close to Brielle. He needs to think this through. For Brielle.

And for the Zodiacs they're trying to bring together.

The back gate creaks and Tristan stiffens. A quick glance over his shoulder tells him there's no time to mull this over right now.

Jareth just arrived.

38

JARETH

J areth almost turns around the moment he sees Tristan by the tree. Of all the people to come across first, it had to be him.

But Jareth said he'd be here.

And the keys to his mother's car are tucked in his pocket. Once this is over, he's out of here.

So, he continues walking forward, nodding at Tristan.

To Jareth's surprise, Tristan relaxes against the tree, smiling a little. "Hey, Jareth."

"Hey." Jareth waits, wondering what the catch is.

But Tristan shakes his head. "When you have a moment, I'd like to talk." His mouth twists. "And apologize."

Jareth's brows shoot up in surprise. "As in, say sorry?"

Tristan grins. "I'd do it now, but…"

"Jareth! You're here!" Sister Agatha's voice rings out, making him wince.

Tristan slaps him on the shoulder as Jareth walks past, his feet suddenly feeling heavy. "Good luck."

Although Jareth's mouth wants to pull into a grimace, he

draws it up into a smile as Sister Agatha rushes toward him. He draws back his shoulders, reminding himself this is the last thing he needs to do before he's gone.

His few belongings are already packed in the trunk of his mother's car. He was worried the old girl wouldn't turn over after all this time. Sunshine, as his mother named the Volkswagen Beetle, is just too…attention-grabbing for Jareth to have driven her around. Catching buses was much more unobtrusive. But she jerked to life with the same enthusiasm his mother had done everything.

Sister Agatha opens her arms in welcome. "The amazing artist himself."

That seems to get everyone's attention, because the low murmur in the cemetery stops. One by one, each face turns to look at him. Jareth suddenly feels like he's under a microscope, and it's not a pleasant feeling.

But he keeps walking, making his way to the daisy sculpture alongside Sister Agatha. He stops in front of it, conscious that the small crowd is contracting around him.

The daisies push up proudly from the soil, all turning their faces to the sun. Each and every one of them a symbol of optimism and hope.

Sister Agatha clears her throat and Jareth's conscious that silence has descended. She smiles a little. "Would you like to say a few words?"

No.

"Of course." He clears his throat. He was expecting this.

Although it doesn't make it any easier.

Jareth keeps his gaze on the colorful daisies. "Everyone needs a family, and the sisters of Grace Orphanage know that. Every orphan that arrives on their doorstep has lost their family. For a while, the orphanage is your family, until you can find someone willing to open their hearts and let you in." He swallows, bittersweet grief rising like a tide. "That's exactly what my parents did. They did it so wholly and so completely, I forgot I was adopted. This sculpture, these daisies, capture what they brought into my life. Light. Love. Beauty. And the belief that we can keep growing during the tough times. Thank you Grace Orphanage, for giving me the opportunity to experience that."

Jareth's throat is tight by the time he's finished, and it's a little hard to draw breath. But he got the words out.

I love you, Mom and Dad.

The clapping comes in a wave, a gentle drum of hands on hands as Jareth looks up to find moist eyes and soft smiles. He blinks. Brielle has a tear streaking down her face, her clasped hands held against her mouth.

Tristan is clapping the loudest.

How strange to feel alone yet connected to all these people. Jareth looks away. It's too late. That speech was the last thing he had to do in Mirror Point.

He glances around the crowd. "Now, if you'll excuse me."

Jareth spins around before anyone can say anything, and heads straight for the back gate. A quiet murmur picks up behind him, but he ignores it.

He said what he had to say. It's time to leave.

Jareth's just striding past the tree, the open gate calling to him , when Tristan grabs him by the arm and yanks him behind the thick trunk. What the—

"Jareth? Jareth."

Sister Agatha's strident voice has him freezing.

Tristan stays where he is against the tree, giving Jareth even more coverage to hide behind. "Sorry, Sister. He went straight out the gate. He was running real fast, like he had to go to the bathroom or something."

Jareth can just imagine Sister Agatha's lips puckering like

a prune. "Well, I was hoping he could talk to some of our sponsors. They're all very impressed with the sculpture."

"I think those daisies and that speech of his might have to be enough. Quite the gift if you ask me."

"Very true, young man," she says, her voice a little softer. "I also wanted to tell him that as long as he has someone, he has family."

Tristan's shoulders tense. "If I see him, I'll pass it on."

Jareth waits with his breath held, listening as Sister Agatha's footsteps recede.

Tristan glances over his shoulder. "You sure you don't want to go back? There are little quiches and pecan pies."

Jareth's mouth waters as he creeps forward to peek around the trunk. "Tempting. Right now, just about anything would beat peanut butter sandwiches."

"I'll trade your sandwich for my ravioli, any day."

Jareth doesn't answer, not trusting this new, friendly Tristan. He sneaks a little further out, seeing that people are back to milling around, Brielle and some of the nuns moving amongst them, holding platters.

Tristan stays where he is, crossing his arms as he leans against the tree. "You know, I miss my parents every day," he says quietly. "Ever since they've been gone…it's like I'm a ship without a rudder."

Jareth turns so his back is against the trunk as he stays out of sight. There's a rawness to Tristan's voice. An honesty. A shared understanding. "I painted the same thing over and over," he admits.

"And yet, the whole time I thought I had everything under control."

"You didn't?" Jareth can't help the surprise in his tone. Tristan seems so…confident.

Tristan half-huffs, half-snorts. "We're supposed to be

friends, Jareth." And until now, they've barely exchanged a pleasant word. "So not so much."

Friends. Like he and Brielle almost instantly became.

They would've discovered they had more in common than Jareth realized.

"I didn't see it," Tristan continues. "That we're all orphans. We need each other." He glances back at Jareth. "That we're each other's someone."

Family.

"Tristan—"

"How did you create the sculpture, Jareth?" he asks quietly, glancing over his shoulder again.

Jareth considers lying, but then decides against it. He doesn't want to leave on a lie. "The same way I create my paintings."

"Is it really so hard to believe you may not be human?" Tristan indicates toward the daisies. "When you can do that?"

Jareth's shoulders sag. "It doesn't matter. I'm not staying here long enough to find out."

"I had a feeling you'd say that." Tristan turns around to face Jareth. "I think you should stay."

Strangely, it has Jareth hesitating. He didn't think anything could sway him from the decision he's made.

Except, if he stays, he's an alien.

If he leaves, he keeps everyone safe from his secret.

Jareth shakes his head. "I'm sorry. I need to leave."

Tristan winces. "I also had a feeling you'd say that."

He jams his hands in his pockets, looking thoughtful. Suddenly, he stiffens, and the next thing Jareth knows, Tristan's surged forward and embraced him in a hug.

Jareth freezes, his arms stuck by his side. But then the warmth of human touch floods him, expanding the sense of connection that had blossomed between him and Tristan.

His arms lift, embracing Tristan back. Their arms tighten, acknowledging the moment.

It's Tristan's "I'm sorry" hug.

It's Jareth's "Goodbye" hug.

There's a stifled gasp. "Oh, I'm so sorry," says Sister Agatha, sounding like she just found them making out.

Jareth stills as he realizes that Tristan was covering for him again.

"Is she gone?" Tristan mutters.

Sister Agatha is striding away, no doubt clutching her cross. "Yeah, she's gone."

Tristan pulls away. "Longest bro hug ever."

Jareth huffs out a laugh. "Thanks."

Tristan steps back with a shrug. "No matter where you are, I'll always have your back, Jareth."

Blinking hard, Jareth nods. He didn't expect this to be that hard.

His cell phone rings, slicing through the heavy silence. Pulling his phone out of his pocket, Jareth glances at the screen.

It's Veronica. His last goodbye.

"Sorry, I've got to take this."

Tristan nods, turning away to face the cemetery again. "I'll let you know if we need to bro hug again."

Jareth presses a button on his cell, his heart heavy. "Hey…" his voice fractures and he has to stop and clear his throat. "I—"

"Jareth!" Veronica's voice is high and panicked. "Don't come! I'll—"

Ice spears through his veins. "Veronica? What's going on?"

But the voice that replies isn't hers. "Veronica's unable to talk right now," says a man dispassionately. It's a voice Jareth recognizes…but can't place.

He hunches around his cell, whispering hoarsely. "Let her go, you bastard."

"We're at your house," the man bites off. "Come alone or she dies."

The line goes dead and it feels like Jareth's heart flatlines for long seconds. The people who've been following him all this time…

They have Veronica.

He spins around, hands clenched so tight he wonders how his phone doesn't crack. It seems there's one more thing he has to do.

It's time to end this.

He turns to find Brielle there, a forgotten plate of food in her hand, looking just as concerned as Tristan is. Does she sense something's up?

Dammit. Now, he's going to have to find a way to lie… without lying.

She frowns. "Is everything okay?"

Such a short phone call. One that's changed everything.

"That was Veronica." Which is the truth. "She's not doing so good with the news." Also the truth.

Brielle frowns. "Is there any way we can help?"

"I doubt it." Jareth shoves his phone in his pocket. "I'll need to go see her."

Tristan straightens, his arms unwinding. "We'll come with you."

"No!" Jareth hurries to modulate his tone. "I need to talk to her alone."

Tristan and Brielle glance at each other, obviously deciding whether they should push this.

Tristan opens his mouth but Jareth has already started walking away. He aims for the gate, his heart thundering with each step. He doesn't know how he can save Veronica, but he's determined that he will.

If anyone's dying today, it's him.

"Where are you going?" Brielle calls out after him.

Jareth doesn't look over his shoulder. He's managed to avoid lying up until now, but maybe if Brielle can't see his face, he can get away with just one.

"We're meeting at her house."

39

BRIELLE

Brielle and Tristan watch as Jareth jogs out the cemetery gate and climbs into the driver's seat of an old yellow bug, then drives off with a trail of dust in his wake.

"Is it just me, or was that weird, even for Jareth?" Tristan asks.

"He lied," she says, still replaying every word he'd said after he got off the phone.

Tristan looks at her. "About what?"

Her brows pinch together. "That's just it. I don't understand why he would lie about something so…small, so seemingly unimportant. His lie was that he was going to Veronica's house."

Tristan frowns. "Maybe he's afraid we'll go after him and try to convince him to stay." He folds his arms over his chest. "He made it crystal clear that he's leaving."

Her heart sinks, and worry balloons it back up into her throat. "What are we going to do about that?"

Tristan sighs, his shoulders bouncing in a brief shrug. "I slipped the onyx into his back pocket, along with a note with the word that activates his suit. The best we can hope for at this point is that he finally accepts what he is and comes back." He looks down and kicks at a tall spear of grass. "We can't force someone's heart to change."

Those words slice right through her. By the way he's avoiding her gaze, she can tell he's not just talking about Jareth.

There's still the unanswered question between them, of whether or not to explore the feelings they share. Is that comment an acceptance of those feelings, or a rejection?

Before she can ask, Frank appears between them. She thought she was imagining it before, but he's definitely glaring at Tristan. And that he's placed himself between them wasn't an accident.

"Your friend sure took off in a hurry," Frank says, his eyes still trained on Tristan. "It's too bad, I would have liked to talk to him about his art. He seems very special."

The urge to break the tension strung tight between Frank and Tristan is almost an itch. "Yes, he is," she says. "I haven't had a chance to take a good look at the sculpture yet, what with helping serve hors d'oeuvres. Will you come with me, Dad?" This is the first time she's called him that, and it definitely got his attention off Tristan.

He snaps his head in her direction, a bright smile on his face. "Of course!"

She sets down the plate she'd been carrying on a nearby table and walks with Frank to the beautiful daisy sculpture.

Frank's posture is so light as they walk, he's practically floating. She's been wanting to call him Dad for the longest time, and feels only the tiniest twinge of guilt that her first use was a distraction tactic. Seeing how happy he is evaporates the guilt pretty quickly.

"What medium do you think he made this out of?" Frank asks, cupping his chin as he examines the daisies. "It's so shiny and sleek, it looks like metal. But it seems more solid than that, like it might be some kind of polished stone. And it must weigh a ton, I can't imagine how he got it out here."

Brielle does nothing but hum at Frank's musings. To be honest, she's curious about the material, too. Jareth must have created this from nothing just as he did his paintings. So what in the world are they actually made of? The materialization of his imagination? Would it even register on the periodic table?

"So, uh, what's the deal with you and Tristan?" Frank asks, still pretending to inspect the tallest flower. "You two seem awfully close."

Brielle's cheeks burn, and even though Frank isn't looking at her, she feels the need to hide behind her hair. "Oh, um. We're just really good friends." She shrugs.

"But you like him." Now Frank does look at her, radiating paternal protectiveness.

The burn spreads to her neck. "Yes," she admits.

He purses his lips and nods.

"You don't," she says softly.

He sighs. "It's not that I don't like him. He seems like a good guy. He's respectful and smart." He shakes his head. "I just don't like him for you."

Brielle never realized how much Frank's approval of Tristan would mean to her, or lack thereof. It stings. Judging by Tristan's closeness all morning, he might say yes to being with her. Would Frank try to stop it if he did?

"Why not?"

"It's hard to explain," Frank says. "What about that Jareth? He's so talented."

She shakes her head, exasperation flooding her. "Jareth is moving away. And he and I are just friends. He's dating someone else."

That whole thing still bugs her. She never got a chance to

talk to Jareth about Veronica before he raced off. And why would he lie about going to her house?

"That's too bad," Frank says.

The seed of concern that has been growing since Jareth left suddenly feels like it's about to burst through her belly. Something wasn't right about Jareth's departure. His attitude had been all haste, and then there was the lie.

What if Veronica is a Skin? There's still Tristan's vision to worry about.

With a sudden bolt of clarity, Brielle realizes the horror of the situation. Jareth is leaving today. Veronica was part of the vision, so the vision has to take place before Jareth leaves. And if Jareth is on his way to see Veronica, it's going to happen right now!

"What's wrong?" Frank asks, concern wrinkling his features as he looks at her.

She hopes her face isn't as pale as it feels. "Actually, Dad, I need to go."

"Go?" he asks, looking confused. "Go where?"

What is she going to say? She hates that she has to keep running out on Frank and Bea. She wants to be a good daughter. But if she doesn't leave now, Jareth will die.

She's a Zodiac Guardian. She swallows as she realizes that, sometimes, that's going to mean disappointing those she loves.

"Jareth," she stammers. "I..." She doesn't want to lie. "I think he's in trouble."

Her anxiety is nearly overflowing as she waits for Frank to object.

"Okay," he says, stunning Brielle into silence. There's not the slightest bit of suspicion on his trusting face. "I'll hold down the fort here. Call me if you need anything."

She's so shocked at his unquestioning acceptance that for a moment, she can't move.

But the moment is brief, stampeded by the urgency to save Jareth. "Will do," she says, then runs to Tristan, who's still standing against the tree.

"What is it?" he asks, clearly noting the expression on her face.

"We have to go after Jareth," she insists. "Your vision, it's going to happen right now."

The same clarity that hit her slaps across his face, and his jaw drops. "How could I not have seen that before? Let's go!"

He starts to bolt toward the gate, but she stops him. "Wait, where do we go? He lied about going to her house. We have no idea where he really is."

His jaw sets, and she can see the calculation in his eyes. "He said he was going to her house, right?"

She nods.

"From my experience, when people lie, they say the closest thing to the truth," he explains. "I think I know where he is. Come on."

He takes her hand, and for a moment, that connection fills her with hope.

That they will save Jareth.

That, together, they can do anything.

40

JARETH

T he front door is ajar when Jareth reaches his house. He glances around, his heart like thunder in his chest.

After all this time, he's about to face the gray-haired man he saw in the alley. The one who shot and killed the guy working for him.

The one who killed Malachi.

The one who killed his parents.

No more living in fear. No more looking over his shoulder.

And all he needs to do is get Veronica out. Then he doesn't care how this ends.

As long as it does.

With a trembling hand, Jareth pushes the door. It silently swings open further, revealing the empty hall. "Veronica?"

"Jare—"

His name is sharply cut off by a sound that has horror exploding through Jareth. A gunshot. From the dining area.

Launching forward, he runs so hard and fast he crashes into the wall, bouncing off it as he turns past the kitchen. He comes to a halt in the doorway, breathing hard like he just ran all the way from the cemetery. He takes in the scenario before him, the wash of relief short-lived.

Veronica is sitting in a chair beside the dining table, eyes wide with terror. She's not bound, but she barely moves a muscle as she mouths one word.

Run.

A man is sitting across the table, slowly placing a gun on the timber surface. Except he's not gray-haired like the man in the alleyway.

A slow, tight smile draws his lips up, seeming to lock into place on his face. "Hello, Jareth."

That's why Jareth knew his voice. They've met before.

"McNally."

The FBI agent who interviewed him after his parents' death. The one who played the good cop.

McNally's smile stretches wider. "I'm touched that you remembered."

There's a creak of wood from Veronica's chair. *Crack.* Another gunshot rings out, making Jareth's heart stop for precious seconds.

"Don't move," McNally growls.

It's then that Jareth sees the bullet holes in the wall just above Veronica's head. They form a loose circle, like a sick halo. She straightens from the instinctive duck, her gaze catching Jareth's again.

Please. Run.

But that's what Jareth's been doing for years. And they found him anyway.

Jareth takes a step further into the room. "It's me you want. Let her go."

McNally watches his movement with detached interest. "Very true, Jareth. It's you I want."

Another step and Jareth is fully in the room. Only a few

more and he'll be beside Veronica. "She's not like Malachi. She doesn't know anything."

"Who?" McNally straightens. "Is he another Zodiac Guardian?"

Jareth stills. "A what?"

McNally's eyes narrow. "Every one of the others said they didn't know what I was talking about, either."

Jareth's breath is shallow as he takes another step. Confusion and fear are battling a war in his mind, making it hard to think clearly.

McNally acts like he doesn't know who Malachi is.

But McNally knows about the Zodiacs…

He inclines his head. "As it turns out, the others failed the test, meaning they weren't Zodiac Guardians. Unfortunate collateral damage, really."

Except McNally doesn't sound sorry. The frigid gleam in his eye freezes Jareth's veins. It's like the man has no soul.

Another slide to the left and Jareth is that little bit closer to Veronica. McNally seems to be too preoccupied with telling his story to notice.

He rubs his chin. "Collateral damage," he muses. "Just like your parents were."

The icy fear is replaced with scorching fury. Jareth's hands clench, trying to contain it. "You bastard!"

McNally acts as if the outburst didn't happen. "And then I was robbed of the opportunity to find out what you really are. Human." His cold eyes glint. "Or something else."

The memories of the fire that stole his parents engulf Jareth. The heat. The screams. The agony as he realized he couldn't save them.

With three quick strides, he's standing beside Veronica. It's the one act of defiance he has right now.

But McNally simply watches him with amusement. "It was quite fortuitous that you two…connected." He waves his gun between Jareth and Veronica, before turning his gaze on her. "Your father is the only one who lifted a fingerprint from one of my crime scenes."

"The Triple Murders," Veronica whispers.

McNally continues before Jareth can try and figure out what she meant by that.

"And with you gone, Jack will be too heartbroken to return now that I've suspended him."

Veronica glares at him, her knuckles white as she grips the chair. Jareth places a hand on her shoulder. He feels the fury rippling through her, but she needs to contain her anger as much as he does his fear.

He squeezes a little, wanting to let her know he's going to do whatever it takes to stop this soulless psychopath from hurting her.

McNally stands, keeping the gun pointed at them. "Neither of you move," he warns as he takes a step toward the kitchen.

"How many?" Jareth grinds out. He needs the truth.

All of it.

"Quite a few," McNally says with relish. "There are thirteen of you, after all. We thought the first Zodiac was in Philadelphia. But she failed the test, then there were two witnesses." He shrugs like those lives never mattered. "Then there was the one whose parents wouldn't give up the search for clues, so they had to go, too. Next thing you know, I had an MO – Triple Murders."

Jareth feels sick. "It's not a badge of honor."

McNally puffs out his chest, like that's exactly what it is. "Which is why they didn't link me to your parents. You were the one who got away, Jareth. You broke my streak."

Which has obviously made McNally angry. Really angry.

"Your score is with me. Let Veronica go."

McNally ignores him, stepping up beside the stove. He

pulls out a silver hip flask from his shirt pocket. As he untwists the top, he smiles. "A Zodiac will be able to escape." Chuckling, he tips it and sprinkles the contents over the stove. "Of course, then I'm going to kill you, anyway, but at least we'll know we're one Zodiac roadblock down."

The unmistakable smell of petrol hits the back of Jareth's throat. "Murderer!"

"Flattery will get you nowhere. What's about to happen is inevitable."

Veronica's out of the chair in a blink, and Jareth just manages to grab her before she shoots past him.

"Bastard," she screams, struggling against Jareth's hold.

The *crack* of the gunshot has them both freezing, the sick thud as the bullet spears into the wall turning Jareth's knees to jelly. Suddenly, Veronica's clutching him as tightly as he is her.

"I said, don't move," McNally snarls.

He pulls a lighter from his pocket, his eyes igniting with their own sick fire as he flicks his thumb. A small flame dances to life, sparking a fresh wave of fear through Jareth.

No. Not again.

McNally's face splits into a grin as he drops the lighter. It hasn't even landed on the stovetop before the fumes burst into flames. The air around the stove goes from empty to roaring fire in a blink. McNally ducks, lifting his arm to shield his face.

He runs to the doorway, stopping to glance over his shoulder. "I'm hoping I'll see you on the other side."

As flames spread over the kitchen walls in the same way Jareth's paintings once did, McNally disappears. The sound of the front door slamming echoes through the shocked stillness.

"Jareth." Veronica grips his arm. "We need to get out of here!"

They can't go out the front door—it won't be long before the fire has swallowed the doorway McNally darted through, plus, he's waiting for them on the other side.

Jareth takes her hand. "This way. We'll go out the back."

Except, the smell that tickles Jareth's nose as they run down the hall is all too familiar. They've just turned a corner when he sees tendrils of smoke snaking along the ceiling.

"No," he moans.

"What? What's wrong?" Veronica asks, panic climbing through her voice.

Jareth yanks open the door to the laundry, expecting to see the flames, but his heart still sinks when he's greeted with a wall of orange and red.

Slamming it shut again, he turns to her. "McNally isn't alone."

Taking her by the hand, he runs to his room. This time the door's open, giving them an unobstructed view of the hot carnage that's already alight. Jareth tries to shut the door, but he draws his hand back when he's singed by the heat. The doorknob feels like molten metal.

Veronica pulls him away. "Leave it. It's too late!"

They try every room, every window. Each time reaching the same conclusion.

There are others like McNally. And they've already set every part of the house ablaze.

Jareth brings Veronica back to the dining room, the place where they started. The crackling of the flames is getting louder. Smoke is flowing like an ashen river above their heads. Pulling her in close as if he can protect her with his own body, Jareth's gaze darts around as he desperately works to think of how they can escape.

But they've tried everywhere.

There's no way out.

Veronica's hands come up to clasp his face, pulling his

gaze to hers. "Is there a basement? Somewhere safe we can go until help arrives?"

Jareth shakes his head, wishing he had a different answer. There's no basement. No safe haven that could buy them some time. "I'm so sorry, Veronica."

The heat is becoming stifling. The walls are dancing with flames. The house will reach flash point soon. And it will all be over.

"There's no way out."

She smiles sadly like she was expecting that. "I was really looking forward to more daisies." She pushes up on her toes, pressing her lips against his. "And more of those."

Jareth clings to her for long seconds. It can't have come to this.

He can't have another death he's responsible for.

If only...

Jareth spears straight again.

The daisy on the wall when they first kissed.

The daisies he created for his parents.

He pulls away from Veronica, looking around them. The flames are only steadily closing in from every direction. They can't go to a safe haven.

But maybe he can make one.

"What is it, Jareth? Do you have an idea?"

Jareth nods, lifting his hands. Four walls. That's all they need.

He's not sure how he created the sculpture for his parents. He just thought about the daisies and they were there.

So, that's what he does again. Closing his eyes, Jareth imagines a wall in front of him. A couple of feet taller, a few feet wide. Made of metal. Thick, impenetrable metal.

Veronica gasps and Jareth's eyes fly open to see that it's

far more than just a figment of his imagination. An expanse of gunmetal gray is now facing him.

"How did you…?" Veronica asks in awe.

But there's no time to answer. He turns ninety degrees and repeats the process. It's a little harder, seeming to take more focus, but a second wall appears. They're now encased on two sides, the coolness a stark contrast to the heat throbbing on their right.

"Two more," Jareth mutters.

"Yes, two more!"

Another half turn, and he focuses on creating the third wall. His head feels heavy and his arms ache as he lifts them again. Sweat trickles down his temple as he strains to focus. But magically, undeniably, the image that forms in his mind grows before them.

"Go, Jareth!" Veronica cheers.

Panting a little, Jareth smiles. "Last one."

Three metallic walls surrounding them, Jareth turns to create the last one. The flames already feel further away. The chance of surviving this is within reach.

His hands tremble. The smoke feels like it's clouding his brain. His head swims and it feels like his legs are about to give out. Creating the walls is far more draining than he expected.

But then Veronica is by his side, propping him up. "You can do this," she says with conviction.

Focusing everything he has, Jareth locks his muscles. Screwing his eyes shut, he concentrates so hard it draws a groan past his lips. When he opens them, the fourth wall is there. Completing their safe haven.

Jareth does a slow spin, trying to process what just happened.

Veronica clasps his hand, her excitement telling him she's

come to grips with this much quicker than he has. "I don't know how you did that, but you're amazeballs!"

Wrapping his arms around her, Jareth pulls her close. "It's no basement, but it'll buy us some time."

Veronica sinks into him, holding him tightly. "That's all we need. The firefighters will be here soon."

They stay like that for long minutes, holding each other in the center of the metal box, the sounds of the fire raging around them. Minutes pass, and the sense of relief wanes. Smoke starts to trickle from above them and Jareth wonders if he has the strength to create a ceiling. Except that would totally box them in…

They wait. But there are no sirens. No voices calling out to them.

Dread blooms like cancer in Jareth's gut. McNally works for the FBI. He's probably delayed any help that would've been sent by now.

"Oh god," Veronica murmurs.

She's just realized it, too.

And now she'd be asking herself the same questions Jareth is. How long before the metal is too hot to touch? For the smoke to clog their lungs and choke them from the inside out? Before they're slowly, painfully roasted?

Jareth's knees almost give out as he realizes it never mattered. Even if they get out, McNally's waiting.

And he'll kill them anyway.

41

TRISTAN

The bright yellow VW is haphazardly parked outside Jareth's house, drawing a sigh of relief from Tristan.

Brielle leans forward. "You were right."

Tristan pulls over to the curb, tapping his fingers on the steering wheel. "He wasn't going to Veronica's house." Thank Pitch. He wasn't relishing rapping on Jack Cadbury's door and asking if Jareth happened to be there. "He was going home."

Which means his hunch was right. After years of searching for others like him, Tristan's learned a few things about human nature, like the fact that when people have to lie on the spot, they find the closest thing to truth. If Jareth's lie was that he was going to Veronica's house, the truth was that he was going to *someone's* house, and he didn't know anyone else. His own house was the most likely outcome.

His gaze scans the house. "Now, we need to figure out why he was in such a rush after that phone call."

Holding his finger to his lips, Tristan creeps out of the car, not bothering to close his door. Brielle follows and they glance at each other when they see the front door is open.

Tristan holds his hand up as he hears a voice. A voice that's not Jareth's.

Brielle frowns as she tries to make out the words, but Tristan hears them. Every word.

Then there's silence.

A second later, Tristan sees it. Brielle must, too, because she gasps.

Smoke.

"Tristan," Brielle breathes. "Jareth's parents were killed in a house fire."

Tristan shoots toward the house, only to come to a halt before he's even reached the porch. A man bursts through the doorway. Holding a handgun.

He pulls to a stop, something lighting in his eyes as he sees Tristan. He pulls a black wallet out of his pocket, flashing the shiny badge inside. "Agent McNally. FBI. Can I help you?"

Tristan's hands clench. What kind of agent runs *out* of a burning house? "Let us pass. Our friend is in there."

McNally pushes away from the post, the light glinting off his weapon. "That would be against orders, I'm afraid."

"And of course, you do anything Chardis asks you to," Tristan bites off.

Tristan feels Brielle tense behind him. Dammit. They're out in the open. Although the neighborhood seems quiet, there's still too much daylight. They can't risk being seen in their suits.

Which leaves Brielle vulnerable.

McNally angles his head, studying them coldly. "His wish is my command."

Every muscle in Tristan's body coils like a spring. He needs this over and done quickly. Jareth's inside and those flames are only going to grow.

Save Jareth. Keep Brielle safe. That's Tristan's job.

His mission was always to unite the Zodiac Guardians. Make them one.

Defeat Chardis.

He lost sight of that.

Pulling his shoulders back, he stares McNally down, his senses arcing out wide as he tries to get a sense of how many others there might be. Skins don't work alone. "Do you want to be conscious or unconscious when I step through that door?"

McNally chuckles just as a man materializes on either side of him. "There are only two Chardis wants alive. The Gemini Twins." McNally shakes his head. "If you ask me, you've slipped through our fingers too many times. Staff or no Staff, you're better off dead."

Tristan's never heard of a staff, but he's not going to let McNally know that. "Except you have your orders."

McNally's mouth twists with the bitter truth. "Doesn't mean I don't get to kill her."

He lifts his gun, his gaze zeroed in on Brielle behind Tristan.

"Stay behind me!" Tristan shouts. "Keep low!"

McNally won't shoot Tristan to get to Brielle. Skins are little more than puppets for Chardis's dark matter.

When Brielle cries out, Tristan spins around to find her being dragged away by another Skin. Her frightened eyes dart past him to stare at McNally. Impossibly, they grow wider.

Making a split-second decision, Tristan turns and runs straight at McNally. As long as he stays in the line of sight, McNally can't pull the trigger.

McNally's face is twisted with frustration as he waves the gun one way, then the other, trying to line Brielle up. Tristan sees the moment he locks onto his target. His eyes flash victory. His chest draws in with an excited gasp.

"No!" Tristan leaps, pushing off the ground with all his strength.

He collides with McNally just as he shoots. The gunshot is loud and harsh. Deadly.

McNally tumbles to the ground, one of the countless flower pots scattered on the porch smashing beneath him. Tristan lands on him, already punching the bastard's face.

Brielle, his heart screams. *Say something!*

"I'm okay," Brielle shouts as if he said it out loud.

Relief courses through Tristan, and he uses it to power his punches. He aims for the face over and over as McNally struggles to block as many as he can.

"Get him off me!" he shrieks.

Hands that grip like steel clamp onto Tristan's shoulders, pulling him off and throwing him backward. He finds his footing, leaping straight back at them. The men step in front of McNally, relishing the prospect of the fight.

And Tristan's going to give it to them.

Not having the time or patience for this, he launches himself at them. The first man cops a flying kick to the chin, the force lifting the Skin off the ground in a graceful arc. Tristan lands in a crouch, instantly pushing up again. The second Skin is already coming at him, swinging. Tristan ducks, grabbing the fist that sails over his head. Using the man's momentum, he slams him into the porch post. It splinters and blood explodes, the man crumpling beside his groaning comrade.

A strangled cry has Tristan spinning around.

McNally has his hands around Brielle's throat as she's being held by the Skin who grabbed her. Tristan can't see McNally's face, but the veins of his hands stand out with the effort he's exerting.

Tristan glances around frantically for a weapon, hoping against hope that McNally dropped his gun. McNally could easily snap Brielle's neck if Tristan doesn't instantly disable him. But there's no gun, and the post has splintered into little more than shards. There's nothing.

Brielle moves before Tristan gets a chance. Just like he taught her, her arms spear between his, one great shove tearing them off her neck. Taking advantage of McNally's shock she jams the heel of her palm into his chin.

McNally roars with just as much pain as outrage. The Skin behind Brielle scrabbles to get a hold of her again as she desperately tries to escape. One hand clamps onto her arm, but it's all the diversion Tristan needed.

Roaring his rage, he runs at McNally, his arms high in the air. It only takes a few steps, little more than a second, and he brings down the flower pot on the back of McNally's head.

Daisies and dirt rain down on McNally as he slumps to the ground, unconscious before his head hits the pavement.

"Duck!" Tristan shouts.

Brielle crunches down in an instant. Using the large shard of terracotta still in his hand, Tristan swings and cracks it across the Skin's face like a giant backhand. The man collapses beside McNally, his face slack.

Spinning around, Tristan's not surprised to find the other two have fled.

They're alone with two unconscious Skins.

Brielle's hands come to grasp her bruised neck. "We did it?"

"You did good," Tristan says, his tone warm with admiration.

Brielle draws in a ragged breath, blinking in disbelief. Seeing the shock sinking in, Tristan reaches out and clasps her just as his knees give out.

Her hands land on his chest, her soft body molding to his.

"You did good," he repeats quietly. She saved herself. She gave him time to take McNally out.

"Tristan…"

The sound of something crashing has them both spinning around. Fire and smoke pour out from the back of the house.

"The roof must've caved in," Brielle breathes.

"Check the perimeter," he tells her. "See if there's any way we can get him out."

His heart thundering all over again, Tristan runs. He streaks through the front door, adrenaline injecting through his system. The heat swallows him like the ravenous monster it is, instantly suffocating.

He lifts his arm to shield his face. "Jareth! Where are you?"

For long moments there's nothing but acrid smoke and crackling fire filling Tristan's ears.

"Tristan!" Jareth's voice calls out from beyond the flames. "We're trapped."

We? As in he's not alone? Pitch. Veronica must be with him.

Brielle comes back, breathing hard. She shakes her head, her eyes watering from the smoke. "There's no way in. The whole place is ablaze."

Flames crackle, the heated air seeming to roar with its own violent anger. It feels like every molecule is on fire.

Tristan grips his own stone. He doesn't know if his suit is fireproof, but he's willing to find out.

Wait! Tristan cups his hands around his mouth. "Use your suit!"

There's a pause. "What suit?"

"The onyx, it's in your pocket." Tristan coughs as smoke fills his lungs. He shakes his head, as if he can escape the cloying cloud. "With a note."

Brielle's hand lands on his arm. "You can't go in there. You don't know if you'll survive."

Tristan's jaw clenches so hard it hurts. "I may have to find out."

JARETH

Tristan slipped the onyx in Jareth's pocket?

The heat feels like it's multiplying by the second as Jareth releases Veronica, fumbling in his pockets. He finds it in one at the back. Small, hard, round.

Pulling it out, Jareth stares at it as it sits in his palm. The slip of paper it's encased in unfurls, exposing the midnight gem beneath. Just like before, Jareth feels its warmth. Its draw.

Its power.

Veronica peers down at it. "What does the note say?"

Clutching the onyx tightly in one hand, Jareth opens the small slip of paper. It's small and rectangular, with one word scrawled on it.

Jareth frowns. It's not a word he's heard before. He mouths the two syllables, barely uttering them as he tries to pronounce the strange sounding word.

"Akash."

The next thing Jareth knows, he's being devoured. By the onyx! Faster than he can process what's happening, a black material, almost a liquid, is spearing up his arm and across his body.

Jareth leaps back, trying to shove it away, only to see his other hand being encapsulated by the strange inky stuff. It's like the onyx is exploding all over his body.

He's about to shout out in alarm when his head is engulfed, cutting off the smell of smoke and the roaring of the flames. For a moment, Jareth struggles to breathe. He feels trapped. Like he's been swallowed.

But his lungs fill as they always have. There's no pain. Just quiet.

When nothing else happens, the panic subsides. Jareth realizes he can barely feel the heat of the blaze, that he can see the cloying smoke, but it's no longer clogging his throat.

"Jareth?" Veronica's voice is incredulous.

Jareth looks down at himself. He's covered from head to toe in an...onyx-colored suit.

"Tristan!" he shouts. "What the hell is this?"

"You found it?" comes Tristan's voice over the flames. "You found the suit?"

"It seems so!"

"Awesome!" Tristan sounds downright jubilant. "Now make like a bird and fly the heck out of there!"

Jareth blinks in astonishment. He can fly?

"Now that's cool," Veronica says in awe.

But he has no idea how to fly! Right now, flying is probably more dangerous than staying here!

Another crash detonates not far away. The sound of wood splintering and beams collapsing shudders around them, only to be drowned out by a renewed roaring of the fire. A part of the ceiling has opened up, giving the hungry beast more fuel—oxygen.

"Jareth!" Veronica cries in alarm. She throws herself

against him, clinging to his shoulders. "We have to get out of here!"

"How, Tristan?" Jareth calls frantically.

But the noise of the fire is too loud. Jareth stills, realizing his hearing is far more acute. He tries to detect Tristan's voice, the one person who can tell him what to do next. Except there's no response. Tristan didn't hear him.

A shower of sparks rains down through the opening of the walls he built and Veronica furiously pats one out when it lands in her hair. Jareth looks up, realizing they have to chance it. He's going to have to fly.

Soar like your spirit was always destined to.

His mother's voice is like a warm caress through his mind. Comforting. Confident.

Jareth wraps one arm around Veronica, hauling her tightly against him. Despite the second skin encasing him, he can feel her trembling. Both of their lives are depending on him being able to do this.

He lifts his other arm above his head. Shield. They need a shield. Round, not too big, made of solid metal. When a weight settles down on his forearm, Jareth looks up in disbelief.

The protection he wished for is strapped to his arm.

"Hold on," Jareth mutters.

Veronica tightens her death grip. "It's getting me to let go that will be the challenge."

Not knowing what else to do, Jareth crouches a little then pushes up. In the same way that he created the walls and the shield, he imagines them lifting up into the air. Up through the smoke.

Away from the flames.

He imagines himself flying, Veronica in his arms. Getting them out of this inferno.

His feet leave the ground…and don't come back down.

They hover for precious seconds, embers raining down around them. It's then that Jareth sees that the walls he created are starting to crumble, to fade away in the same way his paintings used to.

It's only a matter of time before they've disappeared.

Veronica gasps. "Jareth! You're doing it!"

Elation shoots through him like a comet. He's doing it!

Suddenly, they're rocketing toward the ceiling. They wobble as he struggles to find their center of gravity. Jareth tries to slow them down, but their momentum is too much. They're a rocket heading for the roof, whether he likes it or not.

Jareth locks the arm he's holding above them as he curves his shoulders in, trying to protect Veronica as much as possible. The impact of crashing through the ceiling is absorbed by the shield and then, strangely, by his suit. Plaster fractures, wood splinters, beams feel like little more than twigs. Veronica's face is buried in his chest so she doesn't see the explosion of materials, the shards of timber falling into the blaze below them.

Then there's the smashing of tiles as they hurl through the roof, shattering the shield as the collision once again knocks Jareth off balance. He half-tumbles, half-flies into the evening sky, wrapping his other arm around Veronica.

Desperately, he glances around, spotting an alleyway only a few houses behind his. Everything is in sharp relief, as if he's wearing binoculars. Focusing his concentration on where he needs to get to, his body tips forward. His breath is short and choppy as he wobbles through the air, trying to right himself, only to find he's over-correcting.

The ground comes at them faster than Jareth would like. He changes angle, bringing his feet forward just in time. He connects with the hard cement, his legs crouching to absorb the impact. His feet tumble over themselves for a few steps but he manages to keep them upright.

Coming to a standstill, Jareth isn't sure what to feel first. Relief? Amazement? Disbelief?

Everything happened so fast. But Jareth can no longer deny it. From the moment he said the word, a new truth was born in his world.

He whispers it. "Akash."

As quickly as it appeared, the suit withdraws, impossibly retracting back into the onyx. He's left standing in the alley, Veronica looking at him with eyes the widest he's ever seen.

Realizing everything has changed.

43

VERONICA

This is so much bigger than Veronica ever dreamed.

Her father was right. And yet, so wrong.

"What just happened?" she stammers out excitedly after Jareth sets her on the floor of a quiet, dark alley.

"I was so far from the truth," Jareth mutters. "I'm so sorry. If I'd only accepted everything before, this wouldn't have happened to you. McNally wouldn't have gotten to you."

She grabs his face, making sure he can see her eyes in the shadows. "McNally would have come after me eventually. My dad was investigating the Triple Murders. It was only a matter of time."

Jareth nods, but he looks away, doubt wrinkling his handsome features.

"What's going on, Jareth?" she asks, desperately needing to know. He's not normal. She already knew that. She's accepted that. But everything he just did is so far from normal, it demands explanation.

She deserves an explanation.

"Tristan and Brielle were right," he says softly, so low she can barely hear him over the rumble of a nearby passing car. "I'm a Zodiac Guardian."

"What does that even mean?" she hiccups.

His eyes finally meet hers. "All this time, I'd thought different bad guys were after me. Human bad guys. I never in my wildest dreams thought I was part of the craziness Tristan described. But McNally blatantly admitted to it. I'm…" He pauses, struggling so hard to force the words out. "I'm an alien, Veronica."

She knew this was coming. After everything that happened, hell, after everything she'd seen before tonight, she'd known. And she'd still been willing to keep it from her father. But could she keep this from him now? Eye-witness proof that aliens exist and have powers that could endanger the public?

But Jareth isn't dangerous. Of this she's undeniably certain. And she'll do anything to keep him safe.

"What does that mean?" she asks, unable to say anything else.

"Tristan told me a few days ago that thirteen alien royals were sent to Earth seventeen years ago, all to protect us from some menacing creature called Chardis," he explains, looking fixedly away from her, as if the words he speaks are ludicrous and he knows it. "We're destined to destroy him, if he doesn't destroy the Universe first." He shakes his head. "I didn't want to believe him. But I can't deny it now. It's all true. I'm…" He opens his hand, and in the center of his palm sits a small onyx stone, which she can swear is glowing like a blacklight. "I'm the Capricorn Guardian."

"Capricorn?" she asks, dazed and confused. "Like the zodiac symbol?"

"Yes." He closes his hand around the stone, then tucks it away. "There are thirteen Zodiac Guardians, apparently, and I'm the second he's found."

Veronica thinks for a moment. "So...Brielle?"

"She's the Libra," he says.

She thinks some more. Then shakes her head. "Wait, if these alien royals are based on the zodiac, shouldn't there only be twelve?"

Jareth clenches his eyes closed. "I don't know the specifics. I only know what I've been told." His dark eyes find hers in the gloom. "Are you going to tell your dad?"

No! She instantly thinks.

But her family loyalty keeps her from voicing it.

This is all the proof her father needs. To show his colleagues at the FBI that he isn't some lune. That he was right all along and they should believe him.

And yet, he's had it wrong this whole time.

Tristan, Brielle, Jareth. They may be aliens, but they aren't the bad guys. She knows deep in her soul that Jareth isn't, and she trusts that what Tristan told him is the truth. After all, who had Tristan really hurt? No one. Who had Brielle hurt? No one.

Who has Jareth hurt?

Not a goddamn soul.

These alien guardians, as they call themselves. They're not here to hurt *anyone*. They're here to protect *everyone*. But at the same time, she knows her dad will never accept it. He'll never accept that Tristan—and in relation, Brielle, and especially Jareth—aren't the bad guys.

It's this...Chardis, or whatever, who's the bad guy. He's the one who put McNally up to it. She'd heard that confession with her own ears. But that would never be enough to convince her father.

Jack Cadbury. The man who'd dedicated his entire life to exposing aliens. To exposing Tristan Ayers.

To exposing Jareth.

"No," she says finally with unwavering conviction. "I won't tell him about you. I'll protect your secret to the grave."

Jareth shakes his head, and again looks away. "You won't have to. I can't let you get hurt again, Veronica. As long as I'm with you, these people, these *Skins*, as Tristan calls them, will keep coming after you—"

"Then let them come," she demands, stepping so close he can't look away. "You hear me, Jareth Stone, I'm not going anywhere. Aliens and evil creatures be damned. I'm staying by your side no matter what. If you'll have me."

Before she can brace herself, he closes his arms around her and crushes his lips to hers in a kiss that makes her head spin. Even after he releases her, she clutches him for balance.

"You understand what that means, don't you," he says softly, almost a whisper. "You'll be in constant danger. This won't be the last time someone will take you to use against me. I don't think I can do that to you. But..." His arms tighten around her waist. "I *can't* send you away. I can't let you go, if you choose to be with me."

"And I do," she insists without a moment's hesitation. "As the daughter of an FBI agent, I'm in constant danger, anyway. Like I said, McNally would have taken me eventually. If not to use against you, then to use against my dad. And, as I'm already linked to aliens, I might be better off staying close to you." She knows she's being manipulative, but she needs to make this point clear. "I can promise you, I will never be anyone's pawn again. I'll train. I'll do whatever it takes."

He chuckles dryly, sardonically. "I guess I'll have to introduce you to Tristan, then. Apparently, he's quite the fighter."

"Like I said, whatever it takes," she vows, hoping he can see the pure determination and devotion on her face.

"So be it," he sighs. "Like I said, I can't let you go if you're determined to stay, but whenever you want out—"

She cuts him off with her index finger to his lips. "I'm not going anywhere. Ever. Your fight is my fight."

"Even if your dad is dead set against exposing me and my team?"

She can't help but feel the conviction when he says the word "team". He's accepted Tristan and Brielle and his part in this. And so has she.

She finds his hand in the darkness and tangles her fingers in his. "Absolutely. Your secrets are my secrets."

He sighs heavily, but smiles despite himself. "Very well. Let's officially introduce you to the team."

44

TRISTAN

Watching Jareth, all sleek and black, shoot into the sky is one of the most beautiful things Tristan has ever seen. Veronica is glued to him, her arms gripping his shoulders, her legs wrapped around his. They peak a little above the house, smoke whirling around them, before they angle forward and spear away.

Tristan and Brielle stand in the front yard, shielding their faces from the heat of the house fire as they watch. Brielle gasps a little as Jareth wobbles like a lame albatross, but he quickly rights himself. Well, mostly rights himself...

Tristan stands on tippy toes as he strains to see where they go, catching the glint of light off the midnight suit as Jareth angles down. He turns to Brielle. "Looks like he'll land not far away."

Brielle sags with relief. "Thank goodness they got out in time."

Tristan lets out the breath that feels like it's been caught in his chest from the moment they arrived. "It was a close one."

Beside him, Brielle starts to tremble. She turns her pale

face to Tristan "Another few seconds and they wouldn't have made it."

Instinctively, Tristan wraps his arms around her. "Chardis underestimated us," he states fiercely. "We just proved again he has no idea what he's up against."

Brielle nods, her face tucked into his chest. The trembling subsides and she looks up at him, her green eyes moist and yet...warm. "Always the strong one, huh?"

Tristan feels himself flush. "Says the girl who clocked McNally a good one."

But Brielle shakes her head. "I meant with your faith and determination. You have me believing we might just pull this off."

Two things have Tristan stilling. The reminder of who and what he is. And the sweet heat that's kindling in Brielle's gaze.

If they were anyone else, this is the moment they'd kiss. He wouldn't fight the attraction that shouldn't exist. His head would tip down, she would arc up. Their lips would finally touch. Press. Probably never want to let go.

Locking every muscle into place, Tristan steps back. "I... I'm sorry." He swallows. These are words he never wanted to say. "We...I can't do this. We can't confuse our Zodiac bond for any more than what it is."

As he stood in the cemetery with Jareth, Tristan had realized. He can't do anything that could divide the Zodiacs. He'd be letting Zarius and Tess down. The Guardians down.

Heck, he'd be letting the Universe and every life that exists in it down.

And Brielle isn't his soulmate. Someone else is.

Brielle's lashes flutter, matching the stuttering of his heart. "Oh." She frowns as if she's in pain. "Of course."

"I'm the Gemini. I have a...twin." He can't bring himself to say *soulmate* out loud. Not to Brielle.

She swallows. "I know."

The finality in her voice feels like it's shredding him.

"I'm so sorry, Brielle."

Tristan knows the words are lame. That if she's feeling anything close to the tearing that's ripping at his chest, the words won't be enough.

They stand and stare at each other, neither moving as the gulf between them widens. Tristan clenches his hands as he resists the urge to reach out.

The sound of sirens pierces the heavy air, and there's a groan behind Tristan. He spins around, instantly on alert again. The other Skins ran like the cowards they are while Tristan and Brielle were in the house.

But McNally had yet to gain consciousness, which means he got left behind. Although Tristan was tempted to leave him close to the burning house, they'd dragged him into the shrubs. Killing in cold blood isn't something Tristan wants to live with.

Tristan rushes to stand over him, but McNally only manages to turn himself over before blacking out again.

"What are we going to do with him?" Brielle asks. She hasn't moved from where he left her.

Wiping his hand down his face, Tristan realizes this is exactly why he had to say what he did. The pain from the words they just exchanged is clinging to every cell in his body. He has to work to stop it clouding his thinking.

"It's too late to do anything." As he says the words, the sirens hit ear-piercing levels. A firetruck roars up the driveway, police cars right behind.

Tristan and Brielle move themselves to the side as men and women in their heavy yellow uniform swarm around. One of them shouts over the flames, asking whether there's anyone inside.

Tristan shakes his head. "No. We checked."

When another car pulls up with a screech of tires, Tristan almost groans.

Jack Cadbury leaps out, shrewd eyes scanning the scene. They land on Tristan, almost as if he was expecting to see him. Like he was looking for him.

Obviously whatever alerts Jack had programmed in, they included Jareth's house.

Jack strides over, angry triumph stamped on his features. "And here you are again, Ayers. Right outside the scene of the crime."

"No one's been hurt, Jack. The house is empty."

The last thing Jack needs to know is that his daughter was in that inferno.

Jack fiddles with something at his belt, the soft sound of metal clanging slipping through the smoky air. "Your own house was destroyed in a fire, too, wasn't it?"

Tristan grits his teeth. Jack already knows the answer to that one.

Jack straightens, showing what he just grabbed. Handcuffs.

Brielle shifts closer to Tristan. "You can't arrest him. You have no evidence."

"Evidence will only be a matter of time," Jack growls.

As he wonders whether he needs to run or not, Tristan realizes something. He stood outside, he heard every word McNally said to Jareth before setting it alight. Tristan had learned a lot in those few minutes.

Jack's suspended. He has no capacity to arrest him. All Tristan has to do is point that out and he gets to walk away.

Tristan opens his mouth, but the other details McNally shared crowd in his mind. McNally killed Jareth's parents. And others... Tristan inhales sharply. McNally said something about being responsible for the Triple Murders.

Crossing his arms, Tristan angles his head. "I have a better idea."

Suspended or not, Jack won't give up on digging for the truth. And he's getting too close to uncovering it. The fact that he's here proves that.

"I doubt it," Jack scoffs. "I've been waiting for this moment for a long time, Ayers."

"I'd like to propose a truce."

Jack snorts. "No."

"You back off and leave us alone. I tell you who the Triple Murderer is."

Jack's gaze sharpens as he glares at Tristan. "You're bluffing."

Tristan unwinds his arms, allowing a grin to climb up his face. "I'll take that as a yes." He steps to the side, revealing an unconscious McNally behind them. "He tried to kill Jareth the same way he killed his parents—a house fire. You might want to run his fingerprints through your database."

Jack gapes as he sees his boss, hair bloody and face slack, lying unconscious on the ground.

Brielle clasps her hands. "He's telling you the truth, Agent Cadbury. McNally confessed, right before he attacked us."

Indicating with his chin toward her, Tristan strides past him, slapping Jack on the shoulder. "By tomorrow, you should be back at your desk, drinking crap coffee."

And leaving the Zodiacs alone.

Jack spins around, glaring at them. "If I find out you're lying, Ayers…"

Tristan's shoulders drop an inch, the cocky act getting heavy. He doesn't look over his shoulder as he speaks. "The bad guys aren't always who you think they are, Jack."

Out on the road, Tristan knows there will still be questions to answer about this fire. They have to find Jareth and

Veronica. Jareth's house is burning to the ground behind them.

But they've found the next Zodiac.

Jack will no longer be breathing down their necks.

And McNally, a Skin who killed too many before he was stopped, will be behind bars.

Brielle pulls out her cell. "I'll call my parents and get them to pick me up." Stepping aside, she doesn't meet his gaze as she presses the buttons. "There's no need to wait, they're probably still at the cemetery."

Tristan's about to point out that he can give her a lift, but he stops himself. Brielle's telling him she needs space.

It's possible her wounds are all internal, just like his.

Jamming his hands in his pockets, Tristan nods, unable to hold her gaze. The place is crawling with cops, Brielle will be safe until her parents arrive.

This is one thing he can give her right now.

As he walks away, he tells himself today was another win for the Zodiacs.

No matter how much it feels like he lost.

JARETH

"So, this is your bedroom?" Shandra's eyebrows have been permanently hiked up in her white helmet-hair since she started the home visit twenty minutes ago. "You've already unpacked, too."

Jareth looks around the room, noting the handful of books on the bedside table, the shirt that lays rumpled on the bed. In all fairness, the entirety of his belongings were in a duffel bag in the back of Sunshine when the house fire hit, so there wasn't a lot to unpack.

"I chose the one at the other end of the hall in case Tristan snores."

Tristan rolls his eyes from where he's leaning against the doorjamb. "Which I don't."

Shandra spins around. "You have a bedroom, too?"

Tristan shuffles a little. "Of course, I have a bedroom. I live here as well, remember?"

Shandra tucks her arms under her bosom. "I'm not sure where you were sleeping, but it wasn't in a bedroom."

Shoving away from the doorjamb, Tristan talks over his

shoulder as he walks away. "Well, I had to make sure I got the one furthest away from Jareth. In case he snores."

"Which I don't," Jareth calls after him.

Shandra chuckles as she shakes her head. "You know, I tried to introduce the two of you not long after you arrived."

Jareth jams his hands in his pockets. At first, moving into this mansion with Tristan was necessary, seeing as Jareth was homeless. But the first night, as they'd sat down for dinner and he'd swapped his peanut butter sandwich with Tristan's ravioli, he'd realized something.

He was no longer alone.

What's more. Tristan seemed to like having him around, too.

Jareth shrugs, liking the sense of stillness that's finally settled in his chest. "Seems we found each other, anyway." He steps toward the door. "Have you seen everything you need to?"

Shandra does something Jareth hasn't seen before, possibly something a social worker doesn't get to do a lot of. She smiles. "I most certainly have."

Jareth leads her back downstairs, where they find Tristan in the kitchen. He holds up a plate. "I baked. I specifically googled foolproof choc chip cookies."

Jareth almost groans. Tristan's strengths are found outside the kitchen, as his mother would say.

Shandra must have some sixth-sense of self-preservation, because she shakes her head, her unmoving hair seeming to stand still. "Thank you, but I'd better be going."

Except Tristan whips out a zip-lock bag with a grin. "Not a problem, you can take them with you." With a flourish, he tips the entirety of the plate into the bag. "Share them with your family."

"Or use them as fertilizer," adds Jareth.

Shandra's startled eyes shoot to his as Tristan holds out

the bag expectantly. Jareth considers telling her it was a joke, although then she might eat one…

Tristan grins. "Do you have any particularly stubborn weeds you need to get rid of?"

Shandra huffs out a chuckle as she tucks the cookies into her handbag. "I knew you two would have a lot in common."

She's already bustling to the front door, so Shandra doesn't see the she-has-no-idea glance Jareth and Tristan exchange. As Tristan rushes forward to open it for her, Jareth shakes his head.

It's odd to realize that discovering he's an alien gave him a sense of belonging…one he didn't know he was looking for.

Outside, Shandra hikes her handbag further up her shoulder. The weight of the cookies is probably dragging it down… She pulls in a deep, happy sigh. "I'm going to propose we reduce our visits to monthly. What do you think?"

Jareth and Tristan exchange another glance. Jareth smiles. "No offense, but that sounds great."

"None taken," Shandra assures. "With my job, seeing less of me is a sign you're a success story."

A success story. Not how Jareth would've thought he'd be described.

Shandra walks away before they can respond. She stops and smiles at the single pot sitting beside the front door. "I love daisies, by the way."

Only one pot of the sweet little flowers his parents loved survived the destruction of McNally, and it's probably the only thing that Jareth would've wanted to salvage. He'd placed it on the front porch, a testament to the resilience of beauty, even after such carnage.

It was one thing McNally—no, Chardis—didn't take from him.

Jareth nods. "Me, too."

They've been a witness to every moment that's defined his life.

Tristan waves from beside him. "Bye, Shandra. See you next month."

She waves back cheerily, looking like she's leaving Santa's workshop as she jauntily climbs into her car.

Tristan's gaze follows the vehicle as it reverses down the drive. "Did you notice it?"

"Uh huh. She didn't pull out her notebook."

"Not once." Tristan sucks on his bottom lip. "That felt almost as good as Jack's phone call, saying McNally isn't likely to be seeing the light of freedom in his lifetime."

Jareth nods. McNally was linked to every Triple Murder killing they knew of. Which means there are others out there like Jareth and Tristan, living with loss.

Because of Chardis.

Before Jareth can say anything, his cell dings. Glancing at the screen, his heart smiles. "Veronica says she's already there."

Tristan sighs. "Of all the people you could've hooked up with, did it have to be Jack Cadbury's daughter?"

Jareth levels his gaze at Tristan. They've already had this conversation. "It seems not only the Gemini has a soulmate."

Something flickers in Tristan's gaze. During the tours of HQ and dinners and late evening talks, Tristan told him all about the Zodiacs. Twelve sectors of the Universe, each with its Zodiac Guardian. Except for Gemini, which has two, each one half of a whole.

Although Tristan never said it, the fact that he's avoided mentioning Brielle's name for the past three days tells Jareth that maybe that's not as straightforward as it sounds.

"Besides," Jareth adds. "Veronica's using every chance she can get to tell her father we're the good guys. Nice, *human* good guys."

Surely, with the truce, that should be enough to get Jack off their back.

Tristan snorts. "I don't think there are enough daisies in the world to make that happen."

"So, what next?"

Tristan shrugs. "We find the others." He jogs down the stairs and heads to the garage. "Come on, we have a celebration fro-yo waiting for us. And no, we're not going in Sunshine."

Jareth hesitates for a second. Tristan's words were simple. We find the others. But Jareth knows that'll be as straightforward as finding the Gemini Twin.

For the first time in a long time, Jareth isn't scared. He belongs. He has a purpose.

And his family is only going to grow.

Jareth follows Tristan to the garage, a determined smile playing at the edge of his lips.

They need to find the others.

Before Chardis does.

BRIELLE

"Wh at'll you have?" Madge asks behind the counter at Creamy Dreams.

Brielle shakes herself out of her daze. "Oh. Um. Just caramel. No toppings."

Madge fills the cup with the frozen yogurt and hands it to her, and Brielle goes to sit next to Veronica while they wait for Jareth and Tristan to arrive.

"Just caramel?" Veronica asks, eying her cup. "No toppings?" she puts the spoon in her mouth, savoring the taste of her frozen tri-colored treat.

"Yep," Brielle replies simply. "I don't feel like anything extravagant today."

Especially after Tristan's response to her proposal about their relationship. Even though Jareth is part of their family now, and through osmosis, Veronica, Brielle isn't in the festive mood this outing is meant to celebrate.

One of Chardis's trusted pawns is behind bars. Jareth is safe as long as he's living with Tristan, as it seems Chardis is still intimidated by their powers, which are only growing.

This should be a victory meal.

And yet...

Tristan made it clear they need to remain just friends.

After everything, it still hurts. She knows he feels the connection between them. But it's apparently not enough. Maybe being around Jareth has shown him that same bond exists between all Zodiac Guardians.

But she doesn't feel anywhere near the same pull to Jareth that she feels to Tristan. And it's not just because Jareth's heart is firmly owned by Veronica. Brielle is certain that, even if the other Gemini walked in holding hands with Tristan, she'd still want him just as badly.

Maybe even more.

And it would hurt so much worse.

"I don't think I could live without fruit on my froyo," says Veronica as she sticks another spoonful in her mouth.

Brielle doesn't know the girl very well, yet even though she lied about them being friends, Brielle knows it will be inevitable. She likes Veronica already.

Brielle smiles at her, then sees the familiar truck parking out the window over Veronica's shoulder. Tristan and Jareth climb out and approach, and the wound stings with renewed freshness when Tristan immediately averts his eyes from hers.

They enter and Tristan goes to the counter to order while Jareth comes to drape his arms over Veronica's shoulders. She arches her neck to kiss him, and Brielle's insides churn with conflicting emotions. She's happy to see Jareth so happy, so at peace. But...it also reminds her of what she doesn't have with Tristan. What she never will.

"That's not nearly enough gummy bears," she overhears Madge arguing while serving Tristan's cup. "A few more should do it."

Brielle can't help but laugh at the fruitless flirting attempts by the middle-aged woman. It's so cute how she fawns over Tristan. Brielle knows she'd do the same in her shoes.

"I think he has enough gummy bears," an all too familiar and unwelcome voice intrudes on Brielle's musings.

Cassandra flips her golden locks, irritated at not yet being acknowledged behind Tristan. Brielle instinctively rolls her eyes and turns away.

"That girl seems like a real brat," Veronica mutters before licking another spoonful.

"You have no idea," Brielle says, unable to keep her lips from curling downward.

"Ah, that's right," Veronica says, her eyes suddenly bright with recognition. "You know her."

"Know is an understatement." Brielle can't even look at her yogurt, her appetite completely vanished.

"Well, on the bright side, you only have one more year to put up with her before you graduate," Veronica points out.

"Thank God!" Brielle exclaims, finally taking a saluting bite of her froyo.

Tristan suddenly plops down beside her, his eyes practically burning a hole in the table where he's staring blankly.

"What's up?" she asks as she nudges his shoulder, confused but intrigued.

Those intense blue eyes look up at her, swelling with debate like a turbulent sea.

This must be important.

"I think there's another Zodiac Guardian right here in Mirror Point!"

Ready for the next installment in the Zodiac Guardians
series?
Check out LEO RISING!

http://mybook.to/LeoRising

LEO RISING

As long as Cassandra controls her emotions, she's okay. She just needs to focus—excel at school, sports, make her father proud...and suppress the anger that seethes within her.

Except there's always been one person who gets under her skin, the girl Cassandra called her childhood best-friend in the loneliness of the orphanage. Now, when Cassandra can't control her fury, she reveals her powers to Brielle. Powers that Cassandra has hidden for a reason.

The moment Cassandra grips her stone, the truth is undeniable. She's a Zodiac Heir.

And she's about to learn that evil is amassing. Dark matter is being manipulated and a wormhole has opened, releasing an asteroid heading straight for Earth. Tristan has foreseen the death and damage it could wreak.

Cassandra could be their most powerful weapon against Chardis yet. But first there are deep wounds to heal and relationships to be forged. Will the fledgling Zodiac Heir team be able to come together to save countless lives? Or will Cassandra's anger prove to be the most dangerous power yet?

Fans of paranormal and sci-fi romance will love this Sailor Moon meets Avengers series from USA Today Best-Selling authors Tricia Barr and Tamar Sloan!

Grab your copy HERE!

http://mybook.to/LeoRising

MORE EPIC ROMANCE TO FALL IN LOVE WITH!

ALSO BY TAMAR SLOAN

PRIME PROPHECY SERIES

KEEPERS OF THE GRAIL

KEEPERS OF THE CHALICE

KEEPERS OF THE LIGHT

KEEPERS OF EXCALIBUR

DESTINED DEMIGODS

ELEMENTAL GAMES

THE SOVEREIGN CODE

THE THAW CHRONICLES

ALSO BY TRICIA BARR

THE MATING GAMES

THE BOUND ONE SERIES

THE AMARANT SERIES

SHIFTER ACADEMY

HEAVENLY SINNERS

ABOUT THE AUTHORS

By day, Tricia is a full time mom to two beautiful girls and a wife/business partner to a handsome hard-working husband. By night—and nap times—she's a USA Today Best-selling Author of unique and thrilling teen and adult fantasies inspired by her vivid, somewhat creepy dreams and her own adventures around the world.

Tamar hasn't decided whether she's a psychologist who loves writing, or a writer with a lifelong fascination with psychology. She must've been someone pretty awesome in a previous life (past life regression indicates a Care Bear), because she gets to do both. When not reading, writing, or working with teens, Tamar can be found with her husband and two sons enjoying country life in their small slice of the Australian bush.